Puffin Books

WICKED!

Something very weird is happening to Dawn and Rory. And it's not just their new step-family.

Slurping slobberers want to suck their bones out.
Strange steel sheep want to smash them to pieces.
Giant frogs want to crunch them up.
Cruel killer creepers want to squeeze the life out of them.

Their parents can't help them. Gramps wants to, but he's a bit off-the-planet.

Dawn and Rory are on their own.

It's wild. It's wacky. It's WICKED!

Other books by

Paul

Unreal!
Unbelievable!
Uncanny!
Unbearable!
Unmentionable!
Undone!
Uncovered!
Quirky Tails
Unseen!
Tongue-Tied!
The Gizmo
The Gizmo Again
Come Back Gizmo
Sink the Gizmo
Sucked In . . .
Round the Twist
The Many Adventures of
    Singenpoo

Morris

The Other Facts of Life
Second Childhood
Two Weeks with the Queen
Misery Guts
Worry Warts
Blabber Mouth
Sticky Beak
Puppy Fat
Belly Flop
Water Wings
Bumface
Gift of the Gab
Toad Rage
Toad Heaven
Toad Away
Adults Only
Boy Overboard
Teacher's Pet
Girl Underground

Also available by Paul and Morris

Deadly!

Wicked!

ALL SIX BOOKS IN ONE

PAUL JENNINGS & MORRIS GLEITZMAN

PUFFIN BOOKS

PUFFIN BOOKS

Published by the Penguin Group
Penguin Group (Australia)
250 Camberwell Road, Camberwell, Victoria 3124, Australia
(a division of Pearson Australia Group Pty Ltd)
Penguin Group (USA) Inc.
375 Hudson Street, New York, New York 10014, USA
Penguin Group (Canada)
10 Alcorn Avenue, Toronto, Ontario, Canada M4V 3B2
(a division of Pearson Penguin Canada Inc.)
Penguin Books Ltd
80 Strand, London WC2R 0RL, England
Penguin Ireland
25 St Stephen's Green, Dublin 2, Ireland
(a division of Penguin Books Ltd)
Penguin Books India Pvt Ltd
11, Community Centre, Panchsheel Park, New Delhi-110 017, India
Penguin Group (NZ)
Cnr Airborne and Rosedale Roads, Albany, Auckland, New Zealand
(a division of Pearson New Zealand Ltd)
Penguin Books (South Africa) (Pty) Ltd
24 Sturdee Avenue, Rosebank, Johannesburg 2196, South Africa

Penguin Books Ltd, Registered Offices: 80 Strand, London WC2R 0RL, England

First published in six volumes by Penguin Books Australia, 1997
This edition first published by Penguin Books Australia, 1998

20 19 18 17

Designed by George Dale © Penguin Group (Australia)
Typeset in Berkeley Old Style by Midland Typesetters, Maryborough, Victoria
Printed in Australia by McPherson's Printing Group, Maryborough, Victoria

ISBN 014 130047 7

Series editor: Julie Watts
Cover and text illustrations: Dean Gorissen

www.puffin.com.au

Contents

Book One

THE SLOBBERERS

ONE

They all reckon I'm a worm.

A grub.

A monster.

I could tell from their faces as I ran out of the church. And from what they were saying.

'You're a wicked girl,' hissed Mr Kinloch from the Wool Growers' Association.

I didn't blame him. I'd probably think the same if I saw a kid do what I'd just done. Ruin her own dad's wedding. Leave a church in uproar and a bride in tears and a minister in shock.

I wish Dad had listened all those times I tried to talk to him.

But parents don't listen when love's made them dopey. You just have to go along with their mad plans and hope everyone doesn't end up in the poo.

That's what I was telling myself this arvo in church while Mrs Conti from the cake shop was playing 'Here Comes the Bride' on the organ.

'It'll be okay,' I said in my head as Dad and Eileen stepped up to the altar. 'We can get through this. Dad's a really good dad even though his brain has turned to confetti, and Eileen's not a bad person even though she does dribble a bit when she loses her temper. We'll be right.'

I wanted to believe it heaps. But it was no good. My neck was hurting. I always get neck tension when I try and lie to myself.

I thought a curried-egg sandwich might help. I reached for the one next to me on the pew, the one I'd pinched from the caterers when we'd dropped into the Scout Hall on the way to the church to check that the glitter ball had arrived for the reception.

I hoped the bread hadn't gone too hard in the heat. Rev Arnott's voice was pretty quiet and I didn't want to disrupt the ceremony with crunching. I lifted the sandwich to my mouth.

And froze.

There was a slug sitting on the bread.

Looking at me.

It was more of a worm than a slug, slimy and sort of veiny. I'd never seen one like it before, and Dad's a shearer so I've seen lots. You wouldn't believe some of the things that crawl out of sheep's bottoms.

I glared at it and went to knock it off. That's when I saw Rory glaring at *me*.

You'd think grown adults would know better than to put two kids who hate each other side by side on the same pew. Even love-fuddled adults with new shoes that are hurting them a bit should know better than that. But Dad and Eileen were determined.

'She's your step-sister,' Eileen had hissed to Rory when we got to the church. 'Sit next to her.'

'Aw, Mum . . . ' Rory had moaned.

Dad had taken me to one side and given me a pep talk.

'Dawn,' he'd said, squeezing my shoulders. 'I know it's not easy, but we'll all feel more comfortable with each other once we're living together and getting to know each other better.'

I opened my mouth to remind Dad that Rory and me have known each other for eight years and he's hated my guts for five and I've been going off him in a big way for at least four and a half.

Then Mrs Conti deafened us with the organ, and the wedding started.

Two minutes later Rory was grabbing my sandwich.

'That's mine,' I whispered, furious. 'Hands off.'

We struggled over the sandwich.

'The worm's mine,' grunted Rory.

He let go of the sandwich and grabbed the worm.

I chewed my sandwich angrily. How's anyone meant to like a person who keeps worms as pets? Specially when that person's a year older than you and is meant to be setting a good example.

Rory put the worm into a tin.

I stared. Inside the tin was the little troll that Rory

takes everywhere with him. The one with the wooden body and the dried apple for a head. I try not to make jokes about it 'cos his dad sent it to him and it's the only present he's had from his dad for ages.

The troll's shrivelled-up apple head had been dry and dead. Now it was alive. With worms. They were slobbering all over it and wriggling into the mouth and writhing out of the eyes.

It was worse than anything I'd seen on a sheep, even in nightmares.

I looked at Rory.

He wasn't gagging or looking revolted or anything. He was staring at the worms, fascinated.

Then I saw something even more horrible.

The tin.

It was *my* tin. My Milo tin. The one Mum had given me to keep pencils in.

I couldn't believe it. Rory had taken it from my room without asking. The last thing Mum had given me before she died. And he'd put slimy slobbery revolting worms in it.

I felt rage uncoiling inside me. Hot tears stinging.

In the distance Rev Arnott was saying that stuff about how if anyone had a reason why these two people should not be joined together in holy matrimony, speak now or forever hold your peace.

Before I knew it I was on my feet.

'I have,' I shouted. I heard the pews creak as everyone stiffened. I could feel everyone's eyes on me.

'We all hate each other,' I said. My heart was pounding in my ears. Dad's mouth was wider than a sheep chute. 'Not Dad and Eileen,' I continued, 'cos they've got sex, but the rest of us.'

Eileen's face was crumpling and Rev Arnott was clinging to the altar. I ploughed on.

'We pretend we like each other, but we don't. You should see Rory go off when I catch him using Dad's razor to scrape the fluff of his socks. You should see Dad when Rory has a nightmare and gets into bed with Eileen. You should see Eileen when I make friendly jokes about her bottom exercises.'

'Thank you, Dawn,' croaked Rev Arnott. 'Why don't we finish the ceremony and have a family talk afterwards.'

I turned to appeal to the other guests. Rows of open mouths and big eyes. I pointed at Rory.

'I try to be friendly with him and he lets his rat poo in my underwear drawer.'

'I did not,' shouted Rory. 'It was a mouse.'

'Dawn,' roared Dad, storming towards me, 'sit down.'

'Second marriages never work,' I yelled. 'Specially when she's more educated than he is and her son sneaks into his daughter's room and takes precious things.'

I grabbed at my Milo tin but Rory hung on and the tin spun out of our hands and crashed onto the tiles. The apple head bounced across the floor. Worms slithered everywhere.

I turned and ran out of the church. Dad followed for a bit, shouting, then gave up. I wasn't surprised. Eileen's been more important to him than I have for about a year now.

I suppose I was pretty dopey coming here to the old bus 'cos Dad knows it's where I always come when I want to be close to Mum. When the ceremony's over he'll know where to find me.

In fact I can hear someone crashing through the bush now.

Whoever it is, I'm history.

If it's Dad, he'll kill me for ruining his wedding, and if it's Rev Arnott to tell me I'm forgiven, I've still got to live with Worm Boy.

So either way my life's over.

TWO

Big Bad Dawn. Everything is big about her. Big muscles, big head, big mouth. Worst of all she's my sister. Well, step-sister to be exact. It's not the same. A real sister wouldn't have made a fuss in church over a Milo tin. A real sister wouldn't have nearly let my grubs escape. A real sister wouldn't have . . .

THE SLOBBERERS

Oh, what the heck. I knew where she was hiding.

Everyone from the wedding was looking for her. Fancy standing up in church and objecting to the marriage. What a hoot. I have to give her full marks for that. I wished I'd thought of it myself. I didn't want Mum to marry Jack any more than she did.

The bus. That's where she would be. That was her hideout.

I tucked the Milo tin under one arm and walked along the side of the creek for a while. Then I took the short cut through Dead Cow Clearing. I reached the fence of the wrecker's yard and peered in. There it was. A rusting hulk right in the middle of the yard. Broken windows. Grass sprouting out of the petrol cap. Not a speck of paint left. A tree growing right through the bonnet. And the whole thing leaning drunkenly to one side.

The bus had carried its last passenger, that was one thing for sure.

Last passenger. What was I thinking about? I was the last passenger. I had my crook leg to remind me of that.

I climbed through Dawn's secret hole in the bent iron fence. 'I know you're in there, Dawn,' I said under my breath.

Inside the yard I crept past the remains of a '68 Ford and round a pile of dented hub caps. I didn't want Dawn to hear me so I picked my way forward carefully.

I reached the bus and hopped quietly onto the first step. I stopped.

I didn't want to go in. I'd been on that bus when it crashed. That terrible crash that I still couldn't remember anything about. But there was no time for that now.

'Gotcha.' I jumped up the next two broken steps into the back of the bus.

Dawn was sitting in the driver's seat with tears in her eyes. 'You,' she spat out. 'Worm Boy. Where's your rotten apple-man?'

She shouldn't have said that. Like I was feeling a bit sorry for her sitting in the very seat where her mother had drowned. But when she rubbished my apple-man I could feel my face burning with anger.

'My Dad gave me that apple-man,' I yelled. 'Don't you – '

She wouldn't even let me finish. 'Your dad, your dad. Don't give me that. Where is he then? What sort of dad goes off and never writes? Never sends a present. Not even a Christmas card. My dad gives you stuff all the time. The only thing you've ever got from yours is a rotten apple.'

I ran down the aisle between the sagging seats and put my face up close to Dawn's. I shouldn't have said what I did. Not when she was sitting right where it happened. But I was really mad. 'What about your mum?' I yelled. 'She wanted to get away from you so bad that she drove the bus off the cliff into the river and drowned. And nearly killed me too.'

Dawn just about exploded. I had really pressed the right buttons. She jumped out of her seat and shoved me onto the floor. The Milo tin rolled down the aisle and the lid popped off. My little apple-man spilled out and lay there like a wizened corpse.

Dawn sat on my chest and pinned my arms to the ground with her knees. I couldn't move. I could hardly breathe. She was much stronger than me. And she knew it.

'I'm going to get your rotten apple-man,' she said. 'And flush it down the dunny.'

I squirmed and heaved but I just couldn't move her. If she wanted to, she could do whatever she liked. I knew that if she ran off with him, I'd never catch her. She was just too fast. It would be the last I'd see of my apple-man.

It's amazing how they make those little apple faces. They get an extra-big apple and let it slowly shrivel up so that it's all wrinkled and dry. Then they sew it so that it has little eyes and a mouth and a chin. They make a wooden body and, hey presto – a great little troll with an ugly face.

'Don't touch it,' I screamed. 'I'll kill you.' I bucked like a horse but she just pressed down harder with her knees.

'It's got worms,' she said. 'Horrible little slobberers.'

I knew that. I twisted my head sideways and looked at them. I was a bit worried when I first saw them. What if they ate the whole apple-head off the doll? Dad would be sad if his present got ruined. The funny thing is, though, the apple-man never changed. The slobberers must have eaten something, but what? They couldn't have been eating the apple or there'd be none left.

My arms were starting to tingle with pins and needles. Dawn's knees were knobbly. 'Give in, Worm Boy,' she said.

'Never,' I said.

So we just stayed there on the floor of the bus. I stared up into her ugly mug and she glared down into mine. I decided not to look at her so I fixed my eyes on a seat where the skeleton of a dead goat sat like a ghostly passenger from the past. How the heck did that get there? It must have wandered in and died.

The image of the skeleton sort of locked itself in my head.

Suddenly Dawn gave a scream and jumped up. She was looking down the aisle at the slobberers. Typical girl. Tough as an ox but scared of a few little grubs. Then I looked a bit more closely. Oh no. I scrambled up and backed off. The skin of the apple-man had begun to boil. A huge grub erupted from a wrinkled scar on the apple-man's face. It wormed itself out, wriggling, wriggling, wriggling. Tiny veins and purple blood. Little pinpricks of glowing green eyes. Wet fangs and three or four slobbering, sucking tongues coming out of its mouth.

I hadn't seen a slobberer like this before. Maybe they were changing. It crawled towards us, followed by another and another and another. Each one the same. It was weird. They slimed out of the apple-man's eyes and ears and hair. Soon there were twenty or thirty. They advanced towards us in lines like an army of little snakes.

'I'm out of here,' shrieked Dawn.

Suddenly the slobberers stopped. They reared up as one and seemed to look about. Then they turned and slithered in panic towards the door.

'Hey,' I yelled. 'Come back. She won't hurt you.'

It seems funny to say this but I didn't want to lose them. Since they had been living in the apple-man I had come to like them even though they were pretty yucky. They were a bit like tenants renting a house. They lived in the apple-man and they didn't really do any harm. And no one else had anything like them.

I grabbed the apple-man and ran outside the bus. The slobberers were lined up some distance away. They stared at the bus and seemed to be making frightened, slurping noises. Their little tongues flickered in and out. Weird. It wasn't Dawn they were frightened of. She had run out and was already climbing through the hole in the fence. Heading for home as quick as her legs could take her. What a chicken.

No, the slobberers weren't scared of Dawn. It was something to do with the bus. To be honest, I thought it was a bit spooky myself.

I walked up close to them and put the apple-man down on the ground. 'Come on, guys,' I said. 'Come home. Come home to Daddy.'

In a flash they streaked across the ground towards the apple-man. They wormed and wriggled and fought each other in their hurry to get back inside. There was a bit of a traffic jam at the nostrils. After a few seconds they were gone. Everything was back to normal. For now anyway.

I picked up my apple-man and headed back to the bus. I went inside and put him back in the Milo tin. No point taking risks. I couldn't take the chance that my little slobberers might escape again. Things were weird enough already.

I jumped out of the bus and walked towards the hole in the fence. I was glad to be leaving. The slobberers didn't like that bus.

And neither did I.

THREE

Before the wedding I'd been scared three times in my life. Really scared. The sort of scared where people sit you down. Give you hot drinks. Say 'take deep breaths, Dawn' and peek to see if you've wet your pants.

The first time was when I saw Dad crying just before he told me Mum had died.

The second was at Mum's funeral when I heard Mrs Lecter from the newsagents whispering to Mrs Gleeson the librarian. Whispering that Mum had killed herself on purpose.

The third was when Gramps told me that a rotting beam at the Wilsons' place had crushed a shearer and I thought he meant Dad.

What happened in the bus after the wedding made it four.

I ran out of that wrecker's yard faster than I'd ever run, even faster than I'd run after biting Mrs Lecter at Mum's funeral.

When I got home I threw myself onto my bed. I couldn't stop thinking about it. I couldn't stop shaking. I could still see it, there on the floor of the bus.

Worm Boy probably thought I'd screamed because of the slobberers.

I hadn't. I'd screamed because of the shoe.

It was under the driver's seat. I'd never noticed it before, probably because I'd never had my face that close to the floor before.

It was covered in dust and mildew, but I'd have recognised it anywhere.

Mum's shoe.

She was wearing it the day she died.

Even after five years you don't forget your mum's favourite bus-driving shoes. Specially when you used to spend so much time spitting on them and polishing them with the tea towel.

It didn't look polished now. It looked twisted and scraped and sad, and it made me think of what Mum's body must have looked like when the police divers pulled her out of the river.

That's why I had to get out of the bus.

I yelled something and pushed past Rory, who was busy with his dopey worms, and jumped out and ran.

All the way home I told myself the shoe wasn't real. It was the stress I'd been under lately. The stress of a wedding and a new step-family and trying to push Rory through the metal floor of a bus. Stress could make you see things, I'd read it in a comic about an alcoholic astronaut.

But when Rory got home, I was still shaking and still seeing that shoe.

'Chicken,' he said, still clutching my Milo tin. 'Scared of a few grubs. Pathetic.'

I should have got him in a neck-lock and grabbed my tin. I almost did. But I knew Mum wouldn't have approved. So instead I took a few deep breaths and told him how in my opinion Tasmanian souvenir manufacturers who use worm-infested apples should be reported to the health authorities.

Then Dad got home and yelled at me for a bit.

'Children do not disrupt their parents' weddings,' he shouted. 'And they go to the reception whether they like it or not.'

Stuff like that.

When he'd calmed down, we talked.

'I know it's not easy, this step-family lark,' said Dad. 'But I want you to give it a go, love, okay?'

I told him I would.

We hugged each other.

While Dad had his arms round me, I saw Rory watching from the doorway. As soon as our eyes met, he turned away. There was something about his expression that made me feel sorry for him. Just for a sec. Until I saw he was still clutching my Milo tin. And I remembered he's got a mum who's perfectly capable of hugging him if she doesn't mind getting a bit of worm poo on her.

Dad launched into making a lamb stew for him and Eileen to take on their honeymoon camping trip, and I helped him.

I like cooking with Dad. Being a shearer, he's best at peeling, so I get to use the cleaver.

Once the stew was bubbling away, we went out onto the back verandah for a lemonade. I almost told Dad about the shoe, but I decided not to. No point in upsetting him. Not on his wedding day.

Dad spotted Rory skulking about in the kitchen.

'Hey, Roars,' he called. 'Want a lemonade?'

Rory jumped guiltily. He'd probably already had about three cans while we weren't looking.

Then Eileen arrived with Gramps.

'That was the best wedding I've ever been to,' said Gramps. He reached into his pocket. 'Anyone want a curried-egg sandwich?'

I was the only one who did.

Then I helped Dad get the camping things together while Eileen and Worm Boy unpacked their moving cartons and got Rory's room straight. Assembled his bed and hung all the little worm clothes in the wardrobe, that sort of stuff.

Soon it was time for Dad and Eileen to go.

I hugged Dad again. Rory hugged his mum. Then there was the tricky bit. I took a deep breath and gave Eileen a quick squeeze. Luckily I'm taller than her so our faces didn't have to touch.

Dad sort of half hugged, half patted Rory.

Gramps kissed everyone.

'Have you got the shovel?' Eileen asked Dad.

I sighed. It didn't seem very romantic. Most people went to Bali or Sydney or some other exotic place for their honeymoon, not camping on Bald Mountain where there weren't any dunnies. Oh well, I thought, it's what they both like.

'Be good kids for Gramps,' yelled Dad. 'See you in three days.'

It felt really strange, watching Dad drive off with another woman. I mean I'd seen him driving places with Eileen hundreds of times, but this was different because now we were stuck with each other and our lives would never be the same.

The weird stuff started almost straight away.

Gramps said, 'Okay, kids, let's have lunch,' and we had to remind him it was dinner time.

While he and Rory had a look in the freezer, I grabbed

the opportunity to get my tin back.

It was sitting on Rory's bedside table. I took the lid off and emptied that ugly little apple-man onto the floor. Its evil-looking eyes peered up at me.

Then I heard a scratching sound. Another pair of eyes was watching me. From the top of the chest of drawers. Rory's mouse in its cage.

I stuck my tongue out at both of them. Mum used to do her sewing and charity book-keeping in that room and nobody else had the right to invade it.

Back in my room I hid the tin in the bottom of my wardrobe under the abseiling ropes Dad gave me for my birthday.

'Don't say a word,' I whispered to Finger, my goldfish. 'There are invaders in the house and we've got to be on our guard.'

After dinner, while me and Gramps washed up, I took a chance.

'Gramps,' I said, 'have you ever seen a shoe that you thought was there but it actually wasn't?'

Gramps thought about this.

'Once,' he said, 'I didn't see a shoe that I thought wasn't there but it actually was. Work boot, next to my vegie garden, in front of the wheelbarrow. I tripped over it and squashed my sprouts.'

I decided not to continue with the conversation, partly because Gramps was chuckling so loudly, and partly because Rory had stormed into the kitchen, red-faced.

'You stupid idiot,' he shouted. 'You let them out of

the tin. Do you have any idea what you've just done?'

'It's my tin,' I said.

'Tin,' said Gramps. 'That's right. I squashed my tobacco tin too.'

Rory rushed out and I finished the drying up. Stupid idiot yourself, I thought. They're only a bunch of worms. If you're that worried about them, train them to come when you whistle.

Then I went to my room.

As soon as I walked in I could feel something was wrong. It took me two seconds to spot it.

Finger, floating at the top of her tank.

Heart pounding, I scooped her out and peered at her gills. She was dead. It must have just happened because she was still loose and floppy.

Even as my eyes filled with tears I felt rage eating into my guts. That vicious mongrel. Just 'cos I let a few of his crummy worms escape, he kills my pet.

Still holding Finger I headed for the door.

That mouse was dead meat.

Rory appeared in the doorway. I decided to pound him first, then do the mouse.

'You killed my – ' I yelled, then stopped because he was yelling too.

And he was holding something out. It looked like a small brown bag. I was confused. Why would a kid who'd just killed my fish think I'd care that he'd found a bag to keep his dopey worms in?

Then I realised it wasn't a bag, it was a mouse.

Rory was sniffing and blinking. He was still angry but I could tell he was upset as well.

'He's . . . he's . . .' Rory struggled to get the words out. He didn't need to.

I could see what he was trying to say.

The mouse was dead and it didn't have any bones.

FOUR

I stormed out of the kitchen. My head started to swim with red-hot anger. Dreadful Dawn let my slobberers out. On purpose. And Mum and Jack had gone off on their honeymoon and left me in the camp of the enemy.

I went back to my new bedroom (not nearly as good as my old one) and threw myself onto the bed. I silently hoped that their marriage would break up as quickly as possible. Step-families suck. That's what I thought. I hated Dawn for letting my slobberers out. She was so stupid.

Gramps was the only decent one. Out of all of them he was my favourite. He was certainly a lot better than Big Bad Dawn.

Then I started thinking about Dad. And remembering.

My dad was handsome. Mum used to say all the girls were after him but she was the one who got him.

What I remembered was his kind face. He was one of those people who always looked happy. He didn't have a mean bone in his body. Why did he go and leave me?

I tried to push down the tears. 'Don't cry. Don't cry. Be a man.'

I got up and went over to Nibbler's cage to get him out and have a play. He wasn't running around on his wheel like he usually does. He was inside his little wooden nest. I opened the lid and pulled him out.

He was dead.

And flat. And empty. He looked like a tiny possum that had been lying on the road for a couple of weeks. Run over by thousands of cars. Nibbler was stiff and dry. His bones were gone. His innards were gone. His eyes were gone. He was nothing but a flattened dried-up skin.

My little mouse. My friend. The only one in this house who would listen. Gone.

I blinked back my tears.

Dawn. The scumbag. The murderer. She had it coming this time.

I held the remains of Nibbler in my hand and ran out of the room. She was standing there looking at me with hatred in her eyes.

We both shouted the same thing at the same time.

'You killed my – '

Then we stopped. Our mouths hanging open. She was holding her goldfish and crying. It was shrivelled and horrible with no bones and no innards.

I knew straight away that she hadn't killed Nibbler. She's awful, but she wouldn't kill her own goldfish. Someone else – something else – had killed Nibbler and Finger and sucked all of their bones and innards out.

Dawn's eyes grew rounder and rounder. So did mine. What was going on?

Then she pushed past me into my bedroom. I turned and saw what she saw.

My little apple-man was still on the floor where she had thrown him. Slobberers were wriggling all over him. They were wriggling out of my apple-man at an incredible speed. Twenty or thirty of them. Flickering tongues, evil eyes, pulsing veins. Leeches with tongues. That's what they reminded me of.

They looked at us, then reared up like snakes about to strike. My legs turned to jelly. I felt sick and scared. What were they looking at us like that for? Were they hungry?

If they were, they must have decided that we were a bit too big for them. They slithered out of the window before Dawn or I could even take a breath.

A large magpie sat on the lawn pecking at a piece of bread that Gramps had thrown there. It looked with interest at the approaching slobberers and hopped towards them.

Food.

Well, the magpie was right about that. There was food there all right.

Him.

Horrible, horrible, horrible. The slobberers swarmed all over the poor bird. He gave one squawk and flew into the air just above our heads. The slobberers began to suck. Waving tongues and slurping mouths began to empty him out in front of our eyes. Without a sound the bird and his slimy passengers plummeted onto the grass. Feathers fluttered down slowly.

By the time the last feather had landed the magpie was nothing but an empty, eyeless skin.

The slobberers seemed to have grown after their meal. They were definitely swollen. But that didn't slow them down at all. Before either of us could say a word they had wriggled across the lawn and disappeared under the floor of the garage.

It was the most terrible sight I had ever seen. The slobberers had eaten the magpie alive. Gorging themselves like bloated maggots.

I had to tell Dawn what I had done. Mum and Jack were in terrible danger.

The words stuck in my throat but I managed to get them out. 'Dawn,' I said. 'I put some slobberers in their stew.'

Dawn turned on me half in fury, half in horror. 'You put them in the stew? My dad's going to eat that.'

'So's my mum.' I could hardly find my voice. 'You tried to stop them getting married. I wanted to bust them up. You know – have a row over the worms. Then Mum and me could go back to our place. And never have to see you and Jack again.'

'You stupid idiot,' Dawn yelled. 'Did you see what they did to that bird?'

Dawn spun round and looked viciously at the apple-man. She took a step towards him and grabbed my cricket bat. I knew what she was going to do. And I knew what I had already done. Putting them in Mum's stew. They were dangerous and we had to get rid of them. But I wasn't going to let Dawn smash up the apple-man. No way.

Dawn lifted the bat and then froze. So did I. There was one slobberer left. A long one. A very long one. It slithered out of the apple-man's left eye. On and on and on. It seemed endless. Like a worm of rotten black toothpaste coming out of a tube.

Dawn screamed and closed her eyes in horror.

I couldn't stop looking at the terrible sight. The slobberer finally left the apple and started to coil and uncoil on the floor. What was it doing?

It was writing. Yes, writing. It slowly formed its body into joined-up letters. Letters that spelt out a single word:

'Aagh,' I shrieked.

Dawn opened her eyes. But she had missed seeing the word. The slobberer was wriggling towards the window as fast as it could go. 'Take that,' yelled Dawn. She hurled the bat at the slobberer and it skidded across the floor, narrowly missing the horrible creature's tail. In a flash the slobberer vanished out of the window.

'Come on,' yelled Dawn. 'We have to get to Dad and Eileen before they eat that stew.'

She scrambled out of the door. Out of the house. I grabbed my apple-man and shoved him into my pocket. Then I ran out after her.

'Gramps can help us,' I panted.

Dawn looked at me with contempt. 'Gramps can't even help himself,' she said.

She was right about that. Only an hour before, I had seen Gramps put his electric drill in the freezer. He was definitely past it.

We both looked around. In the garage was Mum's trail bike. As we ran towards it, I knew that Dawn was filled with terrible thoughts about the slobberers and Jack and my mum and what might be happening up on Bald Mountain.

I was just as worried. But I also had another horror to cope with.

The word that the slobberer had spelt out. Karl. That terrible, wonderful word was the name of my father.

Stay calm, I said to myself as we sprinted to the garage. Don't panic. When you panic your brain turns into a thickshake.

It wasn't easy.

Dad's overalls and Eileen's bike gear were hanging on the garage wall, saggy and empty like sucked-out skins.

I forced myself to stop imagining things.

Rory pushed me out of the way and leapt onto the trail bike.

'Wait,' I said. 'It's too risky. Sergeant Wallace said if he sees you on the street on that bike again he'll use you as lawn fertiliser.'

Rory ignored me and kick-started the engine.

'Okay,' I yelled. 'Seeing as we're going to end up at the police station anyway, let's just go there now and get them to save Dad and Eileen.'

'No,' he shouted. 'No cops.' He turned the engine off and slumped forward onto the handlebars.

Rory glared at me.

I felt sorry for him. When your mum's a courier and she's got as many unpaid speeding tickets as his mum, it doesn't leave you a heap of places

27

to go in an emergency.

I had an idea. I grabbed Eileen's bike jacket off the wall, put it on, grabbed the helmets and threw Rory's to him.

'Shift back,' I said. 'With this stuff on, people'll think I'm your mum. She's almost as big as me.'

I swung my leg over the bike and started it.

'Have you ridden a two-fifty before?' yelled Rory.

'Course,' I replied.

My neck went into a cramp and I had a sudden urge for a curried-egg sandwich. I couldn't understand it. Dad had let me have a go on a sheep bike once and that was almost a two-fifty.

I jerked the bike into gear and we jolted out of the garage.

Standing in the driveway, watching us, was Gramps.

My guts sagged. I hit the brakes and heard Rory give a groan of despair through his helmet.

Gramps stared at me. 'Eileen,' he said. 'I thought you were on your honeymoon.'

I wanted to tear my helmet off and show Gramps it was me. Then I remembered Dad and Eileen with their stew full of slobbering parasites. The trouble with Gramps is that if you start a conversation he gets off the track and ends up talking about woodwork.

I revved the bike and we hurtled out of the driveway in a cloud of dust and magpie feathers. Halfway down the street I felt Rory's helmet bang against mine.

'How long till we get to Bald Mountain?' he shouted.

'About an hour,' I yelled. 'A bit longer if you keep grabbing my shoulders and we crash and we have to go via the hospital.'

Rory put his arms round my waist. It wasn't a great feeling. At the time I'd probably have preferred a slobberer. I told myself to grow up and stop being squeamish.

The trip went pretty well all the way down our street and round the corner past the library.

Then we had to stop at a red light. I felt Rory stiffen behind me.

'Relax,' I said. 'We'll get there.'

Rory didn't relax. He gave a gasp.

'It's Dad,' he said. 'Over there. Dad.'

He was pointing to a red car on the other side of the road. The windows were tinted and I couldn't see the driver too well, but he certainly looked like the photos I'd seen of Rory's dad.

I blinked and peered and tried to see more clearly.

'Dad,' yelled Rory.

The guy turned and stared at us. Suddenly he didn't look anything like Rory's dad. Rory's dad's face was pretty ordinary and this guy's features were all lopsided and he had a moustache.

I felt Rory sag behind me.

'I thought it was Dad,' he mumbled.

I could feel his heart thumping in my back.

Poor kid, I thought. At least when a parent's dead you know you'll never see them again. When one just nicks off, you're always hoping.

Which made me think of my dad and whether I'd see him again.

When my eyes had stopped stinging I noticed someone else was staring at us. The bloke in the grey car behind us. He was pretending not to, but I could see his beady eyes in my rear-vision mirror.

It was Mr Kinloch from the Wool Growers' Association. He'd been to our place heaps of times 'cos he and Dad both collected wool samples.

'Get ready for a chase,' I muttered to Rory. 'I think he's recognised my socks.'

My guts clenched and Rory's arms tightened round my waist. I wondered if a bike could go faster than a car. Probably not when the person driving the bike didn't know how to get into fourth gear.

The light turned green.

I revved the bike and we screeched away.

Once the front wheel was back on the ground and my heart was back in my chest, I glanced into the mirror. Mr Kinloch was turning down Station Street.

We headed out of town, me hanging on to the handlebars weak with relief, and Rory hanging on to me muttering about the wear on his mother's tyres.

We didn't know it then, but they were about to get even more worn.

It started when we were out on Bald Mountain Road. I'd just got the hang of fourth gear and we were rocketing along. Rory's helmet clunked against mine again.

'Stop the bike,' he shouted. 'Don't look down.'

His voice had the same fake squeaky fear he'd used in the school play when he was a dying general. His acting hadn't been real good then either.

'Stow it, peabrain,' I yelled, and carried on trying to find fifth gear.

That's all I need, I thought, Worm Boy playing stupid tricks to get his own back for the wheelie at the traffic lights. Has the cretin forgotten this is an emergency?

I found fifth.

'Stop!' screamed Rory. He wasn't acting.

Then I saw it. Crawling out of the hollow handlebar where the stopper had fallen off.

The biggest slobberer yet.

It was the size of a human poo and I could see its wet veiny body pulsing and its slimy tongues darting and its green eyes glaring.

I screamed and took my hand off the handlebar. The bike wobbled and started to slow down.

The slobberer slimed its way along the metal and flopped onto my jacket.

I screamed again.

Others were following it. Slithering out of the handlebar and dropping onto me. Crawling up my chest.

I tried to knock them off. My bike glove slapped against slobbery rubbery muscle. They didn't budge. Their angry eyes just got bigger and glared up at me.

It was like they'd noticed me for the first time.

They started jabbing their tongues into my vinyl jacket.

I almost fainted. I waited for them to suck me dry like the magpie.

Then I noticed the tongues were stabbing into the vinyl but not going all the way through.

Relief flooded through me.

'Look out!' yelled Rory.

Suddenly I realised we weren't on the road any more. Branches and leaves were whipping my face and the bike was airborne.

Then we were through the scrub and in the clear, crashing down, the bike on its side, skidding in a shower of dirt and twigs towards a huge sheet of metal.

Metal?

No, water.

I let go of the bike.

As I rolled painfully over grass tussocks and dried sheep droppings and Rory's knees, I heard a loud splash.

As soon as I stopped rolling I tore the jacket off. I checked every centimetre of it and my whole shaking body. Only then did I see that, like the slobberers, the bike had vanished.

Just ripples on the surface of a large dam.

'Great,' yelled Rory, his voice cracking. He had a cut on his face. 'Now we'll never save them. You're as hopeless as your mother.'

I was shaking so much I could hardly get my hands into fists. But I managed it.

And I'd have managed to pound them into his sneering mouth if I hadn't seen the sun glinting off something way down the hill, past the lower paddock, on Ravine Road.

The windscreen of a car. A parked car. A yellow car with a blue door, which was the only one the wrecker had available after Mal Gleeson backed into us at the speedway.

Dad's car.

Getting down there took a while because we were both limping.

By the time we got close it was almost dusk. The car was half in shadow and at first I couldn't see inside.

All I could see was that the front doors were wide open. The engine was running. The bonnet was crumpled against a tree.

Nothing seemed to be slithering over the car. Not on the outside anyway.

'Dad,' I yelled.

'Mum,' yelled Rory.

No answer.

Sobs wanted to come out of my throat. I didn't let them.

Rory handed me a long stick. He was holding one too, like a spear. 'Thanks,' I said, grateful that even cretins have good ideas sometimes.

We looked at each other, then crept towards the car.

Inside the car was the most revolting thing I'd ever seen.

Splattered over the seats, floor, dashboard and roof.
Lamb stew.

Holding our breath, we prodded the lumps of meat
and the globs of soggy potato and the dripping upholstery
with our spears.

No slobberers.

And no Dad and Eileen.

SIX

They must be dead. Mum and Jack.

That's all I could think when I saw the mangled car.
I had to look in that car – but what would I find?

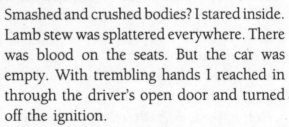

Smashed and crushed bodies? I stared inside.
Lamb stew was splattered everywhere. There
was blood on the seats. But the car was
empty. With trembling hands I reached in
through the driver's open door and turned
off the ignition.

Frantically Dawn and I started to search
through the bushes. My legs didn't want to
go but I forced them forwards. I didn't

know what we were going to find. It could have been the most awful thing ever. Your worst nightmare.

No. Don't think it. Put it out of your mind. Mum and Jack might be lying there under the bushes. Scared but okay. Smiling and glad to see us. That's what I told myself anyway. That's what I hoped for.

We ran from bush to bush shouting wildly.

'Mum.'

'Dad.'

'Mum.'

'Dad.'

'Mum.'

'Dad.'

In the end I didn't find my worst nightmare. I found my second worst.

They were gone.

'Murderer,' screamed Dawn. 'You put those stinking worms in the stew. They must have come out. Like on the bike. And now what's happened. They probably – '

'Stop,' I yelled. 'Stop, stop, stop.' I put my hands over my ears. I didn't want to hear the next bit. I was trying not to think about the sucked-out fish. And my mouse. And the magpie.

'They're still alive,' I said, hoping – oh, hoping so badly that I was right.

'How do you know?' Dawn shrieked.

My voice came out in a scratchy whisper. 'No skins.'

Dawn fell silent.

RORY

Everything fell silent.

In the surrounding bush there was not a sound. Not the croak of a frog or the call of a bird. Not the rub of a cricket's legs. Not even the sound of a leaf falling to the rocky ground.

The whole forest was frozen with terror.

We whispered. Not knowing why.

'I'm going to the cops,' said Dawn.

'No,' I hissed. 'I think my dad's involved with this.'

'What's he got to do with it?' she said. 'That wasn't him back in town.'

I couldn't tell her about the worm spelling out Dad's name. I just couldn't. So I said nothing.

Dawn and I faced each other in the silent twilight.

Until . . .

A sound. Far off. A soft, fearful whooshing. Coming from somewhere off to the left. A slushing, slurping noise. Like a hose in reverse. Sucking up water.

A cold shiver ran over my skin. We stared at each other for a fraction of a second. And then, trying not to scream, we both started scrambling up to the road the way we had come.

We reached the road and started to run downhill. If only a car would come.

My bad leg slowed me down and Dawn disappeared round a bend. She could run so much faster than me even with her bruised leg. Why didn't she wait? Did she hate me that much?

A sudden shriek filled the air. Oh no. I didn't want Dawn for a step-sister, but right then, in the middle of all that terror, she was a million times better than no one.

I rounded the corner and found her staring at a flat dead skin on the road.

'A possum,' Dawn yelled.

'Flattened by a car,' I panted hopefully.

'I wish,' said Dawn.

We crouched down over the possum. It was still warm. No bones or innards. Not even any blood. Slobberers.

We stared down the road into the growing darkness. 'They must be close,' I gasped.

The slurping, slushing, sucking was growing louder, ahead of us and behind us.

'There's only one way to go,' I yelled. 'Down there.' I plunged off the road and into the dense bush. Dawn crashed behind me without a word.

Maybe we would shake them off. Maybe they would rush past our trail and down the road. That was the hope that filled my mind as night began to fall. That was the hope that kept me going. Down, down, down. Clambering over logs. Stumbling. Bleeding from grazed knees and elbows.

Slurp, slurp, slurp.

Oh no. They hadn't rushed past. They hadn't been fooled. They were somewhere behind us now, not far back in the darkness. Loose, wet tongues slithering into every crack and crevice. Following our trail like boneless bloodhounds. Dragging their hungry bellies over the ground.

Fear. Fear was numb inside me like a lump of ice. I could tell by the growing noise of the slurps that the slobberers were getting closer.

There were so many things to think about. So many questions. But only one that really mattered at that moment.

How were we going to escape?

We ran and jumped and fell. But all the time, in the gum trees, somewhere behind, always within earshot, *slobber, slobber, slobber. Slurp, slurp, slurp.*

'They're going to catch us,' said Dawn. She grasped her spear tightly. 'We'll have to fight them.'

'Don't be mad,' I said. 'You saw that sucked-out possum. How would you like – ?' In the moonlight I saw her face crumple and I stopped in mid-sentence.

'Maybe they won't attack in the night,' she said.

I gave a snort. 'I don't think so,' I said. 'Look.'

Not far behind, dozens of glowing green specks blinked through the black trees.

Eyes.

Eyes were seeking us out. The slobberers could see in the dark. I was sure of it.

We crashed onwards in blind panic. My sides ached and my bad leg was hurting. Ever since Dawn's mum had driven me and that bus into the river I couldn't walk or run properly. My knee was killing me.

But it wasn't far to the bottom of the gully. I had a

plan. Desperate, but it might work. Dawn was stronger. Dawn was bigger. Dawn was faster. But I was smarter. That's what I thought at the time anyway.

'There,' I said as we burst out of the trees. 'The river. We must be close to the Wilsons' jetty.'

We stumbled along the river bank.

There it was. A small dinghy tied up to a tree. With not so much as a word to each other we jumped in. Dawn untied the rope without even being asked and I pushed us into the centre of the stream. The bank was just dark shadows. Not even a glimmer of moonlight.

But through the gloom it was not hard to see our nightmare. Green glowing eyes. Dozens of them. Staring out into the river from the receding bank.

The current was strong and we drifted downstream quickly. The eyes blinked, growing smaller as we moved away. Soon they were only little pinpricks. Like a bank of unfriendly glow-worms in the dark.

Relief flooded through me. We were leaving the slobberers behind. 'You know what?' I screamed into the night. 'You guys suck.' I laughed hoarsely.

Dawn started to laugh with me. Hysterical laughter.

At that very moment the eyes went out. Yes, I swear it was the exact moment we laughed. Just as if someone had thrown a switch.

'We'll call the cops,' said Dawn. 'They'll get the army. They'll wipe them out with flame-throwers or snail-killer or something.'

This time I said nothing about Dad and the cops. We

were safe for now but I had a feeling that the slobberers or the apple-man or some other nameless thing was not going to let us tell anyone. I wondered what lay ahead. Waiting in the dark.

'They might be able to swim,' I said.

'Then why didn't they jump into the river after us?'

'Maybe they're going to cut us off somewhere.'

We both shuddered.

'There must be somewhere we can hide,' I said. 'The water will be covering our trail.'

Dawn didn't answer. She was funny like that. Sometimes it was really hard to know what was going on in her weird mind. She was probably thinking everything was my fault.

As we drifted silently in the darkness my thoughts turned to Dad. He gave me that apple-man.

Was Dad behind all this? Was he a crook? Why did he and Mum bust up? Just because he had gone off didn't mean he'd stopped loving me. Did it?

I didn't care. I loved him. He was still my dad no matter what he might have done. He couldn't have sent the slobberers. Not to suck out his own son. Dad's face floated into my mind. His kind, laughing face. The one that watched me so proudly when I rode my dirt bike. The one who always called me mate and told weird jokes.

I missed him.

I thought about how Mum had taken all of Dad's photos out of the family album. She said she didn't want to hurt Jack's feelings. But what about mine? All I had to remind me of Dad was my little apple-man in my pocket. And the slobberers. Had they been part of Dad's present? Nah, they couldn't be. They killed animals. They were dangerous.

Why had Dad gone, leaving just me and Mum?

I didn't even have *her* to myself. She had fallen in love with Jack. Then I really only had half a mum.

And now I had no mum at all. She was gone. Dead for all I knew. Unless I could find her.

And how could I do that? I was only a boy.

I cried silently and hoped that Dawn couldn't see my tears in the night.

SEVEN

I cried silently and hoped that Rory couldn't see my tears in the night.

Oh, Dad. Please. Not you too.

If Dad was dead, there was just me.

Well, as good as.

I tried to imagine life with Gramps and Worm Boy.

DAWN

One person who didn't know which planet I was on and one who didn't care.

As I stared at the black water swirling round the little boat, another awful thought wormed its way into my guts.

Perhaps we were cursed. A horrible family curse that Mum and Dad didn't know anything about. Perhaps one of our ancestors did something really bad and as a result two wonderful people had to die in the prime of life. With all their teeth. With hardly any wrinkles. With sparkling eyes that could spot me pinching a biscuit from a hundred metres . . .

I made myself stop.

Don't give up, that was Dad's motto. In my head I could hear him. 'Don't give up till you've searched the back paddock.' It was an old farmer's saying he used when a mob of sheep or a can-opener went missing.

Don't worry, Dad, I said silently. I'll find you if I have to search every back paddock in Australia.

'Aaghhh!'

Worm Boy was yelling.

Our boat was drifting close to the river bank. Overhanging branches were nearly taking our heads off.

'Push,' he shouted.

We rammed the oars into the roots and heaved ourselves back out into the main current. Rory peered anxiously into the dark trees.

'That was close,' he panted. 'We're lucky we didn't end up with a boat full of slobberers.'

He looked so small and frail and anxious sitting there, eyes big in the moonlight. Suddenly I wanted to make him feel better.

'Don't be a dope,' I said. 'We're miles downstream. Slobberers can't travel that fast.'

Oh, how wrong I was.

How very very dead wrong.

Even as I was pretending to roll my eyes at Worm Boy's dopeyness, I saw the green specks of light overhead.

Not in the trees.

In the black sky.

I must have gasped. Rory saw them too. We stared up, gripping the sides of the boat.

'They're just stars,' I said. 'They just look green 'cos of atmospheric conditions.'

I wanted to believe it, but my neck was killing me and I would have crawled over sheep's poo for a curried-egg sandwich.

'They're moving,' croaked Rory. 'I think they're watching us.'

'As if,' I said. 'Slobberers can't fly.'

Wrong again.

Something splashed into the water.

I gripped my oar as hard as my shaking hands would let me, ready to make slobberer schnitzel. But it wasn't a green-eyed slime-slug floating next to the boat.

It was a fruit bat.

I turned it over with my oar.

A big dead fruit bat without a bone or blood vessel in its flat floppy carcass.

We stared at it.

More splashes further down the river.

Suddenly I heard wings beating overhead and realised what was going on. 'The slobberers are flying in on bats,' I yelled, 'and sucking them dry when they want to come down.'

We looked at each other, then peered frantically into the black water. There they were. Slimy torpedoes with green eyes. Speeding away from us.

'Why aren't they attacking?' said Rory.

'Dunno,' I said. 'They must have another plan.' Up ahead, more splashes.

Rory groaned. 'There's a bridge before we reach town.'

'So?' I said.

'So have you ever seen a spider drop off a roof?'

My guts clenched. We rounded a bend. In the distance, friendly street lights. I went weak with relief. Then I saw it. Spanning the river ahead. An arc of green lights. A miniature Sydney Harbour Bridge at night.

'Row,' screamed Rory. 'Row for the bank.'

We thrashed the water with our oars. When the boat rammed into the bank we leapt out, slipping on mud and grabbing at tree trunks.

Tree trunks supporting a canopy of dark branches.

And an army of evil green eyes.

'Run,' yelled Rory.

'Where to?' I shouted as we ploughed through dry grass.

Behind us I could hear the horrible thud, thud, thud of soft things hitting the ground.

'Dunno,' shouted Rory. 'Yes I do.' He veered to our left, towards Dead Cow Clearing. 'The bus. The slobberers are terrified of the bus.'

I knew how they felt. For several hours I'd been feeling sick every time I thought about Mum's shoe on the bus. I kept having a crazy thought. Drunk people lost their shoe. Mad people. What if the things people said about Mum and the accident were true?

Now, as the jagged iron fence of the wrecker's yard loomed out of the darkness, I knew I couldn't go back on that bus.

'Not the bus,' I pleaded, 'Somewhere else.'

'There isn't anywhere else,' yelled Rory, wide-eyed and frantic.

'There's a caretaker at night,' I said. 'He might have a gun.'

'He's even older than Gramps. He'll think we're burglars and blow our heads off.'

We reached the fence. I glanced back across the moonlit paddock. Green eyes were coming. Slimy bodies hissing over the long dry grass. Tongues slobbering.

I froze.

They were getting bigger.

I stared, terror thudding in my head at their swollen bodies.

'Okay,' I whispered desperately. 'The bus.'

I hurried along the fence, Rory close behind. I tried

not to look at the bus standing wrecked and rusting in the yard.

We reached my secret entrance.

'Hurry,' said Rory. 'They're getting closer.'

I couldn't hurry. I couldn't even move. The hole in the fence had gone. Someone had nailed a sheet of iron over it.

There was no way in.

EIGHT

There was no way in to the wrecker's yard. The fence was just too high.

Dawn and I searched around desperately for something – anything that might get us over the top. 'Ah ha,' I shouted. 'Just the thing. A big oil drum.'

I rolled it over to the fence and stood it up on its end. 'You first,' I managed to gasp.

They were coming. They were coming. The slobberers were coming. And they were bigger than ever. Maybe the darkness would hide us. Maybe they would lose our trail. Maybe their horrible, horrible tongues would not pick up our scent.

Maybe.

The top of the fence had been cut to form sharp points. Dawn scrambled onto the drum and pulled the sleeves of her jumper down over her hands. Then she hoisted herself over the razor points in one bound. I heard her land on the other side of the fence. How did she do that? She was so fit.

I couldn't even get onto the oil drum. It rocked from side to side every time I tried to haul myself up.

Slurp, slurp, slurp.

'Aagh. Someone help. Someone come. Anyone.'

'Rory, hurry up.' Dawn's urgent whisper seemed like thunder in my ears.

'Shhh,' I said. 'They'll hear you.' Finally I managed to get onto the drum. I knelt there on my knocking knees. The drum trembled, threatening to upend itself and me onto the hard ground. Carefully I rose to my feet. I pulled my sleeves down over my fingers and gingerly felt the sharp edges of the iron fence.

Slurp, slurp, slurp.

'Aw, gees. Aaghh . . .' The drum skidded off beneath me leaving me dangling by my hands. The steel points of the fence cut through my sweater, scraping the skin off my fingers. I hauled myself up and felt the jagged points tear along my legs. Blood spilled down the fence in a sticky trail.

Slurp, slurp, slurp.

I dropped to the ground inside the wrecker's yard, a bloody bundle of terror spread-eagled on the oily ground. I groaned in pain as I saw Dawn run towards the bus.

Over in his little office the caretaker looked up and scowled. I could see his face glowing dimly in the light of a desk lamp. His dog was curled up by the open door. It gave a low growl and lifted its head.

'My fingers,' I groaned. I held up my cut hands and stared in horror at the blood pouring down my arm. The pain was terrible.

I looked down at my knee. Something inside me seemed to die. Suddenly I didn't care any more. I was like a wounded soldier wanting to be put out of his misery by a friend's bullet.

It was all too much, the running, the pain, the terror. Let them come. Let them come.

I didn't care any more.

Maybe I was slipping into unconsciousness. Just like after the bus crashed. Then I felt something soft and soothing wipe the blood from my left hand. Like a nurse gently wiping a patient's wound. For a second I couldn't take it in. A long, wet, veined tongue slid through a hole in the iron fence. It slithered over my injured fingers, licking up the blood.

A slobberer's tongue. A horrible blue tongue was feasting, slurping, sliming over me. It slid up and touched my face.

I froze. I couldn't move. On the other side of the fence

I heard horrible gobbling squeals as the other monsters fought over the bloody trail I had left behind on the fence.

'Aagh.' I tore my hand away and fled after Dawn towards the bus. I snatched a glance over my shoulder. Hideous slobbering tongues, like the tentacles of a monstrous sea anemone, were waving over the top of the fence. Some were pausing at the sharp points. Some were even licking the patches of blood on the spikes.

Aarf, aarf, aarf. The caretaker's dog had sensed us. He stood barking, staring into the gloom.

Dawn had reached the bus. 'Rory,' she called. 'I can't go back in there . . .'

'You have to,' I yelled.

Dawn looked over her shoulder. The dog charged towards her. Its lips pulled back over terrible teeth. Growling and howling it leapt. With a scream Dawn ran into the darkness. But the dog wasn't after her. It hurled itself at the gate, springing furiously up at the blue-veined, slithering tongues of the slobberers.

I started up the steps and stumbled. There was something there. Something alive – wedged on the step and blocking the door. A sheep. A stupid sheep. I grabbed it wildly and pulled. My cut finger went right up its wet nose. Oh yuck, yuck, yuck.

As I wrestled with the sheep the caretaker ran out to see what the barking was about. His pot belly jiggled up and down as he lurched across the compound. I stared out from the steps. The moon shone on my face. The caretaker stared right at me and carried on. He must have seen me. But he ran right past. And I couldn't see Dawn anywhere.

The sheep gave one loud baa and scampered off into the night.

Suddenly the gate fell and an army of enormous slobberers poured into the yard. The first slobberer lunged forward and closed its mouth over the dog's jaws. It shoved its tongue straight down the poor animal's throat. There was a horrible sucking noise like the sound a bath makes as the last of the water drains out. Then the dog collapsed, boneless on the wet ground. It shook for a moment, still alive. A furry handbag of jelly. Its legs no more than quivering ropes.

The dog's eyes rolled for a second and then closed. There was a gurgle and it lay still.

I gave a shudder. For the dog's sake I hoped it was dead.

The caretaker fled howling into the night. Most of the slobberers ignored him. They had other prey. It was me they wanted. But one big grey brute turned and rumbled after the caretaker. It looked like a seal galloping forward into battle.

In the darkness there was a yell. Then silence.

The other slobberers surged in my direction. Fighting with their tongues for the red drops I had left behind me.

They tasted the trail and followed.

Was there anything that could help me? Anything at

all? The only thing I had with me was the apple-man. Squashed down in my pocket. With bleeding fingers I pulled him out and stared at him.

My head swam. It felt as if it was filled with a million bees.

I scrambled into the bus and collapsed.

I was alone.

Outside, somewhere in the darkness, I heard a girl scream . . .

Book Two

BATTERING RAMS

ONE

It was night. I was miles from home in a lonely wrecker's yard. Next to me was a bus with the only remaining part of my mother in it. Giant slobbering worms were straining at the battered yard gate, desperate to suck out my bones.

And what was it that made me run blindly into the darkness in terror?

A dog.

Dawn the chicken, that's what Rory would have called me. Well he'd have been wrong.

The dog was a killer. It had a savage snarl and huge teeth. Its saliva had bubbles in it, not from eating soap, from being so vicious. When it charged at me with its huge jagged mouth wide open, I ran.

Scary broken-down farm equipment loomed out of the darkness. I crashed into something, scraping my arm on rusty metal. I kept running until I tripped and sprawled painfully in the dirt. I scrambled up, heart thumping, expecting to see dog-food-stained teeth

coming for my throat at any second.

But the dog was over by the gate, leaping up at the slithering tongues of the giant worms. My heart slowed down to very fast. The dog hadn't been going for me, it had been going for the slobberers.

There was enough moonlight for me to see my hands trembling with relief.

I heard feet scampering towards me.

'Rory,' I tried to yell, but all that came out of my parched throat was a croak.

I strained to see if it was Rory. He was about as hopeless a step-brother as you could get, but at that moment I really wanted it to be him.

It wasn't. It was a sheep.

We looked at each other, startled. Then the sheep grinned.

I blinked. Was I imagining it? Had terror scrambled my brain? Sheep didn't grin.

Get real, I told myself. It's just got wind.

A screech of twisting metal rang out across the yard and the sheep bolted. I turned towards the sound. The gate was slowly groaning inwards. Then it fell.

A sea of slobberers poured in.

I stood frozen with terror. I knew they'd been growing, but I was shocked to see how big they were. Most of them were fatter than the sheep. In the moonlight they looked like angry, slurping vacuum cleaners without the wheels.

I didn't want to see what they did to the dog, but I

was too slow turning away. The horrible image burned into my brain and I felt sick. No dog deserved that, not even a vicious one. No step-brother did either.

'Rory,' I tried to scream, but my vocal cords were in shock and all I could do was squeak.

I looked frantically over at where I'd last seen him. That part of the yard was alive with slobberers. Green eyes glinting. Wet tongues sliming.

A sob forced its way out of my throat.

The slobberers started moving towards me.

As I turned and began running again, I heard other running feet nearby.

Thank God. Rory was okay.

I sprinted in the same direction. Soon I could see the shape of a figure up ahead. I tried to yell but I had no breath.

Neither did the running figure. He was wheezing and gasping. His white hair was flopping. His pot belly was rising and falling with each step.

My guts fell too. It wasn't Rory. It was the old caretaker.

'Wait,' I yelled, sucking in air. 'Rory's back there. You've got to help.'

The caretaker lumbered on. I forced my legs to go faster and caught him at his car door as he fumbled with his keys.

'Please,' I gasped. 'Please help.'

He turned, saw me, and gave a yell.

'Arghhh.'

I'd never had an adult yell at me in fear before, and

for a couple of seconds I didn't know what to say.

Then I did. 'You're our only hope,' I pleaded. 'My mum's dead, and Rory's dad's nicked off, and my dad and Rory's mum have had an accident on their honeymoon and disappeared and they could be dead too.'

Panting, I waited for him to digest this and then get some really high-powered slobberer-strength guns out of his boot.

Instead he glared at me.

'I know you're not real,' he said, and blew a raspberry at me.

I was stunned. But I didn't have time to be stunned for long. 'I *am* real,' I said, and kicked him in the ankle to prove it.

He winced and rubbed his ankle with his other foot.

'That wasn't real either,' he said, scowling. 'Lousy doctor. What's the point of heart pills if they make you see stuff and get palpitations.'

He hurled a bottle of tablets into the darkness. Then he got into his car, slammed the door and started the engine.

'Wait,' I begged. 'We're just two kids. Probably only one now.'

The caretaker spun his tyres in the dirt and the car took off, flattening a second rusty iron gate and skidding over it in a cloud of tyre smoke.

As I watched his rear lights getting smaller in the darkness, I suddenly felt small too. And very alone. Suddenly I wanted Mum and Dad, both of them, with their arms round me and their soft voices in my ears. I crouched in the dirt and squeezed my eyes tight so the tears wouldn't sting so much.

At first I thought the sound of mucus bubbling was me crying. Then I opened my eyes and saw it wasn't.

A slobberer, the biggest of the lot, was writhing slowly about a car's length away from me. Its green eyes were fixed on mine and I could see the blue veins in its slithering, hungry tongue.

I screamed.

The slobberer's eyes glowed brighter and it slimed towards me like a big vinyl bag on a luggage carousel with all its shampoo and moisturiser oozing out.

I stepped back and scraped my leg on something. A steel fence post sticking out of a pile of scrap. I grabbed it and raised it above my head and closed my eyes and swung it down onto the slobberer with all my strength.

It was a shock.

I expected a squish and what I got was a thunk. The slobberer was solid muscle. The fence post vibrated and so did my hands and arms and shoulders and major internal organs.

I opened my eyes.

The fence post was bent.

The slobberer was slithering backwards. Then it stopped, shuddered and suddenly went sloppy like liver when you cut open the plastic bag.

I didn't take my eyes off it.

After a bit I chucked a metal bolt at it. The bolt sort

of sunk in. The slobberer didn't move. Its eyes were grey.

I peered over at the other side of the yard. The rusty hulk of the bus was completely surrounded by slurping, tongue-waving slobberers.

Mum's bus.

Suddenly my fingers weren't numb any more. Blood tingled through my body. I thought of Dad, my only remaining parent, who was probably next on the slobberers' menu. One scrawny kid and a dog wouldn't keep them going for long.

I gripped my fence post and walked slowly towards the slobberers.

Okay, there were heaps of them. Okay, there was only one of me.

But now I was as angry as they were.

TWO

As the slobberers poured into the wrecker's yard, I slammed the door in a panic and stared out of the bus window with wide, terrified eyes. They were still sucking their way after me – looking for a meal. Ever since I'd cut my hand on the fence trying to escape them, they'd followed the bloody trail I'd left behind me.

A few metres from the bus they suddenly stopped. They sniffed and sucked at the air, their green eyes glowing in the dark of the wrecker's yard as they stared in hatred.

At first I thought they were going to charge. But no. Something held them back. They seemed frightened of the bus, but not to the point of giving up. Instead of charging they slid and slithered around each other like piles of slime-filled garbage bags. Finally they surrounded the bus. I was trapped.

Why didn't they come for me?

I looked around. The shoe. Dawn's mother's shoe. She had died in that bus. And I had been there. But I couldn't remember what had happened. I had tried to remember a thousand times. But the memory of it was gone. Knocked out by the crash.

Had Dawn's mum been drunk? Had she crashed the bus on purpose like some people thought but didn't like to say? I had *her* to thank for my limp and my twisted leg. If it wasn't for her I'd have been able to run faster than Dawn. If she hadn't died, Dawn wouldn't be my step-sister. My mum would still be married to Dad. And we all would have been happy. It was all Louise's fault.

The shoe made me angry. It was a rotting reminder of Dawn's mum and how she had crashed the bus. With me in it.

I picked up the worn shoe and held it in front of my eyes.

Outside in the night I heard a huge swooshing noise. Almost as if a hundred mouths had sucked in breath at the same time. It was the slobberers. They were blinking their eyes and sighing.

They didn't seem to like the shoe either.

Without thinking I ran over to the door and threw the shoe out like a hand grenade. 'Cop that,' I yelled.

The shoe bounced right through a bunch of slobberers and landed next to the remains of a clapped-out Land Rover. The slobberers squealed and wriggled away backwards. I laughed hysterically to myself. They didn't like it. The shoe had them worried.

Except for one little group that had other problems.

They were stretched out in the shadows. Groaning. Almost as if they were sick. The very sound of their wailing sent waves of revulsion through my shaking body.

I looked around the bus. There was no way out. Sunrise was a long way off. And so was Dawn.

If she was still alive.

I was alone. Outside were the slobberers. And inside – terrors as yet unknown.

I slumped down onto the floor and sunk my head into my hands. My cut fingers ached and throbbed. I felt as if I had an awful bout of the flu. The inside of the bus seemed to warp and bend. Strange things were happening.

My whole body was racked with wild, uncontrollable shaking.

I turned to my little apple-man for comfort as I had done many times before. The way a child turns to a teddy bear in the darkness of the night.

I stared down at him and tried to focus. My father's last gift. But this time there was no comfort. Was it my eyes, or was my apple-man changing?

Yes, he was changing. Slowly at first so that I couldn't quite make out what was happening. Then faster.

His face began to squirm and boil. It warped and bubbled and re-formed itself. The eyes became evil slits. Sharp, cruel teeth erupted from its lips. Pointed ears sprouted from the head. The mouth opened and a mocking, blue, forked tongue flickered out.

Oh, horror of horrors. Something else. Worse. Oh, so much worse.

A whining, high-pitched, cackling laugh came from its mouth. Like a tortured chainsaw squeal, the sound filled the air.

The contorted head began to swell, larger and larger, until it was the size of a football. *Whang, sploosh, cackle*. The head exploded and filled the bus with the stench of a thousand farts.

Then there was nothing left except a dry skin which began to smoke and burn.

Oh, no, no, no. I dropped the shredded remains of the apple-man to the floor and screamed.

Was there no end to this nightmare?

Everything was changing. Even in the moonlit shadows I could tell that the bus had more sick secrets to tell. The seats were no longer torn and cracked. And the smashed speedometer now had a sparkling new face. I stared out through the windscreen. The tree that had grown out of the bonnet was still there. But it was smaller. Not broken or pruned. Just smaller.

I stared at it. It was shrinking. Slowly, slowly, slowly, the tree was shrinking.

'It's un-growing,' I gasped to myself.

I heard something above me and looked up. A moth buzzed at enormous speed around my head. So fast that I could hardly see it.

I looked down. Beside me on the floor a tiny lizard scampered quickly away and into a small rust hole. Backwards.

I shook my head in disbelief. 'What the heck is going on?' I yelled.

No one answered. There *was* no one.

On the wall of the bus a patch of rust was disappearing and being replaced by red paint. A faded poster was growing brighter and renewing itself. The photo of a doctor stared down. Underneath in bold letters it said ARE YOU SICK? WE'RE HERE TO HELP.

I looked along the aisle. There was no one there. No one to help me.

The goat's skeleton still sat in the seat where it had died. But now it was different. Its bones were no longer bleached. And small pieces of dried flesh and skin clung to some of the ribs.

I stared at it with widening eyes. Last time I was there, those bones were as dry and smooth as old wood. I backed away – unable to even scream.

Another foul odour started to fill the air. A disgusting, dead-flesh smell. My eyes watered and my stomach heaved as the revolting smell choked the inside of the bus. I pinched my nose with my fingers and ran to a broken window and started to gulp in fresh air.

I only managed a couple of gasps. The shattered window un-shattered. Pieces of broken glass flew up from the floor and from the ground outside. In an instant the window was whole and re-made. I fell back into a seat and began to scream and scream and scream.

Every cell in my body begged me to leave that bus. That stinking jail. That terrible refuge. Making itself new.

I stared at the goat. I couldn't take my eyes away from the skeleton as flesh slowly re-formed on the bones.

Slobberers. An un-rotting goat. A window re-made. A bus becoming new.

Terrible, terrible, terrible.

But all made small next to the one sight which had burned itself into my frenzied mind. A vision which would remain with me for ever. Like the worm spelling *Karl* in my bedroom . . .

The face . . . The wicked face on the apple-man when it exploded . . .

Had been the face of my father.

THREE

Keep a clear head, I told myself as I strode across the wrecker's yard. You need a clear head when you're going to beat a hundred slobberers to death with a steel fence post.

My head wouldn't listen. It kept filling up with Dad. And how I didn't know if I was ever going to see him again.

That thought should have made me even angrier. Even more determined to pulp the slobberers. It didn't. It just made me sadder.

As I got closer to them I felt my anger draining away. My legs started to feel heavy. So did the steel fence post.

Then I realised the dopeyness of what I was trying to do. One kid, forty-eight kilos in her boots. A hundred assorted slobberers, eighteen thousand kilos not including the slime.

How many could I kill before they sucked out *my* bones?

Fifty?

Twenty-eight?

Three?

And what if Dad *was* still alive? How'd he feel coming along afterwards with the army and finding me tossed onto the roof of the bus, just an empty bag of skin?

Suddenly my whole body started shaking and I wondered if I could make it to the gate before the slobberers attacked.

I looked at them sprawled around the bus in the moonlight. Then I stared. They weren't moving. Not even their eyes. They looked like they were asleep. Why not? I thought. Maggots sleep.

Then I had another thought. What if Rory was in the bus? Cowering in there now, too terrified to come out? Waiting for me to rescue him?

I took a deep breath.

I didn't want him in my life but I couldn't leave him to die.

Perhaps I could make it. Perhaps I could get to the bus if I crept really quietly. Making sure I didn't kick any scrap metal or tread on any tongues.

I gripped my fence post tighter and tried to spot a clear path between the dozing slobberers.

Then I saw it. Lying next to the axle of a wrecked four-wheel drive. Slobberers all around it. Scuffed and mouldy and dirty but unmistakeable.

Mum's shoe.

My stomach lurched.

The last time I'd seen it, it had been on the bus. Under the driver's seat. Right where she died.

How did it get out here?

The slobberers must have slimed onto the bus and

dragged it off, hoping there were human bones in it.

I shuddered at the thought of filthy slobberers squabbling over Mum's shoe. Well, they weren't having it any more. If Dad was dead, it was the last remaining bit of both my parents and it was mine.

Heart pounding, I started picking my way between the slobberers.

Closer.

Closer.

Please, I silently begged the giant grubs. Don't be light sleepers.

Closer.

Closer.

Got it.

I pressed Mum's shoe to my chest and squeezed my neck muscles really hard to stop a sob coming out. It wasn't easy. For a second it was like Mum was there with me but I knew she wasn't and that was almost more than I could bear.

Then I remembered I was surrounded by slobberers.

I pulled myself together. But only for a second. A horrible thought hit me. This was what it must have been like for Rory when the slobberers flooded into the yard. All around him like this. Except worse. Charging at him, slurping, ravenous.

That's when I knew Rory must be dead. I started shaking again and I had to squeeze my neck muscles as hard as I could. I hoped it had been even quicker for Rory than it had been for the dog.

Then I concentrated on getting out of there. The longer I hung around being sad and wobbly, the more chance I'd wake up the slobberers.

Halfway back they woke up anyway. Or at least I thought they had. I caught a glimpse of movement. My heart stopped. Movement all around me. My head spun. Then I realised it wasn't bodies that were moving, it was skin.

While the slobberers slept, their skin was starting to fester and bubble like cream cheese past its use-by date.

I hurried on, trying not to look. What was happening? Perhaps it was just because they were adults. Eileen always complained that she got dry painful skin at night.

I stepped past the last slobberer, hoping desperately it wouldn't wake up and be as grumpy as Eileen was in the mornings.

Then I ran for the gate.

My plan was to get back to town and find a phone and raise the alarm and the armed forces of several nations.

In the middle of Dead Cow Clearing another awful thought hit me. The slobberers on the bridge over the river. What if they weren't all sleeping and having skin problems? What if some were guarding the roads into town?

I decided to go cross-country and head into town through the paddocks behind Agnelli's dairy.

It wasn't easy, going bush at night. In less than an hour I was scratched and sore and exhausted. I wasn't even sure I was going in the right direction. Dad had taught me to use the stars, but now the clouds kept getting in the way.

I hung onto my fence post just in case. At about three a.m. I was glad I had. I'd just painfully unhooked myself from a thorn bush when I saw movement ahead in the gloom.

I froze.

Several slobberer-sized shapes were watching me.

Then a cloud shifted off the moon and I saw it was only a mob of sheep. They had weird expressions on their faces, just like the one in the wrecker's yard. My neck prickled. Must be an imported breed, I thought, with unusual jaw bones.

'Dunno why you're grinning,' I said loudly. 'You won't find any feed here under the trees.'

The sheep turned and trotted off. Then stopped and looked back at me. Then trotted some more. Then looked back again.

I had the crazy thought that they wanted me to follow them. It was my turn to grin. Dopey sheep. But I didn't grin for long. Suddenly they all came back and surrounded me and several started butting me behind the knees. When I tried to free myself they closed in tighter. Then they started herding me towards an open paddock.

As the shock wore off I tried to stay calm. Relax, my desperately tired brain told my desperately tired body. You're being rescued by a mob of sheep. They're grateful for the considerate way Dad always warms the shears first.

After a fair bit of herding I saw the dark shape of a building and recognised where the sheep had brought me.

The Piggot place. Ernie Piggot had tried to run sheep too far up Bald Mountain and he'd gone broke and got into a big fight with the bank. Eileen had done heaps of courier trips out to him with legal documents before he'd got evicted.

Dad had told me that when Ernie had gone he'd left the phone on with a rude answering-machine message to the bank. When I saw it was his place my heart gave an exhausted thump of joy. 'Thanks, guys,' I said to the sheep.

The door was open. I blundered around in the dark. Finally I found the phone socket.

No phone.

I was too tired to cry. I just lay down on the bare boards with the fence post next to me. I hugged Mum's shoe and thought how normal my life had been until twelve hours ago and how sad and weird and scary it was now.

As I fell asleep I thought I heard a strange sound from outside. No, it couldn't be. Sheep didn't laugh.

FOUR

Dad, Dad, Dad. Why did I see your face just before the apple-man exploded? And why was it twisted and horrible and ugly?

'You don't look like that. You don't, you don't, you don't,' I screamed to myself.

I had no time to figure it out. Another horror was about to start. The retreat of the flies.

In they flew. Buzzing in reverse gear. Settling like a black, boiling blanket near the rotting flesh of the goat.

Why was this bus set on rewind? Was it really happening? Or was I mad?

I couldn't tear my eyes away from the goat. Now, where the flies had been there was a mass of pale-coloured things. A moving mass.

My head hurt terribly. I found it hard to focus my eyes. What was going on?

No, no, no, no, no. The pupae were slowly turning back into maggots. Hungry maggots. Wriggling towards the rotting body of the goat.

At first there were just a few. Then a couple of dozen. Then hundreds. And thousands. And millions. They were centimetres deep crawling right across the floor. Squirming and squiggling by the barrow-load.

As they seethed on the carcass of the goat, it filled with more and more rotting flesh. The maggots were disgorging, not eating their meal – but un-eating it.

I gagged and retched as the foul stench filled the air. I had to get out. I threw up on the wall. Gasping in agony I stumbled to the door.

Suddenly I stopped.

I couldn't leave and face the slobberers. Never. And I couldn't stay either. Think, think, think. I pulled my windcheater over my head and blocked out the ghastly sight of the maggots.

Inside my own little black space I stole a second or two and tried to clear my head. For all I knew the waiting slobberers had killed Dawn. And my mum.

Poor Dawn. She didn't seem so bad now. Not now that she was gone. I would have given anything just to have seen her ugly mug again. She would have been someone to talk to. She was a pain in the bum. But she was human. And she was strong. A little reminder of home.

Home. It seemed so far away. Normal. Hamburgers. Cereal. My bed. Milk in the fridge. Arguments about photos and Milo tins.

It seemed so wonderful. So unreal. So distant.

The thought of it gave me a speck of courage and I pulled the windcheater down off my head. Through watering eyes I peered at the great carcass. It stank as much as ever but there weren't as many maggots. Shoot. Was this really happening? Each maggot was being replaced by a small, white egg.

The maggots were going back into their eggs.

Bzzzz. Now what? The number of flies was building up. Oh no. A billion buzzing blowflies blackened the air and filled it with an ear-splitting whine. Flying furiously backwards. The parents of the first lot. The ones that laid the eggs. They were coming back for what they had left behind. Each fly stopped for an instant on the pink flesh and took its eggs, one by one, back into its body. The flies were un-laying their eggs.

The stench was bad. I choked and staggered. I covered my mouth and tried not to breathe in the hideous fumes. My head seemed to float in space. My hand throbbed. But I could still work out what was happening.

The bus and everything in it was being made new. Growing younger. Renewing itself.

The dials. The seats. The dead goat.

They were going back to the way they once were. Before the bus crash.

The goat was now fully fleshed and covered in a white, hairy coat. Flies still buzzed backwards but there were fewer of them. The goat's empty eye sockets seemed to be staring at me. Then, slowly but surely, the sockets began to fill, almost as if some invisible sculptor was re-making them. Dead, black pupils appeared and then the yellowy brown of the eyes.

The smell began to weaken and then it was gone. So were the flies. There was just me and the goat. And my throbbing hand, which was growing more and more painful.

The dead goat seemed to mock me from its seat. I hated that goat. I hated it.

As the hate grew inside me I noticed that a bruise was spreading up my arm. Almost as if the anger was feeding it.

It was a silly thing to do. A stupid, weak thing. But it was all I could think of. I stuck my fingers into the air. 'Nick off,' I yelled.

Oh, why did I say that? Why, why, why? The goat gave a loud bleat, jumped to its feet and ran past me down the aisle backwards. It slipped and skidded and then wriggled bum-first through the door, back the way it must have come when it had entered.

I couldn't believe it. The goat was alive.

But I was nearly dead. With fear. I fell back against the seat and stared around the bus. I was alone. Thank goodness for that. My rotting companion had gone.

The inside of the bus stopped warping and bending and grew still. My head began to clear.

Everything in the bus was back to new. The paintwork was fresh. The vinyl seats were shining. The floor was clean. The steering wheel and instrument panel were in perfect condition. The ignition key was in the lock.

The tree that had been growing through the bonnet had disappeared.

The bus was ready to go. And outside the sun beat down from high in the sky.

One lonely fly circled above my head. Forwards. The backward journey was over.

I heard a footfall on the step outside. Someone was there. Someone was coming. My heart leapt in my chest. Thump-fear. Thump-hope. Thump-fear. Thump-hope. The aching bruise washed up and down my arm like a purple wave on a beach.

The driver's door opened and someone stepped in. Was it Dawn? Was it Dad, come to save me? I couldn't see at first in the glare of the midday sun. It was a human. Oh yes, a person, not a slobberer. Someone else to share the terror. Maybe even someone to make it go away.

I peered more closely. The visitor was wearing a uniform. And shoes that I had seen before.

The bright sunlight made the new arrival into a silhouette against the windscreen. Who was it? I watched the shadowy form sit down in the driver's seat. I stared at those familiar shoes as the left foot depressed the clutch. A gloved hand turned the ignition key and the engine sprang to life. The bus began to rock gently as if it was parked at a bus stop waiting for passengers.

Then the driver turned. And smiled.

I didn't return the smile. I screamed.

The driver was Louise. Dawn's dead mother.

I dreamed I was asleep on a hard wooden floor and someone was shaking me.

Then I woke up and someone *was* shaking me.

'Dawn,' she was saying. 'What are you doing here? You look terrible.'

I blinked in the daylight. A woman was bending over me. A woman I knew.

'Mum,' I screamed.

I staggered to my feet. My neck and back were so stiff from the floor that I could hardly get my arms up to throw them round her, but I managed.

Then I stopped.

It wasn't Mum, it was Eileen.

My guts dropped with disappointment. The kind of disappointment you feel when you think your mum's come back from the dead and then you find it's just the woman your dad's replaced her with.

'What's going on?' Eileen was saying, concerned. 'Is Rory here?'

I stared at her. She had twigs in her hair, lamb stew on her face, and her arm was in a sling made from

Dad's camping shirt.

'Dad,' I gasped. 'Where is he? Is he all right?'

'He's fine,' said Eileen. She sat on the floor with a groan. 'We had an accident yesterday and I was concussed so he went back to town to get help.' She frowned. 'For some reason he didn't come back.'

My heart stopped beating, partly because of what might have happened to Dad, and partly because of what I could see charging through the door behind Eileen.

A sheep.

With a rusty dinner fork in its mouth.

Prongs aimed at Eileen.

I pushed Eileen one way and dived the other. The sheep tried to turn towards Eileen but its hooves couldn't get a grip on the floorboards and it skittered over to the other side of the room. It dropped the fork, sneered at us and ran out the other door.

'What are you doing?' Eileen was shouting. She sat up, holding her hurt arm.

'Sorry,' I said, dazed, not sure if it had really happened. 'A sheep tried to stab you with a fork.' I realised how dopey that sounded. 'It was probably just trying to be playful,' I added uneasily.

Eileen didn't look playful. She took a deep breath. She had the expression she got first thing in the morning if she found there was no coffee.

'Listen,' she growled, standing up. 'I've got a sprained shoulder, badly bruised ribs, I've just spent the night sleeping in a ditch, I walked two hours to use the phone here and it's gone, and I'm not in the mood for stupid games.' She grabbed my arm. 'So why aren't you at home, and where's Rory?'

I gulped. My mouth was dry. How could I tell her? How could I just announce that her son's innards had been sucked out by giant worms and that his skin was probably flapping somewhere in the morning breeze?

I turned away, struggling to find the words and keep the tears in. Then I saw something out of the window. A sheep running across the paddock with an electrical cord in its mouth, dragging a phone and answering machine behind it.

'Look,' I yelled. 'There's the phone.'

We dashed out of the house. The sheep tried to run faster but we soon caught it. As we took the phone the sheep tried to bite us, but we pushed it away. Then we ran back into the house and plugged the phone in.

It didn't work. The whole thing was covered with teeth marks and the cord was half chewed through.

Eileen swore. I stared at the cord and felt dread seeping through my guts. Eileen turned to me.

'Well?' she said.

I knew I couldn't put off telling her any longer. I tried to prepare her for it by starting at the very beginning. The slobberers in the church. In the stew. On her bike.

'Great,' she exploded. 'That's really going to help my courier deliveries, having my bike at the bottom of a dam.'

I couldn't look her in the eye, so I squinted out the

window. Several sheep were struggling across the sunlit front yard, dragging an old garden rake. 'Look,' I whispered in alarm.

'Don't try and change the subject,' snapped Eileen, not taking her eyes off me.

Miserably, I carried on with my story. I told her about finding the car, the boat trip, the airborne slobberers and finally, in a tearful whisper, what had happened at the wrecker's yard.

Eileen listened without saying anything. Then she said a lot.

'I'm disgusted with you, Dawn,' she said angrily. 'Taking my bike and crashing it into a dam is one thing. Coming out with a heap of disgusting and hurtful and ridiculous lies to try and wriggle out of it is ... is ... I'd have expected more of you than that.'

'It's true,' I sobbed. 'It is.'

She looked at me with narrow eyes for what seemed like ages. 'All right,' she said at last. 'Looks like there's only one way to handle this, young lady. We'd better go to Lumley's Wrecker's Yard and have a look at these slobberers of yours.'

'That wouldn't be a good idea,' I whispered.

'Oh, yes it would,' she said. 'Come on.' She strode out of the house.

I grabbed Mum's shoe and hugged it to try and make myself feel better. Then I went through the door after Eileen.

She was glaring at me over her shoulder and yelling

'hurry up' and not seeing that she was stepping on a garden rake lying on the overgrown path. The handle flew up, just missed her head and smashed into the wall of an old shed.

My guts tightened. It was the rake the sheep had been dragging.

Before I could say anything, Eileen grabbed me by the arm and yanked me after her in the direction of the wrecker's yard.

'Step it out,' she said. 'We've got a long walk.'

'Eileen,' I pleaded. 'You don't realise how dangerous the slobberers are.'

'Don't worry,' she replied. 'Nothing gets in my road. I'm a courier.'

Okay, I thought bitterly. Have it your way. You're the adult.

She obviously didn't believe a word I'd told her. So I didn't even bother telling her what I'd just seen behind the old shed.

Four grinning sheep sitting on a tractor.

SIX

Dawn's mum was dead. Yet there she was, sitting in the driver's seat of the bus. Smiling at me. Had she come back to life like the dead goat? Was she a ghost?

There was one thing for sure. Whatever she was I wasn't hanging around to find out. I charged down the aisle of the bus and leapt out after the goat. My feet didn't even touch the steps. I crashed onto the ground and rolled over and over and over. Finally I came to rest next to a pile of old steering wheels in the wrecker's yard.

The sun was starting to peep over the horizon. The first rays of morning scratched their way across the sky. But I had no time for the view. I could think of only one thing. The slobberers.

The slobberers would suck me up for breakfast. I remembered the caretaker's dog and what they had done

to him. I wanted to run but I couldn't get up. I was exhausted, weak and alone. This was it. This was the end of my life.

Now that the moment had come I felt calm. My hand and arm stopped aching. The panic fled from me and my thoughts turned to other things. Actually, if the slobberers sucked me up I would be famous. The adults could get my skin and stuff it. Like Phar Lap, the racehorse.

I would be the boy who gave up his life to the slobberers.

I lay there on the ground next to the clapped-out Land Rover and waited for the slimy tongues to come for me.

I waited.

And waited.

Nothing happened.

Nothing at all. I slowly lifted my head and looked around. The wrecked cars littered the yard like ghostly chariots. The bus rusted away and the tree that grew through its bonnet stood still and silent in the morning mist.

The slobberers had gone. Not a sign of them.

Yes. Gone. My heart leapt and I felt my energy return. I was safe. It was all over.

But where were they? An image of Dawn fleeing through the night filled my mind. Had the slobberers gone after her? Were they hunting her like a pack of hungry seals?

I suddenly felt sad. I had no right to be safe while she was in danger. Okay, she was a pain. But she didn't deserve to die like that. Sucked out into an ugly mat. Even a step-sister didn't deserve to end up like that.

My arm felt warm and the ache fell away completely. Almost as if my thoughts were healing it. But the angry purple bruise was still there.

I stared at the rusting bus. The rusting bus? A few minutes ago it had been covered in fresh paint. Its engine had been running. But now it just sat there on its flat tyres. Battered and broken and wrecked. The motor looked as if it hadn't run for years.

And wait a minute. When I was in the bus the sun outside had been high in the sky. And now it was only just peeping over the hills.

What was going on? The sun can't go backwards. A bus can't be made new again. My fingers began to throb and the wound started to weep.

I wanted to run home. Every nerve in my body was stretched to breaking point. I looked at the bus. What was that on the step? It couldn't be. But it was. The apple-man.

I tried to swallow but my tongue was dry with fear. The apple-man's face had become the face of my father. Horrible and distorted. Then it had exploded. And yet here it was, whole and intact.

Slowly and in a daze I walked back to the bus. I picked up the apple-man and with knocking knees climbed the steps and looked inside. The goat's skeleton sat there, its dry white bones glowing in the red rays of dawn. Dust covered the seats and spider webs barred the broken windows.

There were no maggots. No flies. There was no Louise. Just an empty, decaying cabin of dreams.

Was it a dream? Never.

Nightmare? Maybe.

Had any of this happened at all?

A thought crept into my mind. If it hadn't been a nightmare or a dream what was it? Maybe I was ill. My nervous system might be collapsing. All the pressures of Dad going out of my life and Dawn coming into it could be weakening my brain. Making me see things. Was my step-sister driving me crazy?

I sat there on the steps of the bus in misery.

Think, think, think. Some things might only be happening inside my head. I hit my forehead with my good hand and tried to get my brain back into gear.

Go back over it all. Pick out the bits that are real and the bits that aren't.

Louise – starting up the bus. Dead people don't drive. Maybe she didn't die after all.

The apple-man. Did it explode? No. Because it was still in one piece in my hands.

The shoe. Was there a shoe? I looked around near the Land Rover. No sign of it. There was some dried-up blobs of cow dung on the ground but no shoe. No, there couldn't have been a shoe.

The slobberers. Not one in sight. They must have just been in my head, my insane mind.

Dawn. Was there any such person as Big Bad Dawn? Yes, because she had been at my school since the bubs' class. But her mother mustn't have died. Fantastic. Maybe Dawn's dad Jack wasn't married to my mum. Maybe we were all together still. Me and Mum and Dad. In our old house. Our real house. Yes, yes, yes.

RORY

Oh, someone wake me up. Or take me home.

I looked down at the apple-man and my joy fled. Dad had sent me that apple-man after the bust-up with Mum. Louise *had* died. The step-marriage *had* happened. Dawn *was* my step-sister.

I wandered slowly around the wrecker's yard trying to work out what was real and what wasn't.

The caretaker. He would help me. I made my way over to his little hut and looked inside. His reading lamp was still on but the room was empty. A dog chain and a bowl of dog food lay on the floor. There was no sign of the dog. I felt so lonely and scared.

And my hand had started to hurt again.

My hand. I had cut it climbing over the fence. And . . . A shudder ran down my spine. Slobberers had licked my fingers and sucked the blood. Hadn't they? I wasn't sure about anything any more.

I limped over to the fence. Yes, there were traces of blood on the rusting metal.

The climb over the fence had taken place all right. But the bit in the bus hadn't. Half of the mad things had happened. And half hadn't. Maybe I was only half mad.

The marriage was real. The apple-man was real. And Dawn was real. The blood on the fence was real. But had slobberers licked it or were they invented by my warped mind?

I decided to leave the wrecker's yard for good. It was time to go home. It was time to get help. I needed a shrink to put me on the right track.

As I moved something caught my eye. A dark shadow on the ground. That sent me screaming down the road. It was the flat, empty body of the caretaker's dog.

SEVEN

I had something on my mind all the way back to the wrecker's yard.

Sheep.

I knew sheep pretty well, and I'd never seen them attack a person before. Not with a garden rake. Definitely not with a table fork.

What's going on? I wondered anxiously as I plodded along behind Eileen.

Were the sheep just grouchy because Ernie Piggot had upped and gone and left them?

Or were they out to get us like the slobberers?

A shiver of fear ran through me. I thought about the sheep on the tractor. Could sheep get a tractor started? I told myself to stop being dopey.

Then I realised Eileen had turned and was yelling at me. 'Stop dragging your feet,' she snapped. 'I want to get this charade over with. The sooner we knock this giant worm nonsense on the head, the sooner I can find out what's going on.'

She grabbed me by the arm and I had to trot to keep up with her. Then we both crashed to the ground.

There was a length of fencing wire stretched across the dirt track. As I tripped and fell forward I noticed something glinting in the dust. When my head cleared after the impact I saw what it was.

Glass. Jagged pieces of brown glass. Luckily I hadn't landed on any of them. Neither had Eileen. Having her arm in a sling had made her fall to one side. She lay on the grass verge, swearing.

Then I recognised a torn label on one of the pieces of glass. Sheep dip. We'd been tripped up so we'd cut ourselves on broken sheep-dip bottles.

I sat up in a panic and looked around. Sheep were watching us from each side of the track. I was just in time to see one of them open its mouth and drop an end of the fencing wire.

'Eileen.' My voice was a whisper. 'These sheep are out to get us.'

The sheep grinned menacingly.

'Bulldust,' yelled Eileen, struggling to her feet. She dragged me up. 'It's just kids playing stupid tricks, and if I catch them they'll suffer almost as much as you're going to. Now come on.'

She dragged me along the track. I glanced nervously over my shoulder. The sheep had gone. I was almost disappointed. If they whacked Eileen round the head with a fence post, then she'd know I wasn't a liar.

You'll see, I thought helplessly. When we get to the wrecker's yard and a hundred slobberers suck your innards out, then you'll see I was telling the truth.

At that moment I remembered I'd left my fence post back at Ernie Piggot's house. I tried to turn back, but Eileen's grip was unbreakable.

At least I had Mum's shoe inside my shirt.

I held it tight through the cloth. It made me feel better even though it wasn't much good as a weapon.

We were close to the wrecker's yard. I strained my ear for sounds of slobberers. My heart was pounding so loudly I couldn't hear much. Just some birds screeching and Eileen muttering about kids and their warped minds.

At the gate I stopped. 'Let's go to the police,' I pleaded. 'They can come and take photos of the slobberers and you can see those.'

Eileen looked at me grimly. 'If we're going to be a family, Dawn, we've got to start being honest with each other.'

She dragged me through the gate.

'No,' I yelled desperately. 'We don't stand a chance. They haven't eaten for hours. We'll be – '

I stopped and stared. The yard was empty. There wasn't a slobberer to be seen.

I tore my arm free and ran around the piles of scrap and the bus and the four-wheel drive and the big wrecker's crane, looking wildly.

Nothing.

'Okay, young lady,' yelled Eileen. 'Come here and start talking.'

I ignored her. I ran back to the bus and peered in, not caring if a tidal wave of slobberers poured out. At least then she'd know.

The bus was empty. Just the torn seats and the smashed speedometer and the goat's skeleton.

'Dawn,' roared Eileen.

Slowly I turned to face a life of not being believed and possibly being accused of killing and eating Rory.

Then I noticed something. On the ground. Big patches of what looked like cow poo. Dry and cracked. But not crumbly like cow poo. Hard like dried leather. When I kicked one I hurt my foot.

Of course. I remembered the slobberers' festering skins. They must have been dying. But what could have made them decompose so fast?

My thoughts were interrupted by Eileen grabbing me.

'I said,' she hissed, 'start talking.'

'They've died and shrivelled up,' I explained desperately. 'Look, you can see where they were. There and there and there and . . .'

'Cow dung,' said Eileen icily. 'It's dried cow dung,

Dawn. Just like you're feeding me. Now tell me what's going on. Where's Rory?'

As I blinked back tears of rage and frustration, I was tempted to just make something up. 'He's run away from home because you're such a pain', something like that. But I knew Mum wouldn't have approved. She was a stickler for the truth. Even if it meant admitting she was five minutes late with the school bus because she'd got one of her uniform buttons jammed in my high chair.

'There's something weird and scary going on,' I said to Eileen. 'Maggots turning into bone-sucking monsters and sheep behaving in a very unfriendly manner. I don't know why and I don't know how, but it's happening.'

Eileen looked like she was going to explode.

She didn't. 'I shouldn't blame you,' she said, taking a deep breath. 'Not when your mother had so much trouble telling the truth.'

I felt like *I* was going to explode.

Before I could, I heard a loud creak above us. And a whoosh. I looked up. Swinging towards us was the big metal ball hanging from the end of the wrecker's crane.

Except it wasn't a ball of metal, it was a ball of sheep. About six of them, all with evil grins, clinging to the end of the chain.

I couldn't move. I stared horrified as the sheep hurtled towards us. Then I noticed something even worse. The sheep were glinting in the sun. Their wool wasn't soft and fluffy any more, it was hard and metallic.

Steel wool.

EIGHT

I ran screaming down the country road away from the remains of the dog. The glow of dawn and the morning mist meant nothing. My mind was a whirlpool of doubt, fear and horror. Was I mad? Did a goat's skeleton really come to life on that bus? Was Dawn's dead mother really there?

The whole thing was crazy, crazy, crazy. Even now slobberers could be waiting for me in the trees beside the road. Waiting to pounce and suck.

My bad leg ached. And my hand and arm were inflamed again. The purple bruise had spread. Pain filled my whole arm and part of my chest. Was my arm infected? The slobberers had licked me. Did I have some new illness? Slobberers' disease. Maybe I was dying.

I ran until I could run no further. I fell down exhausted in the middle of the road next to a slimy pond.

Eventually I got my breath back and sat up. I looked around me. All seemed quiet in the early morning light.

I still clutched the apple-man. I stared down at him. He was a bit grimy so I wiped him on my sleeve.

I loved the apple-man. He might have been the home of the slobberers. He might or might not have exploded on the bus. But he was still a gift from my dad. And even though he was an ugly little doll made out of a dried-up apple I was not going to part with him.

I think I knew, deep down inside me. Even way back then, at the beginning of it all. That the apple-man held the answers to all the questions I was too frightened to ask.

My feet stirred up the dust on the road as I slowly headed for home. Home? It wasn't really my place. Dawn's dad owned the house. And Dawn thought she owned it too. And Gramps, even though he was a nice guy and harmless, wasn't really *my* Gramps. Okay, Mum lived there now. But she always seemed to stick up for Dawn. Like that first time me and Mum went over to their place.

I don't know what all the fuss was about. Just because I made a double slingshot out of Dawn's bra. It could fire two tennis balls at once. Right over the house.

'Golf balls,' I told her. 'One on each side. That's all it would hold.'

Okay, so I lied a bit. And I ruined the bra. But Mum shouldn't have grounded me. Not her own son. Not her own flesh and blood.

I felt hurt. And angry. Really angry. And as I trudged along the road my arm hurt more and more. It was so painful that tears pricked behind my eyelids.

If only Dad were there. He would know what to do.

He would know whether I was insane or not. He would stick up for me. He would help.

I looked down at the little apple-man with a bit of a smile and continued to force my aching legs towards the house. 'I'll show them,' I thought. 'You can't treat me like that.'

My arm and chest throbbed more and more. My bad leg ached. I had to rest again. I sank down on a log, exhausted, and closed my eyes.

Something cold and wet moved across my hand. What, what, what? A slobberer's tongue? I was too scared to move. Too scared to open my eyes. But I had to.

Two eyes blinked back at me. Not a slobberer. Only a frog.

I laughed with relief and picked him up gently. 'Hello, little fella,' I said.

The frog shot out his tiny tongue and tickled my cut hand. I could feel the small wet flick of it on the seeping scab of my wound. Suddenly the frog's eyes rolled back in his head and then quivered back into view. Like the symbols on a poker machine when you hit the jackpot.

The frog sat shivering on my palm. Why was it shivering? Frogs don't get cold, do they? Maybe it was scared. Like me.

Then the frog crouched. For a second it was like a coiled spring. Then its eyes rolled, and POW. It shot up into the sky with an enormous leap. Talk about the cow jumping over the moon. It disappeared over the top of the trees. *Splash*. It must have landed back in the pond.

What a jump. Incredible. I had never seen anything like it.

My mind started to tick over. The frog licking me. It reminded me of something. Something similar. What was it?

Then it clicked. The slobberers had licked my bleeding hand. And then there was the sheep. On the step of the bus. I had stuck my cut finger into the sheep's nostril.

Maybe there was some sort of disease going around. Maybe we were infecting each other. Like the Black Death. I needed help. I had to get home.

I staggered on down the road. On and on. It seemed such a long way home. Finally I reached the bridge. Not far now. I stopped and listened to the water gurgling below. And heard something else. Behind me in the bushes.

Plip, plop, plip, plop. Like tiny spoonfuls of jelly falling onto the road. Dozens of them. No, hundreds. *Plip, plop, plip, plop, plip, plop.* No, thousands. As if an unseen hand was throwing stones into the air.

There. Stretched across the road. Little green lumps with small blinking eyes. Suddenly they lifted into the air like a swarm of grasshoppers. Up, up, up, up. Way above the treetops. They stopped, paused in mid-flight and began to fall. A hailstorm of frogs in the forest.

Whoosh, they landed together. As one. The sound reminded me of a huge bucket of water sloshing on the road. A million frogs, all landing at once.

They blinked at me. Unfriendly. My legs felt so weak

I could hardly stand. But somehow I managed to back away from them across the bridge. Not for one second did I take my eyes off the fearful plague.

The frogs, as one, crouched down and then sprang. Way, way over my head. Right across the river in one – no, not one. But one million identical giant leaps. They sloshed down onto the road and jumped again. And again.

The shower of frogs disappeared into the distance along the dusty road.

Towards our house.

I stumbled after them as fast as I could go. I was nearly there. Home at last. Suddenly it all seemed silly. A nightmare. Unreal. There were no frogs. It was all a mistake. All my tiredness fell away. Even my arm didn't hurt quite as much as I trudged the last few steps up to the gate. Now I could get adult help. They could take over.

Slobberers, a skeleton goat, Dawn's mother back from the dead, an exploding apple-man and frogs that can jump trees. They were all just in my head. Part of my sickness. None of that would matter any more.

A shadowy figure moved in the kitchen window. Mum? Maybe Mum was there by now. And Jack. Oh, I hoped so much that they were. I let out a sob and opened the gate.

A thunderous roar filled the air. It was almost as if the movement of the gate had been a signal for it to start. I clapped my hands over my ears and started running for the front door. What *was* that noise? So loud.

It was an ordinary old noise made bigger. A noise from a peaceful morning in the country. But amplified like a rock band out of control.

Frogs. A billion frogs croaking together. I couldn't see them but there was no doubt that they were there. Hiding in the trees that surrounded the house.

NINE

'Look out,' I screamed at Eileen.

She just stood there, in shock, staring.

I didn't blame her. Most people, if they had a choice between paying attention to a step-daughter screaming at them or to six sheep hurtling towards them on a wrecker's ball, would choose the sheep.

Specially if the sheep had razor-sharp steel wool.

I grabbed Eileen's sling and dragged her out of the way. The ball of sheep whooshed past, scowling. I thought how many layers of skin their wool would rip off us if it touched us. Suddenly my legs were pumping.

'Over here,' I yelled at Eileen as I ran towards the bus. I looked back. Eileen was still rooted to the spot, staring at the sheep, stunned. The sheep landed on the roof of the caretaker's office. One lost its grip on the ball and slid across the roof in a spray of rust and metal shavings. The others launched themselves at Eileen again.

I found I was rooted to the spot too. For a fleeting second all I could think about was that Eileen believed the evil gossip about Mum being a liar and the bus crash being Mum's fault. For a fleeting second I almost wanted the sheep to get her. Then I remembered Dad loved her, so I sprinted over and pulled her out of the way again.

'This can't be happening,' she croaked as the sheep whizzed past her head.

'If you think *this* is scary,' I muttered grimly, 'you should have seen what the slobberers did to the dog.' I remembered they'd probably done it to her son too, so I changed the subject. 'We'll be safer in the bus,' I said.

It was too late. The sheep were on the roof of the crane cab preparing for another swing. I looked wildly around. Near us was a pile of scrap. I grabbed Eileen and we tried to squeeze in between a stack of flattened cars and a big old industrial fridge. There wasn't room.

I looked frantically up at the sheep. All six pairs of bloodshot eyes were fixed on Eileen.

That's when I realised the sheep weren't interested in me. They wanted my step-mother.

I pulled Eileen out of the cubbyhole and stood her next to the fridge, directly in the path of the swooping sheep. 'It's you they're after,' I explained, then I squeezed in alongside the fridge.

Eileen didn't move. She must still have been in shock. The sheep hurtled towards her. Just before the ball of sheep gave her the worst skin problem of her life, I flung open the fridge door. The ball, and the sheep, slammed into it.

After the dust had settled, and my heart had dropped back down into my chest, I checked none of the sheep on the ground were moving. Then I checked Eileen.

'Are you okay?' I asked.

She nodded, shaking. I was shaking too. If I'd been any later opening that fridge door, Dad would have killed me.

'We've got to get back to town,' I said, 'and find Dad and tell the cops what's going on. They'll believe it coming from you.'

Eileen nodded again. She didn't look as though *she'd* believe it coming from her.

We set off back to town on foot, me keeping a nervous eye out for sheep. Eileen didn't say anything for about ten minutes. I understood. My nerves were a mess too. Plus adults took longer to adjust. It was the same with Dad when I dyed my hair green.

As we plodded along the dusty road, I tried not to worry about Dad. It was hard with his shirt wrapped round Eileen's arm and my dazed brain so full of scary questions.

Was the whole world being attacked by giant worms and killer sheep? Or was it just us?

If it was just us, why?

Suddenly Eileen started talking. 'Those slitherers or blubberers or whatever you called them. Where did they come from?'

I told her how they'd started out as normal grubs in the souvenir apple-man Rory's dad had sent him.

Eileen stopped walking and her face went even grimmer than the time I dried my hair on her white towel. The time I discovered the dye wasn't permanent.

She started pacing around and muttering to herself, the way adults do when they're wrestling with a really difficult thought.

'He wouldn't,' she said. 'Surely not. No, I'm being stupid.'

'What?' I said.

Eileen stared at me as if she'd forgotten I was there. 'Rory's father,' she said quietly. 'I've been worried he might try and pull a stunt on account of me getting married again. Try and get Rory away from me. But this . . .' She winced and shook her head as if the thought was too big even for someone like her who'd finished Year 12.

I stared at her. What did she mean? That Rory's father was a giant worm? Or a vicious sheep? That was dopey. But hang on, how did I know it was? I didn't know anything about Rory's father, except that he'd nicked off when Rory was five. Rory never wanted to talk about him. He could be a Martian for all I knew. Or a really skilful sheep trainer.

Suddenly the stress of the last day and a half got to me. Something snapped in my head and my brain went woolly with rage. It wasn't fair. Me and Dad had been happy till he'd got involved with Eileen and Rory and their psycho family.

'Why me?' I screamed. 'I'm sick of this.'

Eileen didn't reply. She was straining to hear something. Then I heard it too. It sounded like a tractor, accelerating towards us at speed.

I turned and couldn't believe what I was seeing. Roaring towards us round a bend in the road was Ernie Piggot's tractor. Riding it were four sheep. One had its front legs on the steering wheel. One was sitting on the accelerator pedal. One had the gearstick in its mouth.

The fourth was sprawled on the engine cover. Jutting out from under its tummy, like a knight's lance, was my steel fence post.

Its jagged point was speeding towards us.

We screamed and ran. Ahead I spotted a small shack that had once been a roadside fruit stall. Juicy Melons said the sign. Behind us I could hear the tractor getting closer.

We dived in and slammed the ricketty door. The shack shuddered and dust and splinters showered down on us. Then I realised Mum's shoe wasn't inside my shirt. Desperately I peered through a crack in the flimsy wall. There was the shoe, on the road outside. And there, thundering towards us like angry knights in steel-wool armour, were the sheep.

I couldn't look. I buried my face in Eileen's sling, and as we waited for the walls to cave in I realised this was the first time I'd ever hugged my step-mother.

TEN

Home. Safe at last, I hoped.

I lurched down the garden path and crashed through the front door. It hadn't even been locked but I soon took care of that.

'Rory,' croaked a friendly voice.

It wasn't Mum's voice but any human voice would have been friendly at that moment. Especially an adult voice.

'Gramps,' I yelled.

Although he wasn't really my Gramps I was starting to feel as if he was. I ran across the room and threw myself into his arms. I tried really hard not to cry but I was so upset that I couldn't say anything for a second or two.

'I was worried about you,' said Gramps. 'Out there all night in this thunderstorm.'

I fought for breath, trying to control the sobs that were trying to escape. I ran and peered out of the window. 'That's not thunder,' I said. 'It's frogs.'

Outside, the racket was so loud that it almost drowned us out.

'Frogs?' he said. 'Frogs didn't sound like that when I was a boy.' He looked sad. 'But then nothing seems the same any more, does it? I'll make you a nice cup of tea. You look terrible. Then you can tell me where Dawn is. And what's going on.'

'I don't want tea,' I yelled. 'Those frogs are dangerous. I think they're after me. We have to board up the windows. We have to keep them out.'

Gramps ambled over to the stove and put on the kettle. The roar of the frogs suddenly stopped. All was silent outside. But I wasn't fooled. Not after everything that had happened. Anything was possible. The frogs were up to something. I just knew it.

'The thunder has stopped,' said Gramps. 'Now you just settle down and tell me all about it. I won't hear another word until you've got some tea into you.'

Gramps picked up two shoes from beside the door and put some sugar and milk into them. Then he poured the boiling tea into them and handed one to me. He started to sip his tea from the shoe.

'Hey,' I yelled. 'What are you doing? You don't drink tea from a shoe.'

This terrible nightmare was going on and on and on. Surely there was no other weird thing left to happen.

Gramps looked at his shoe of tea and his eyes started to brim with tears. 'You don't, do you,' he said. 'You put feet into shoes. And . . . tea into cups.'

He stood up and fetched two clean cups and poured us some more tea.

'What's wrong with you, Gramps?' I asked gently. 'Yesterday you put a drill in the freezer.'

He just sat there and blinked at me for a bit. I could tell that he was trying to make up his mind whether or not to tell me.

'I'm sick,' he said.

'So am I,' I yelled. 'So am I. We've got the same thing.' I held out my purple arm and waved it in front of his face. 'I got licked by, by, by . . . slobberers. I keep seeing things. Exploding apple-men and, and . . . and a goat came to life. And millions of frogs are – '

'No,' said Gramps. 'We haven't got the same thing. What I've got. You only get it when you're old.'

'Did the slobberers lick you? Did they? Did they?'

He shook his head. 'No,' he said. 'In my day there was no such thing as slobberers. At least I don't think there was.' He scratched his head. I could tell he was trying very hard to think straight. To remember something. 'We had cobblers, though,' he said. 'Yes. They made these.' He held up a cup.

I started to feel really sad. Cobblers made shoes, not cups. 'How did you catch your disease?' I asked slowly.

'No one knows,' said Gramps. 'Some people say that you get it from cooking with aluminium saucepans. But no one really knows.'

I suddenly stopped feeling sorry for myself. Okay, I was seeing things that weren't there. But somehow it was different with Gramps. It was as if he was wearing out. Like an old car or a shoe.

'What's your disease called?' I asked in a whisper.

'I've forgotten,' he said. 'I keep forgetting things. Did I really put a drill in the freezer? I've never been that bad before.'

I didn't know whether or not to tell the truth. In the end I said, 'Don't worry about it. It was only an old drill. No one wanted it.'

His eyes filled with tears and he just sat there. I must have said the wrong thing.

Gramps put a hand on my shoulder. 'Your mum thought I was still well enough to look after you,' he said. 'But soon you'll be looking after me.'

At that very moment the frogs started up their roaring croaks.

I backed away from the windows. *Splat, splot, splitter, splatter.* The frogs started throwing themselves against the glass.

'It's raining cats and dogs,' yelled Gramps.

'No,' I shrieked. 'Frogs.'

The sound grew louder and louder. Every window was

under attack. The frogs were hurling themselves against the house like bullets from a machine gun. In broad daylight they were mounting a crazy attack. Limp, stunned bodies mounded up like green snow on the window-sills. The glass above shivered under the blows.

But the windows were strong. And they held. Gramps sat down and shook his head. 'I know this isn't happening,' he said.

Suddenly everything fell silent.

The frogs had fallen back across the lawn. Their first attack had failed and now they were planning something else. Those that weren't dead.

The frogs were getting into a line. It was a terrifying sight. Intelligent frogs. They looked like people queuing up at a bus stop. Except that the line was too long. It wound across the lawn and out of the gate. It stretched down the dusty road and into the forest. I could see it winding over the hill way in the distance on the other side of the trees. Thousands and thousands of little green frogs. Waiting their turn.

What were they up to?

What was their plan?

What did they want?

At the head of the line one large frog stood facing the others. Like a general reviewing his troops.

What were they lining up for? Lunch?

Yes.

The frog at the front – the general – opened his mouth. And the first frog in the line jumped into it. The general gave a gulp and the poor little creature was gone. The frog general opened his mouth again and the next little victim jumped straight in. The general chewed a couple of times and swallowed. Then he croaked and stretched open his jaws. The next frog obeyed orders. In it went.

One by one the queuing frogs jumped into the gaping mouth. The general munched and crunched. He burped and slurped. And the line shuffled forward. Each little leaper moving anxiously on, impatient to be eaten.

Faster and faster the meal progressed. In they went. Hopping to their doom. Kamikaze frogs. At this rate they would be gone in no time.

And with each swallow, I noticed something happening to the frog general. Something that made the hair stand up on the back of my head.

He was already the size of a dog. Swelling with each swallow like a monstrous balloon. Soon the tiny frogs would not be enough to satisfy him.

He turned his eyes greedily towards us and a loud croak belched out of his mouth.

'Meat,' I said. 'He wants meat.'

Gramps ran to the fridge and threw open the door He started to chuckle. 'I ate the last sausage yesterday, he yelled. 'There's not a bit of meat in the house.'

I stared at Gramps' skinny legs.

'Yes there is,' I said . . .

Book Three

CROAKED

ONE

My new house had never seemed less like home.

Gramps and I stared out of the kitchen window. The plague of frogs was still there.

The frog general ate his little soldiers one at a time. He chewed and chomped and sucked and swallowed. And with each mouthful he grew bigger.

The line of frogs shuffled forward like troops waiting for the firing squad. They jumped into his gaping gob without complaint. Without protest. They were sacrificing themselves. But for what?

The frog general was as big as a dog and still growing. The smaller frogs had failed in their attempt to get into the house. So now they were joining forces. Making one big frog. That could ... could ...

Break down the door.

This was crazy. Crazy, crazy, crazy. The frogs could have attacked me on the road. But they had gone right past. Jumped over my head. So who were they after?

It could only be one person. Gramps.

'We have to stop that frog,' I said in a trembling voice.

'Rory,' said Gramps, 'did you know I was a Rat?'

Oh no. He was rambling again. Out of his mind. Now he thought he was a rat.

'The Rats of Tobruk,' he said proudly. 'In the war. We held Rommel off for months. I was in the Tank Corps.'

I tried not to get upset by Gramps' nonsense. The frog general had grown to the size of a sheep. And the line of frogs was leaping faster and faster into his gaping mouth. They reminded me of bullets being loaded into the breech of a gun.

'I wouldn't mind a tank right now,' I said to Gramps. 'We could blow the frog general away.'

Gramps began to chuckle. 'I've got one,' he said. 'I've got a tank. Out the back.'

Oh, it made me sad. It really did. Poor old Gramps.

I had been seeing a few things myself lately. But that was because the slobberers had licked my cut hand. The infection had spread right up my arm and onto my chest. Sometimes it made my head spin and sent me crazy. I saw things that weren't there.

But Gramps had some other problem. He was off the planet all the time. I never knew what he was going to do next. Not that it made any difference to how I felt. I really liked him. He was a great guy. He was Dawn's gramps, not mine. But he and I were growing close. In the heat of battle. Comrades in arms.

My thoughts turned to Dawn. She was really gutsy.

Big, strong and bold. And dead? Oh, I hoped not. I would have given anything to see her walk through that door. I started to feel really mean for calling her Big Bad Dawn. After all, the step-family was just as bad for her as it was for me.

'This'll fix him,' said Gramps.

I looked up and saw Gramps holding a large sack of salt.

'Frogs and snails and things don't like salt.' He started to laugh and chuckle like a madman. 'We'll lob it into his gob.'

I peered out through the green-splattered windows. The general was still cannibalising the company of frogs. His webbed feet were as big as hubcaps. He certainly wouldn't have any trouble smashing through a window.

'Not a bad idea,' I said slowly. 'But how will we get the salt out there without them attacking us?' The thought of the general's slimy mouth made me shiver. We had to do something though. Sitting waiting for the general to invite himself to dinner wasn't my idea of fun.

Slam. The back door banged.

'Gramps,' I screamed. 'Gramps. Don't go out there.'

I was too late.

I rushed to the back door and threw it open. I couldn't see any frogs because they were lining up in the front yard. And I couldn't see Gramps. Where was he?

'Come on, Rory,' said a muffled voice. 'Start her up. We'll let him have it.'

Where *was* Gramps? What was he up to?

The voice was coming from the vegetable garden. The wheelbarrow. A large metal dustbin was sitting in the wheelbarrow. Suddenly the lid of the bin popped open and Gramps' head poked out. He was wearing a pair of goggles and pointing towards the front yard. Oh, weird, weird, weird. Gramps thought the wheelbarrow was a tank. He was back in the Second World War. Attacking the enemy.

'Oh, what the hell,' I yelled to myself. 'We've got to do something.' I raced into the garden and pushed Gramps' head back inside the bin. 'Stay there,' I said. 'Until I tell you.'

'Charge,' came Gramps' excited voice from inside the bin.

I grabbed the handles and started to push the bin around to the front yard. Gramps was heavy but there was a slight downhill slope. And the cement path made it fairly easy. Faster and faster. There. There they were. The tiny frogs were still leaping to their doom. The general frog was still gorging himself. I gasped. He was as big as a full-grown cow.

The general took no notice of me. Neither did the line of frogs. They must have been too intent on what they were doing. Or hadn't they seen me?

I had no time to think as I headed down the path towards the general. The wheelbarrow started to wobble from side to side. I couldn't keep it upright. 'Tank traps,' came Gramps' muffled voice. 'Keep going.'

I was nearly there. I stared into the frog general's huge,

gaping mouth. I looked into his cruel eyes. They were as big as soccer balls. They swivelled and he fixed me with a wet glare. He started to roll his tongue back into his mouth. I knew without a doubt what he was going to do. He was going to slurp me up and slide me down his throat.

'Now,' I screamed. 'Fire.'

Gramps' head popped out of the bin and the general forgot all about me. His rolled tongue was already coiled like a spring. Gramps' shaking hands held the sack of salt in the air but it was too heavy for him. He began to sink down into the bin. *Thwack*. The frog general cracked out his tongue like a giant whip just as Gramps' head disappeared into the bin.

The general's tongue plucked the sack from Gramps' hands as if it was no more than a fly sitting on a leaf. In a flash it was gone. Swallowed.

The wheelbarrow tipped over and we both fell sprawling onto the ground. 'Land mine,' he yelled. 'A blasted landmine.'

We stared up at the frog. For a moment the world seemed to stand still. Nothing moved. Then the general began to moan. His pimpled green skin started to stretch. His bloated body bulged and quivered.

Bang. The frog general exploded like a monster balloon that had been pricked by a pin.

Thousands of bits of green muck hurtled into the air. Then they began to fall. Green and brown goo dripped down over the lawn and the house. Shreds of dead frog covered my hair and windcheater. The gum trees seemed to bear rotting green fruit.

'Yahoo,' yelled Gramps. 'We got him. The general's croaked it.' He did an excited little rain dance on the lawn.

There were a few thousand frogs left still standing in line. They seemed paralysed by the loss of their leader. For a few seconds they just stood there. Like a queue at McDonald's that's just heard the hamburgers have run out.

Gramps danced away in front of them. But he was celebrating too soon.

I stared at the blasted bits of the frog general which covered the landscape. They began to writhe and squirm. They were growing little legs and eyes. The pieces of the general were turning into more frogs. Thousands of them.

'Quick,' I screamed. 'Back to the house.'

But I was too late. The frogs were already heading there themselves. Leaping and bounding like a swarm of lumpy locusts, they spread across the lawn and poured into the house.

They ignored Gramps. They ignored me.

So what were they after?

Gramps and I waded through the door. The frogs were swarming into Mum and Jack's room. They were into the clothes cupboard. They were all over Mum's jeans and wedding dress.

Then it hit me.

The frogs were not after me. They were not after Gramps.

They were after Eileen. My mum.

TWO

I was huddled in a rickety roadside fruit stall, about to die. Killer sheep with razor-sharp steel wool were thundering towards me on a bone-crushing tractor. To make things worse, I was hugging a step-mother I didn't even like.

I should have been praying.

I should have been screaming for Dad.

Instead I was having shameful thoughts.

I remembered the earlier sheep attacks. With the fork. And the rake. And the wrecker's ball. All aimed at my step-mother.

It's Eileen they're after, I told myself, not me. I could run for it. I could sprint down the road and they wouldn't even see me go. They'd be too busy stabbing Eileen and ploughing her into the ground.

I peeped through a crack to see if I had enough time to get out. Yes. The tractor was several seconds away. If I flung open the door and ran, I could make it.

Now.

Do it now.

I didn't move.

Instead I stared at Mum's shoe, lying where I'd dropped it on the dusty road in front of the advancing tractor.

I couldn't leave Eileen. She might be a pain. She might have stolen Dad from me. But she was Rory's mum.

Then an amazing thing happened.

The sheep saw the shoe. Their eyes widened. Their stiff steel wool, gleaming in the morning sun, seemed to bristle.

Just before the tractor ran over the shoe, one of the sheep pushed at the steering wheel with its front legs and the tractor swerved.

It thundered past the fruit stall. The walls shook. Eileen swore. We were showered with dust and old price tickets.

I kicked open the door and peered out, just in time to see the tractor veer across the road and hit a large rock.

All four sheep flew through the air. Three of them crashed down into the undergrowth. They scrambled to their feet, leaves and twigs impaled on their wool, and glared at me. Chest thumping, I waited for them to charge. But they didn't. They glared a bit more, then turned and ran off down the road.

I looked around anxiously for the fourth sheep. At first I couldn't see it. Then I heard grunting and looked up.

The sheep was halfway up a large tree, the steel wool on its back embedded in the trunk, its legs sticking out in surprise. It started to kick and snort. After a while it tore itself free and fell to the ground.

From that height it should have been history. It wasn't. It stood up, gave me an evil look and came towards me.

My insides went rigid with terror.

Then I had an idea. I picked up Mum's shoe and pointed it at the sheep.

The sheep stopped. It took a step backwards. For a few seconds it seemed to be frozen. Then it turned and ran off down the road, a large scab of bark still stuck to its back.

I hugged Mum's shoe, weak with relief.

But I was puzzled. Why had the sheep swerved? Why had they all run off? Was it just that they didn't like dead people's footwear? Or did Mum's shoe have some sort of special power?

My thoughts were interrupted by Eileen staggering out of the fruit stall. She had a price ticket in her hair – 2.99 a kilo. She looked shocked and dazed and her sling was crooked and I felt pretty bad that I'd thought of nicking off and leaving her.

Sometimes you had to take responsibility for people even though it was your dad who'd invited them into your life.

'The sheep have gone,' I said. 'For now.'

Eileen nodded slowly, her eyes darting around. She seemed to be having trouble taking stuff in, even really short sentences.

I went over to the tractor. It had flipped over and was sitting in a puddle of diesel, wheels still spinning. I'd thought perhaps we could ride it back to town, but the engine looked pretty crumpled.

Then I heard a faint sound.

Soft and high-pitched.

Baa.

I tensed and gripped Mum's shoe.

Baa.

I looked around frantically. Was there a fifth sheep with a dodgy voice, about to drop out of a tree?

Then I saw it. Huddled near the tractor. A tiny lamb, about three days old. It had something wrong with its leg and looked like it was in pain.

Normally I'd have picked it up. I'd nursed quite a few injured lambs in my time. Dad reckoned I had the touch.

But when those sheep on the wrecker's ball had turned to steel, part of me had too.

'Go on,' I said to the lamb. 'Shoo.'

The lamb didn't move. Eileen came over. 'Poor little thing,' she said. The lamb baaed pitifully and looked up at her with big eyes.

Eileen picked it up.

'Be careful,' I said, wondering if I was turning into one of those people who couldn't feel sympathetic even in sad movies.

'You poor love,' said Eileen to the lamb. 'What's wrong?'

I saw instantly what was wrong. As Eileen cradled the lamb, its soft fluffy white wool was turning hard and grey and steely.

'Eileen,' I yelled. 'Let go.'

I swung Mum's shoe and knocked the lamb out of Eileen's arms. It landed on four strong and perfectly healthy legs. The needle-sharp coils of its steel wool glinted.

'You little scumbag,' I hissed. Before I could point Mum's shoe at it, the lamb sniggered and ran off down the road in the same direction as the others.

'Are you okay?' I asked Eileen anxiously.

She was dabbing at her neck. She looked at her fingers. There was blood on them.

'I'm okay,' she said. 'It's just a scratch.' She wiped the blood off.

I waited for my own blood to stop pounding in my ears.

'Come on,' said Eileen, heading off down the road. 'I want to get home and find out what's happened to Jack and Rory.'

I hurried after her. How could she be so calm? I'd already explained to her that Rory was probably dead. And the fear slicing through me was that Dad was too.

Suddenly I felt sick with grief.

I squeezed my neck muscles and decided that Eileen was right. No sense in panicking till we knew for sure.

'Good idea,' I said. 'They're probably fine.' My neck

knew I was lying and cramped up. I had a sudden urge for a curried-egg sandwich to make it feel better.

I made myself think about other things.

'Eileen,' I said, catching her up, 'the sheep are after you, so you should carry this.' I pushed the shoe into her hand. 'It was Mum's. She was wearing it when she died.'

Eileen stared at it. 'Yuck,' she said, and dropped it.

Okay, it was dirty and mildewy, but what did she expect from a shoe that had been to the bottom of a river and then in a wrecked bus for five years?

I picked it up and tucked it inside Eileen's sling. 'It'll protect you,' I explained. 'The sheep don't like it.'

'*I* don't like it,' said Eileen, thrusting it back at me.

I saw in her face what she really meant. 'I don't like your mum,' was what she meant. 'I don't like her because she was a drunk or a mental case or both and she crashed a school bus with my son on it.'

I took the shoe back. 'One day,' I said, my eyes pricking with tears, 'when we've sorted out all this weird stuff, I'll find out the truth about my mum's death and then you'll have to apologise.'

We trudged towards town, not speaking.

Two things happened on the way.

After about ten minutes I noticed some piles of brown powder on the road. Five of them. Each pile was about the size of a sheep, except for one which was much smaller.

I bent closer.

It was rust.

I struggled to make sense of what I was seeing. Could Mum's shoe have done that? Turned the sheep into rust?

The second thing happened close to the house. I'd just noticed that Eileen's neck seemed red and swollen where the lamb had scratched her.

Eileen suddenly turned to me, wide-eyed and scared.

'What's this?' she said, pointing to her sling.

At first I didn't understand what she meant.

'What is it?' she shouted.

'It's a sling,' I said, suddenly scared myself. 'You and Dad had a car crash and you hurt your arm and made a sling out of one of Dad's shirts.'

Eileen stared at the shirt. Then she gave a relieved sigh. 'That's right,' she said. 'I remember.'

Poor thing, I thought. She must have concussion. At least we'll be home soon.

To calm myself down I thought of our place, just over the next rise. At the top of the hill I stopped to gaze down at the familiar cosy house nestled among the trees.

Instead I stared in horror.

The last time I'd seen the house it had been white. Now it was green. Green walls, green roof, green guttering, green windows.

And even at that distance I could see that the green was alive.

THREE

It was awful. Disgusting really. To see those frogs swarming over Mum's clothes. The foul green plague filled sleeves and legs and pockets. The frogs filled out flat jackets and jumpers and made them ripple and flow with a dreadful life of their own.

'The mongrels,' yelled Gramps. 'They've got us out-numbered.'

He wasn't wrong there. I started kicking and jumping and squashing the frogs under my shoes. But it was useless. There were just too many. The green tide grew higher as the frogs climbed on each other's backs to get at Mum's outfits.

Gramps tugged at my shoulder. 'Come on,' he said. 'We need to talk.'

We waded out to the kitchen where there were fewer frogs.

'The first question is,' said Gramps, 'are they really there? Or am I getting confused again?'

'You see them,' I said. 'And I see them. So they must be there.'

'Well, the next question is,' said Gramps. 'What do they want?'

'Mum,' I said. 'They are all over her clothes. It's *her* they want.'

Gramps looked terribly upset. And I was scared. For some reason it was worse now that Mum was in danger and not me. Scared for yourself is one thing. But scared for someone you love. That's different altogether.

By now almost all of the frogs had swarmed into the bedroom. We could see them from the kitchen. They were piled up in one huge seething mass that reached to the ceiling. They reminded me of a heap of tiny green sumo wrestlers struggling for prizes.

I started to tremble and shake all over. Like someone who has malaria. It was all too much. I just couldn't take any more. I needed someone to wake me up. And hold me in their arms. I was only a kid. Mums and dads are supposed to fix things up. To look after you. To make the nasty things go away.

But how could they help me? I had driven them all away. Suddenly I felt all alone in the world. Everything seemed to be my fault.

Dad had gone away and left me years ago. Why didn't he come back? Was it because my leg was twisted and I couldn't walk or run properly any more? Was he disappointed because I'd never play football for Essendon like he wanted me to?

And Dawn's mum. Dead. Drowned in a bus. I couldn't remember what had happened but I probably caused that too. No wonder Jack and Dawn didn't like me.

But that wasn't all. No – I had to go and put some

slobberers in the stew and cause Jack and Mum's car to run off the road. They were probably dead as well.

Was there anyone I hadn't hurt? I had run out on Dawn. Left her to be chased off into the night by the slobberers. She was probably nothing but a sucked-out scruffy doormat by now. All because of me.

I was no good to anyone. No one wanted me. And I didn't blame them. Right then I wished I was the one who was dead.

Without warning two arms grabbed me. It was Gramps. He hugged me close to his chest. Tears ran down my cheeks and soaked into the wool of his jumper. I could smell that musty odour that all gramps seem to have. We just stood there hugging each other without speaking.

A hug doesn't need words.

Finally I stopped shaking. I opened my eyes and wiped my damp cheeks. 'Look,' I shouted. 'Look.' I saw something wonderful. Fantastic. Better than winning the Lotto. Better than a Ferrari. Better than anything. I was so happy.

I could see two figures walking down the track towards the house.

So could the frogs. They started to pour out of the bedroom and into the hall.

I was filled with joy and terror. It was Mum. And Dawn. They *weren't* dead.

'We have to keep the frogs in the house,' I shrieked. 'We have to. They'll kill Mum. It's her they want.'

I ran through the frogs to the back door and slammed it. Then I ran back to the window. 'Stay away,' I yelled desperately at the distant figures. 'The frogs are after you.'

The frogs surged towards the windows and doors. Gramps started kicking at them. He slipped and slid around on the greasy floor. His legs were tottery but he stomped and stamped like crazy. 'We need reinforcements,' he yelled in a horrified voice. 'I can't hold the line. The scumbags are breaking out.'

But he was wrong. We didn't need help. Even through the mist of my terror I could see that something was happening. The frogs were not their old selves. The fight seemed to be going out of them. I noticed that some were already dead, while others waved their legs at the ceiling like huge green beetles turned on their backs. The fittest of them were hopping half-heartedly towards the door.

'I don't believe it,' gasped Gramps. 'They're giving up. Just when they had us beaten.'

I tried to work out what was happening to the frogs. It was almost as if they had lost interest in Mum.

By the time Mum and Dawn reached the garden gate every frog was dead.

I rushed out of the door and threw myself into Mum's arms. 'You're alive,' I screamed. 'You're alive, you're alive, you're alive.'

'Where's Dad?' Dawn shrieked at me. 'Is he with you?'

I wished I could tell her that Jack was alive, but I didn't know where he was. And anyway, I couldn't speak. Mum was kissing the top of my head and pushing my face into her soft body.

Gramps started hugging Dawn. 'He'll turn up,' he said. 'He's missing in action. Probably a prisoner of war.'

'Slobberers don't take prisoners,' said Dawn. 'Neither do killer sheep.'

'Killer sheep? Killer frogs, you mean,' I said.

Mum frowned at me. 'Don't you start on that nonsense too,' she said. Then she turned to Gramps and hugged him. That was really nice to see but I couldn't really enjoy it. It is a terrible feeling when something wonderful happens at exactly the same time as something awful. I was so happy to see Mum. She was thrilled to see me. Dawn was pleased that Gramps was okay. And I was rapt that Dawn had not been slurped up by slobberers. Dawn even looked as if she might be glad that I was still alive.

But none of us could be really happy while Jack was missing.

We all walked slowly towards the house, Mum hanging on to me. And Gramps hugging Dawn. We stared at the goo that dripped from the eaves and gutters. It looked as if a furious green snowstorm had attacked our home. In amongst the slime you could make out an occasional bit of frog – an eye or leg or a bit of rotting curled tongue. But mostly it was just slimy gunk draped over everything.

'What happened?' whispered Dawn.

'Rommel's green panzers,' said Gramps. 'But we licked 'em. Me and Rory and the other Rats of Tobruk.'

'Frogs,' I said. 'They were after Mum.'

'Like the sheep,' said Dawn. 'They were too.'

'Don't you start on that,' said Mum angrily. 'I've heard enough about slobberers and killer sheep and . . . other nonsense for one lifetime.'

At that very moment I saw something that made my heart fill with fear. As Mum grew angry, a purple bruise started to wash up her neck.

Mum sat down in a slimy green chair.

'Oh, yuck,' said Dawn.

Mum didn't seem too worried about the goo. 'Where's Jack?' she mumbled. 'My head feels funny. I can't remember things.'

I felt a hand in mine. A soft warm girl's hand that sent a pleasant little shiver up my spine. I looked up at Dawn. It was funny. If you sort of half closed your eyelids and squinted at her from the side, she really was quite pretty.

'Come on,' said Dawn. 'We have to talk, Worm Boy.'

Worm Boy? I pulled my hand away and stomped outside after her.

We went into the garage and Dawn sat on the wood pile and glared at me. 'My dad's missing,' she said. 'I want to know what's going on.'

'Okay,' I yelled. 'Okay, okay. I know it was my fault. But he still might be alive. We have to do something. We're the only ones who know the truth. No one will believe us.'

'What is the truth?' she said.

'Slobberers,' I said. 'And frogs and maggots. And a dead goat come back to life. And . . .'

Dawn's eyes grew wide as I told her everything that had happened. Well, almost everything. I couldn't tell her that I had seen her mother in the old bus. That couldn't have been real. We all knew she was dead. That bit must just have been my sick mind.

Then Dawn told me about the giant slobberer. And the killer sheep. And everything else she had gone through. Her story was worse than mine. She was pretty brave was Dawn. You had to give her that.

What had happened was awful. But she left the worst till last. 'Your mum can't remember about the sheep,' she said. 'Even though she saw them. And she doesn't believe me about the slobberers. Or you about the frogs. She's sick.' Dawn pointed at my hand. 'And so are you.'

I gave my head a shake and tried to clear my muddled brain. 'We have to stick together on this,' I said. 'Mum's in trouble. Jack must be too. We have to stop fighting each other and start thinking.'

'Yes,' said Dawn slowly. 'We have to piece the bits together. Where did the sickness begin?'

I held up my aching arm. 'The slobberers licked me,' I told her. 'I've got slobberer's disease.'

Dawn looked at me carefully. Did she shuffle back a bit? Was she scared of catching something? Or was that just my imagination?

'Yes,' she said. 'You've got an infection all right. But what about the sheep? The slobberers licked you. And . . .'

'I could have infected the sheep. I stuck my cut finger

up a sheep's nose. Then other sheep might have been infected.'

'And gone off hunting for Eileen.'

'Like the frogs,' I yelled. 'A frog licked my cut hand. Then infected frogs came searching for Mum.'

'The lamb,' shouted Dawn. 'The lamb pricked Eileen. That's how she got infected. The disease goes from person to creature. And creature to person. The slobberers infected you. You infected the sheep.'

Suddenly Dawn grabbed a stick and started scratching in the dust on the garage floor.

'What are – ?'

'Quiet,' she said. 'This is complicated.'

I bit my tongue and watched her as she drew.

'The worms infected you,' she said. 'And you infected sheep and frogs. And now the sheep have infected Eileen. And now she'll infect other animals. Maybe cats or dogs or . . .'

I couldn't take it in. I didn't like the sound of it.

I didn't want to believe it. 'Why are the infected animals all dying?' I said.

'It's like sperm,' Dawn blurted out.

I blushed. Even in the middle of all that trouble I blushed. Jeez, she had a big mouth.

'What are you talking about?' I said.

Dawn drew again in the dust. Just like a sex-education teacher at the blackboard. 'Thousands of sperm go for an egg,' she said. 'But only one gets through.'

'I know all that stuff,' I said gruffly. I did too. In fact I'd been thinking about it a fair bit lately.

'And,' said Dawn. 'Once the egg is fertilised all the other sperm just die.'

'So?' I said.

'So it's the same with slobberer's disease. Once the person they are after has been infected, the germs have no target and the creatures all die. Their job is done.'

I thought about it. She could be right.

'Then the infected person passes it on to another creature,' I said slowly. 'And a whole lot more of them catch it. And they go looking for . . .'

'Someone else in *your* family,' said Dawn, sounding a bit relieved.

A shiver ran through me. My family? Who else could that mean?

Dad, that's who. Was I going to kill him too? With my germs?

I held up my bruised arm. 'Do you think I will keep passing it on?' I said. 'Can I still infect animals that will go searching for my relatives?'

'I don't know,' said Dawn slowly.

Suddenly I had an idea. I ran over to Jack's tool shelf and picked up an old plastic box. I ran outside and searched around in the bushes. 'Got you,' I yelled.

'A snail?' said Dawn. 'What do you want that for?'

I put the snail under the tap and watched it as it stuck out its little eye stalks. I rubbed the snail's face into my wound so that it would catch the germs. Then I placed it in the box and put on the lid. We could see what the snail was up to because the lid was made of clear plastic.

We both peered down at the snail. It moved around for a bit and then pulled its eyes back into its shell.

'We'll watch it,' I said. 'If I'm infectious and can still pass on the disease . . .'

I didn't finish the sentence so Dawn did it for me.

'The snail will start to change,' she said.

FOUR

I felt a bit better, knowing Dad couldn't be infected.

But only a bit.

He could still have had his bones sucked out by a

slobberer or his skin scraped off by a mean-minded sheep. I was aching with worry. Where was he? Why wasn't he here?

I did what Dad always did when he was worried sick. Kept myself busy.

Rory and I went back to the kitchen and I made everyone their second hot drink in a row and tried to occupy my mind by wondering what exactly the infection was and whether Eileen would turn into a slobberer.

I could see Gramps was worried too. He kept looking at Eileen and Rory, his face crumpled with concern. But he didn't want to alarm them, so he tried to stay cheery.

'Top tea,' he said after a couple of sips. 'Better than the pot I made.'

'Thanks, Gramps,' I said. He was right, mostly because he'd used gravy powder.

'Goes right through you,' he said, 'tea. 'Scuse me.' He shuffled off to the bathroom.

I was in the middle of wondering which I should do first, ring the police or make Eileen and Rory have a lie-down, when a familiar voice filled the kitchen.

'Jeez, am I glad to see you lot.'

I spun round.

Dad was leaning against the door frame, face streaked with dirt, shirt torn, jeans filthy, smiling wearily. He opened his arms wide.

'Dad,' I screamed, and rushed at him.

But it wasn't me he wrapped his arms round, it was
Eileen. I stood waiting, grinning, heart thumping with
joy, desperate for my turn.

'Where have you been?' asked Eileen tearfully.

That's exactly what I would have asked.

'Twisted my leg,' said Dad. 'Tried to take a short cut
back to town along the old fire break. I was that ropeable
with myself for pranging the car I didn't watch where I
was going. Stepped in a wombat hole. I've done more
crawling in the last sixteen hours than all the pollies in
Canberra put together.'

I grinned even wider. Good old Dad. Now he was
here everything would be okay.

Eileen stepped back and anxiously checked Dad over
and I slid in for my turn. I put my arms round him and
hugged. He ponged of B.O. but I didn't care. My eyes
were watering anyway.

'Oh, Dad,' I whispered. 'I thought you were a goner '

He didn't reply. I looked up at him. He was staring at
Eileen, concerned. She did look pretty crook. Her neck
was red and blotchy and her face was sort of grey.

There was so much to tell him, I hardly knew where
to start.

'Something weird and terrible's happening, Dad,' I
began. 'There's an infection and Rory and Eileen have got
it and it turns grubs into monsters and sheep into killers.'

I realised he wasn't even listening. He was still staring
at Eileen. 'Jeez, love,' he was saying to her. 'We've got to
get you to a doctor.'

'I'm okay,' she said. 'It was only a scratch.'

I pulled at Dad's arm. 'Listen to me,' I pleaded. 'We were attacked by giant worms. Huge giant worms. And sheep on a tractor.'

Dad was staring at me now. Not with concern, with irritation. 'Dawn,' he said sharply. 'You can see what Eileen and me have been through. We're having the world's crookest honeymoon and this is no time for games.'

'It's not a game,' I yelled. 'It's real.'

I heard Rory stand up at the kitchen table behind me. He'd been quiet till now. The infection seemed to do that to people. Now he stopped being quiet.

'She's right,' he said angrily. He pointed to the purple bruise on his arm. It was growing even as we watched. 'The slobberers did this,' he said.

Dad stared. 'Jeez,' he said. 'You look worse than your mum. Must be some sort of stress reaction.' He spoke softly to Eileen. 'Has your family ever had a skin complaint like this before?'

My head felt like it was going to explode. What was happening? Why wouldn't Dad believe me?

I turned frantically to Eileen. 'Tell him about the sheep,' I pleaded. 'The tractor. The wrecker's ball.'

Eileen stared at me, puzzled. There was a long pause. 'Tractor?' she said finally. 'Wrecker's ball?'

'The sheep on the wrecker's ball,' I yelled. 'You were there. You saw it. You were infected by a steel lamb. Tell him.'

Eileen looked confused. 'Steel lamb?' she said, staring at the floor. 'I can remember the explosion, and the car skidding . . .'

'Dawn,' said Dad with rising anger, 'this is not the time for these games.'

Frustration and panic exploded in my guts.

'Come on,' I screamed at Eileen. 'Get real. It was less than two hours ago.'

'Dawn,' roared Dad. 'You do not speak to Eileen like that.'

'Leave her alone,' Rory yelled at Dad. 'She's just trying to tell you what's going on, you stupid idiot.'

Eileen slammed her coffee mug onto the table.

'Rory,' she said furiously. 'Apologise to Jack this instant.'

Suddenly everybody was shouting at everybody. I yelled at Dad that he was pig-headed. Then I stopped. I realised what was happening. Another type of disease was sweeping through the family. We'd been infected with it the day Dad and Eileen got the hots for each other, but we'd never had as bad a dose as this before.

I saw what the anger was doing to Rory and Eileen. The more worked up they got, the more the purple blotches on their skin quivered and bloated. And it was making their faces change too, just for short spells. A couple of times I could hardly recognise them.

Then Rory yelled at Dad that he was pig-headed, and I wasn't going to put up with that.

'None of this would have happened if you weren't such a grub, Worm Boy,' I yelled. 'Carrying around rotting apples and pockets full of filthy worms.'

Eileen glared at me icily. 'That's good,' she said, 'coming from a kid whose bed is a dumping ground for half-eaten biscuits and mouldy toast crumbs.'

'Fair go,' said Dad. 'The first time you and Rory stayed here I found half a pizza in his bed.'

Eileen's blotch gave an angry twitch. 'Why is it,' she said, 'that when Rory and Miss Perfect here do exactly the same thing, Rory always gets bad-mouthed?'

'Because,' said Dad heatedly, 'pizzas stain and biscuits don't.'

Eileen laughed bitterly, 'Oh yes, you'd know all about that. You who haven't made a bed once in the fifteen months we've been together.'

'Haven't made a bed?' roared Dad indignantly. 'The first time I slept at your place the sheets had so many holes in them I had to go out and buy a new pair.'

Eileen stared at him.

'You never bought new sheets,' she said.

'Two pairs,' he said.

Eileen frowned. 'No, you didn't,' she said.

I stared at Eileen. I'd seen those new sheets with my own eyes.

'I see,' said Dad, furious. 'And I suppose when I hopped into bed and you said I looked like the bloke in the sheet ad, that didn't happen either.'

Eileen frowned again, then glared. 'No,' she said.

'My mistake,' yelled Dad, pulling open the back door. 'You must have thought I was someone else.' He hobbled out, slamming the door behind him.

I followed him out.

He was sitting on a stump staring at the lawn. I put my arm round him.

'Let's go somewhere,' I said. 'Start a new life. Just you and me.' I hadn't planned to say it, but when it came out I realised I meant it.

Dad gave me a squeeze. 'Love,' he said softly. 'I know all those tales about monster worms and crazy infections are your way of telling me you're not happy. I get the message you think Eileen and Rory are a bit of a plague. But I need her. After Mum died I was as empty as this poor blighter.'

He picked something up and brushed ants off it. I realised with a stab it was the dry flat body of the magpie that the slobberers had sucked out.

'There was nobody around to save this poor bloke from the ants,' said Dad. 'I was lucky. I had Eileen to save me.'

I opened my mouth to tell him it wasn't ants that had emptied out the magpie. But before I said a word I knew I wouldn't be able to convince him. Not about the slobberers or leaving Eileen.

A cry came from inside the house.

'Help.'

It was Gramps. I rushed in. Gramps was sitting on the dunny, the door open, yelling hysterically. 'It attacked me,' he shouted. 'A giant worm.'

Eileen and Rory got to him first. By the time I'd

sprinted down the hall, Gramps' cries had turned to quiet sobs.

'A giant worm,' he sniffled.

'It's okay, Wilf,' said Eileen gently. 'It's just the draught excluder.' She held up the cloth tube filled with sand we used to stop draughts whistling under the dunny door.

'Don't worry, Gramps,' said Rory. 'It's scared me a few times too.'

While they comforted Gramps, I noticed an amazing thing. The blotches on their skins were shrinking.

'I'm just a dopey old man,' sobbed Gramps.

'No you're not,' said Dad, hobbling along the hall. 'Anyway, a bloke doesn't have to be old to be dopey.' He turned to Eileen. 'Sorry I blew my stack,' he said softly.

Eileen looked at him and frowned. 'Did you? I don't remember.'

Dad put his arms round her. As I watched them hug and kiss, I realised that for all their good qualities, me and Rory couldn't depend on them to get to the bottom of the weird and scary stuff that was happening.

And if our own parents wouldn't believe us, the police and the army certainly wouldn't.

It was up to us kids.

FIVE

For a second or two I had thought that Mum and Jack were going to bust up. But no such luck. After the big row everyone settled down and went back to abnormal. Mum and Jack were as thick as thieves again. All lovey-dovey.

I showed Mum the remains of my mouse and she just said, 'Poor thing. Must have died of stress, listening to you two fighting.'

Dawn didn't fare any better when she showed them her sucked-out fish. 'That's a shame, love,' said Jack. 'But the only slobberers around here are you two at tea time.' Mum and Jack both laughed like crazy. Parents can be maddening sometimes.

Dawn and I went outside and dug two little graves. I put my mouse skin in the bottom of one and Dawn slipped her flat fish into the other.

'Say a few words,' said Dawn.

I bowed my head over the graves. 'Nibbler,' I said. 'You were happy until you got into a step-family.'

'So were you, Finger,' said Dawn.

'You didn't really want a step-fish but

141

you put up with it,' I said.

'Same for you, Finger,' said Dawn. 'A step-mouse is just like a step-brother. Painful.'

I cleared my throat. 'But then you both got sucked out by slobberers. We know you had a terrible end to your short lives. But now you can rest in peas.'

'Peace, idiot,' said Dawn. 'Rest in peace.'

'I know that,' I said in an embarrassed voice.

I picked a white onion-weed flower and threw it into Nibbler's grave. Dawn threw a buttercup on top of Finger and we filled in the two small holes. Then we went into my bedroom where we could talk.

The snail box was on the bed next to my apple-man. Dawn stared at the snail. It was safely tucked up inside its shell and nothing was happening.

'It doesn't look infected,' said Dawn. 'I don't think you're contagious. But I reckon your mum probably is. She's going to infect an animal, and then it's going to go looking for another one of your relatives. Who will it be?'

I didn't want to think about that. 'What will carry the germs?' I said. 'Mosquitoes? Or ants? Or wombats? Or kangaroos? Or elephants? It could be anything.'

'What *I* want to know, Worm Boy,' said Dawn, 'is where this germ or whatever it is came from in the first place.'

I felt sick in the stomach. I couldn't think about that either. I didn't want to face the thought. When you don't want something to be true you can pretend that it's not.

But in the end it gets to you. Like a slobberer in an apple. In the end it will come for you.

Dawn was never one to beat around the bush. She took a deep breath. 'Your dad,' she said. 'Your dad sent the slobberers in your apple-man present.'

'He didn't,' I screamed. 'The slobberers were only normal grubs. They probably got infected in the mail. Or after I got the apple-man. Dad wouldn't send slobberers after me. I'm his son. He wouldn't. He could be the next victim. We have to find him.'

'Okay,' said Dawn. 'Keep your shirt on. You could be right. But it's up to us. We are the only ones who know what's real.'

'But some things *aren't* real,' I said.

'Like what?' said Dawn.

'Like the bus getting new again. Like the goat coming to life. Like the flies and the maggots. Like me seeing your mum.'

It slipped out. It just slipped out.

'What?' shrieked Dawn. She sprang up into the air like a demented cat. 'You saw my mum? Don't be ridiculous. How dare you. You must be out of your mind.'

'That's what *I* thought,' I said. 'It's the disease. It makes you see things when you get upset. Hallucinations. Like a nightmare. That's what happened on the bus.'

Dawn calmed down a bit.

'My mum's dead,' she said sadly. 'I saw her body in the funeral parlour. Her hair was all wrong. And they put a horrible shade of lipstick on her lips. But it was her all right. She looked peaceful and ...'

A little tear ran down her cheek before she said the last word.

'... dead.'

I didn't know what to say. What can you say?

'Dawn,' I said after a bit. 'In the dream she was her old self. She had the right lipstick. And her hair was the same as always. And she wore both shoes. And those leather gloves you gave her.'

Dawn suddenly gasped as if she had swallowed something that wouldn't go down. 'Mum only wore those gloves once,' she yelled. 'The day after her birthday. The day of the last bus trip. The one you can't remember. When Mum died. You must have been re-living the last journey.'

That made me stop and think. The germs in my mind must have made me believe that the bus was growing new again. And then I'd started to remember the last journey.

'What happened next?' Dawn yelled. 'Tell me.'

'I don't know,' I said. 'I jumped out of the bus and everything was back to normal.'

Dawn started to punch my pillow. I think she was pretending that it was me. 'Trust you,' said Dawn. 'Trust you to wake up just at the wrong moment. Can't you do anything right? You're just like your useless father.' She picked up my apple-man and threw him across the room.

'You ratbag,' I yelled. I grabbed her by the arm and gave her a bit of a shake. In a flash we were scratching and pulling and rolling over and over on the floor like two fiends.

She was too strong for me. She always got the better of me.

'Ugly step-sister,' I shouted.

'Ugly?' she yelled. 'Ugly? You should take a look at yourself.'

She suddenly let go of me and started backing away. Staring at me as if I had just landed from Mars.

'What's up now?' I spat out.

'Look in the mirror,' said Dawn in a horrified voice.

I stood up and stared into the mirror.

It wasn't me. The reflection belonged to someone else. A mean face. Sort of like a bully. A snarling, hateful vision of what I was feeling.

'Aagh,' I screamed. 'Aagh . . .'

'Calm down,' said Dawn. 'Calm down. It's the infection. Feeding on the anger. Think of peaceful things.'

I closed my eyes and tried to think of something relaxing. It's hard to be calm when you have just turned into a monster. 'Think,' I said to myself. 'Think peace.' I tried to force pleasant images into my mind. The moon reflected in a silver pond . . . a hamburger . . . gentle sea breezes . . . a trail bike roaring through the forest . . . a waterfall . . . a bucket of ice-cream. Gradually my breathing slowed and my heart stopped its hammering.

'That's better,' said Dawn. 'Keep it up. It's working.'

I opened my eyes and examined my reflection. The hateful face was draining away. I was coming back to normal. I felt a little better. I couldn't get rid of the fear though. And it still showed in my face. But fear isn't as ugly as hate and I didn't look nearly as bad as before.

'Dawn,' I said. 'Whenever I get angry the illness starts to spread in my body and changes my looks. It's the same with Mum. Did you see her ugly face when she told you off?'

'You'll have to keep your cool,' said Dawn. 'Otherwise you'll stir it up again.'

'Then don't rubbish my dad,' I said. 'He wouldn't send germs. He doesn't know anything about it.'

Dawn was staring down at the floor with a startled look on her face. 'He might not know anything about the slobberers,' she said. 'But the slobberers sure know about him.'

She pointed to a silvery trail on the floor. It looked like a snail's track. But we both knew that it wasn't. It was the trail left the day before by the last slobberer out of the apple. The long, long one. The one that had spelt out a word with its body.

We both stood there in silence. My secret was out. The silvery trail spelt out the word Karl for anyone to see.

'He didn't send the slobberers,' I shrieked.

'All right, all right,' said Dawn. 'Maybe he did and maybe he didn't. But there's one thing for sure. If he didn't, the next creature that gets infected is going to go looking for him.'

She was right. She was dead right. If Mum infected

any living creature, it was going to make Dad its victim. The slobberer's message said so.

I jumped to my feet and ran to the window. Outside in the forest were all sorts of animals. And insects. Mum could infect any of them.

I felt like a paper-clip between two big magnets. I wanted to stay and protect Mum. Keep creatures away from her. But I wanted to go to Dad too. Mum might already have infected something that was on its way to Dad.

Mum. Dad. Mum. Dad. How could I choose? In the end I decided to try and help Dad. After all, Mum had Jack to look after her. Dad might not have anybody. And I hadn't seen him for so long.

'We have to find him,' I said. 'We have to find Dad before it's too late.'

'Does Eileen know where he is?' said Dawn.

'No. He never told us. We'll have to find him ourselves. Let's go.'

A hand grabbed my arm. A powerful hand. It was Jack. 'The only place you're going, young man,' he said, 'is to hospital.'

The staff at our local hospital were having a quiet afternoon. Until we walked in.

'Yuck,' said the young doctor in Casualty when he saw Rory and Eileen's skin, which I thought was a bit slack for a person with years of training.

The doctor asked Rory and Eileen if they'd been in contact with acid or crop-dusting spray or sewage. Eileen looked bewildered. 'I don't think so,' she said.

Rory didn't say anything. I could see he was trying hard not to get angry, but he looked pretty trapped and unhappy.

He put his mouth close to my ear, which felt a bit strange. 'Help me get out of here,' he hissed. 'Please.'

Dad explained about the car crash and the step-family and the stress. 'Stress-induced skin complaint, I reckon,' he said to the doctor. 'Plus Eileen's probably got a bit of concussion.'

'From the war,' said Gramps. 'Against the green army.'

The doctor asked Dad if Gramps had concussion too. 'No,' said Dad, 'he's just old.'

I squeezed Gramps' hand.

The doctor took Rory and Eileen off for tests, and Dad for a leg X-ray. As they were going, Rory grabbed my arm. 'Please,' he whispered desperately.

I didn't say anything.

As I watched them go I struggled with my second shameful thought that day. What if the doctors couldn't find out what the infection was? What if Rory and Eileen were shut away and kept under observation for weeks or months or years?

That would just leave me and Dad and Gramps. And Dad would go back to hugging me first.

I tried hard not to feel too happy. It didn't seem right in a place where there were people with tubes up their noses. But I did feel my heart beat a bit faster and I did have a sudden urge to hug Gramps.

Then, as Rory was being led away down the corridor, he turned and looked at me. The look only lasted a few seconds, but it left me shaking. It was the look of a kid who wanted to save his dad. Not just a bit. Not even quite a lot.

Desperately.

And even though I didn't want to, I knew exactly how he felt.

I felt the same way every time I pictured myself sprawled on the floor watching a dopey TV show while Mum was drowning. Chuckling my head off. Instead of hurling myself out the door and sprinting to the river and diving in and saving her.

If only I could turn time back.

But I couldn't.

All I could save now was her good name. And my memories of her.

'Gramps,' I said. 'We've got to get Rory out of here.'

Gramps looked disappointed. He was fiddling with the postage stamp machine in the hospital foyer. 'I wanted some of that chocolate,' he said as I led him away. Then he frowned. 'Rory can't leave, he's sick. He needs to be cured.'

'He will be, Gramps,' I said. 'But first we've got to find out what type of infection he's got and I reckon the person to tell us that is Rory's dad.'

Gramps peered into the distance as if he was struggling with a memory. Perhaps it was just the chocolate.

'I dunno,' he said after a bit. 'Doctors are the ones that know about infections. And vets.'

'Gramps,' I said, looking hard into his milky grey eyes. 'I think Rory can help us find out about Mum.'

Gramps' wobbly jaw was suddenly set hard. 'My daughter is dead,' he croaked, 'and I won't hear a bad word against her.'

'Me neither,' I said. 'That's why we've got to get Rory out of here. You know how the infection is taking Eileen's memory away? Well I think it's bringing Rory's back. He's started having memories of being on the bus just before it crashed. If we can give him the chance, he might be able to tell us why Mum died.'

Gramps' eyes shone. Then his shoulders slumped. 'It's hopeless,' he said. 'This place is like a fortress. The staff have all got guns.'

I reminded him about the difference between guns and pagers, then told him my plan. His eyes shone again.

'There's an op-shop next door,' he said. 'We can get the stuff we need there.'

After we'd been to the op-shop, we waited in the hospital foyer until the nurse on reception ducked out to get some afternoon tea. Then we hurried along the corridor. I looked at the signs on the walls and doors.

'What's the word,' I whispered, 'for the place people are put when they've got an infectious disease?'

'Dunno,' said Gramps. 'I'm no good at crosswords. How many letters?'

I saw a sign on a side corridor saying QUARANTINE. It looked like the word.

Small country hospitals like ours didn't have many patients with infectious diseases, I could tell. The hand-written sign was one give-away. Another was the precautions they'd taken to keep the germs in. I'd seen on telly once how big city hospitals had double air-lock doors with a special microwave oven for your handbag. Our hospital just had big sheets of plastic sticky-taped across the corridor.

Holding our breath, Gramps and I squeezed through the plastic. No alarms went off. We gave each other relieved looks. Then suddenly a trolley burst through a door. Wheeling it was a bloke in a white smock. He stopped and looked at us suspiciously.

'What are you doing in here?' he demanded.

I turned Gramps around. 'Come on, Gramps,' I said

crossly. 'You know you're not meant to be down here. The old people's ward is the other way.'

'Eh?' said Gramps.

I turned to the bloke. 'After you,' I said. 'He's a bit slow.'

The bloke gave me a sympathetic grin and clattered off through the plastic. We waited till he'd turned the corner, then hurried on down the corridor.

'Sorry,' I said to Gramps. 'You're not really slow.'

'That was a close one,' said Gramps. 'Ernie Piggot went on one of those trolleys and lost his prostate.'

I took Mum's shoe out of my shirt and held it out to Gramps. 'Hang on to this,' I said. 'In case there are infectious germs in the air.'

Gramps took it. 'Thanks,' he said.

We started peeking through the glass panels in the doors. The first two rooms were empty. Then someone called my name. 'That sounded like Rory,' I whispered. The door of a nearby room clunked shut. 'In there,' I said.

We stepped into darkness. A tiny thread of sunlight peeped through the curtains. I could just make out the shape of a figure in the bed. I went over. Rory didn't move. I gave him a shake. Instead of flesh and bone, all I could feel were folds of something soft.

Skin.

I gasped and jumped back. Oh no. The infection had done what the slobberers hadn't been able to. Eaten out Rory's insides.

'Don't look,' I mumbled to Gramps, my head swimming with nausea and grief.

'That's right,' said a voice. 'Or the light'll hurt your eyes.' We spun round. A light blinked on and Rory stepped out of a little bathroom. 'They're just blankets,' he said, pointing to the bed. 'So they'll think I'm asleep after I've gone.' He sighed. 'Except I can't go 'cos they'll recognise me. Every doctor, nurse and handyman has been sticky-beaking through that door at the kid with the yucky skin.'

My heart had calmed down enough for me to speak. 'It's not that yucky,' I said, which wasn't true. I tried to ignore my neck cramp and all thoughts of curried-egg sandwiches. 'Anyway,' I went on, 'we've got a plan.' I handed him the op-shop bag. 'Put these on.'

Rory stared. 'That's a *woman's* coat,' he said indignantly. 'An *old* woman's coat.'

'That's right,' said Gramps. 'It was Ivy Bothwell's.'

'And this,' I said, 'is an old woman's hat. If you want to get out of here, put them on.'

Scowling, Rory put them on. 'This is pointless,' he said. 'They'll still recognise my face.'

'No they won't,' I said.

Rory rolled his eyes. 'You're so dumb,' he said.

I took a deep breath. This was the riskiest part of the plan. 'Not as dumb as you,' I said. 'You think the sun shines out of your dad's bum, but a two year old could see he's the evil mastermind behind everything that's happened.'

Rory's eyes flashed angrily. 'No he's not,' he snapped. His face was starting to change.

'It's obvious,' I said. 'Your dad's using this infection to get back at you and Eileen for being in a new family.'

'Bull,' hissed Rory. Already he was hardly recognisable.

'He's out to get you,' I said as harshly as I could.

'Shut up,' gritted Rory, furious. His face had crumpled into a creased, wizened mask of anger. In the hat and coat he looked like grumpy old Mrs Creely from the school tuckshop.

I felt terrible that I'd done it to him. But this was no time for guilt.

'Quick,' I said to Gramps. 'Let's get him out of here.'

I grabbed Rory's overnight bag and turned the light off and we crept out and hurried down the corridor and through the plastic. Gramps was great, keeping an eye out for doctors so I could concentrate on saying awful things to Rory about his dad to keep him angry.

Only once did Gramps lose it. Just as we were hurrying out to the car park, he looked at Rory, confused. 'Mrs Creely,' he said, 'what are you in for?'

By the time we got to Gramps' car, Rory was back to normal. Well, as normal as a kid with a monstrous infection could be.

He looked at me. 'Thanks,' he said. 'I know you had to do that, and I know you didn't really mean it.'

I didn't say anything.

'Thanks, Gramps,' said Rory. 'I don't know what I'd do without you.' He and Gramps hugged each other for a long time. I looked away. Sometimes, I thought, too much hugging goes on in this family.

Rory suddenly had a thought. 'I should say goodbye to Mum,' he said.

'No,' I said. 'That wouldn't be a good idea.' I'd had the same thought about Dad but it was too risky. 'They're in good hands,' I said.

Then I had another thought. I almost kicked myself.

'Worm Boy,' I said. 'You don't know where your dad is, do you?'

Rory stopped hugging Gramps. 'No,' he said. 'You know I don't.'

'So how are we going to find him?' I asked.

Rory gave one of those grins small kids give when they've had a really good idea. 'We'll get ourselves a guide,' he said, and then grinned even wider because I didn't have a clue what he was talking about. 'If my mum infects something,' he continued, 'that thing will go straight to Dad, right? To try and infect him.'

'Probably,' I said.

'So we get my mum to infect something,' he said, 'then follow it.'

I stared at him. The germ was obviously getting to his brain. Even Gramps could see how dopey that idea was.

'What do we follow it in?' I said. 'A helicopter? You saw how fast those slobberers moved.'

'Yeah,' said Rory. 'That's why we need something slow.'

He opened Gramps' car door, groped around on the

floor and held up the plastic box with the see-through lid.

'Something slow like this,' he said. Inside the box, the snail looked at us, bored.

'Clever boy,' said Gramps. I scowled. The trouble with old people was they were too easily impressed.

'Two things, Wonder Boy,' I said. 'One, this snail will take about eighteen years to get anywhere. Two, it'll infect every other snail it meets on the way.'

'Not if we keep it in the box,' said Rory. 'The infected snail will be quarantined in here, and we can use it like a compass. Whichever direction the snail crawls, we drive.'

'Brilliant,' said Gramps. It was sickening. But I had to admit it was clever.

Except for one thing.

'How do we get your mum to infect it?' I said. 'We can't just go up to her and say, 'Excuse me, Eileen, can we put this snail on one of your scabs?'

'You and Gramps will have to do it,' said Rory. 'I can't go back in there.' He sighed. 'Do it gently.'

I sighed too, for my sake rather than Eileen's. Then I took Mum's shoe back from Gramps and told him to stay in the car with Rory. No point in us both being arrested for illegally touching a public hospital patient with a gastropod.

Eileen's room was down the corridor from Rory's. When I got there and peeked in, it was empty. I crept in, made sure nobody was in the bathroom, took the snail out of the box and started searching the room for blood samples or scabs.

Nothing.

Then I heard voices coming down the corridor.

I looked frantically around for a hiding place big enough for a girl and a snail. The bathroom was too risky. Coffee drinkers always had over-active bladders. I climbed into the wardrobe and hoped Eileen wasn't planning to change for dinner.

I'd just got the wardrobe doors closed when Eileen and a nurse came in. Through the crack I saw the nurse settle Eileen into bed and give her a tablet. 'This'll help you sleep,' she said. I hoped she was right. My heart was pounding and the snail was feeling very slimy in my hand.

After about ten years, Eileen's slow breathing told me she was asleep. I crept out of the wardrobe and checked her over. All her cuts and scratches were bandaged. I swallowed nervously. I'd have to make one of my own.

I searched among the nurse's stuff on the bedside table for a scalpel. Nothing. Not even a pair of scissors. Then I remembered something.

Mum's shoe had a loose nail in the heel. After a bit of a struggle I got it out with my teeth. It was pretty rusty but the tip was still fairly sharp. I rubbed it on my shirt so Eileen wouldn't get tetanus and wondered if I could get it through her skin without waking her up.

Eileen murmured something and rolled over. I could

see her bare bottom through the crack in her hospital gown.

'Sorry, Eileen,' I whispered, and placed the point of the nail against her buttock.

I couldn't do it.

It was dopey. All the times I'd imagined stabbing my step-mother, and now I had the chance I couldn't even prick her skin.

Then I remembered something else. Eileen's feet. She was always complaining how her shoes rubbed her feet.

Carefully I lifted the sheet at the bottom of the bed. Perfect. Raw patches on both Eileen's heels.

'Sorry, snail,' I whispered and put it onto one of the raw spots. I'd never infected a snail before so I didn't know how long it would take. I counted to ten, lifted the snail off, put it in the box, found band-aids on the bedside table, stuck one on each of Eileen's heels and slipped out of the room.

I hurried back to the car park with the world's first living compass inside my shirt. I tried to forget that the snail clinging to the thin plastic next to my skin was infected. I tried to forget what that could mean.

The whole way, though, I gripped Mum's shoe tightly. Just in case.

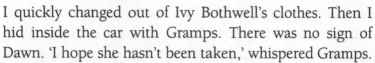

SEVEN

I quickly changed out of Ivy Bothwell's clothes. Then I hid inside the car with Gramps. There was no sign of Dawn. 'I hope she hasn't been taken,' whispered Gramps.

'She wouldn't tell the doctors what we're up to, would she?' I asked.

Gramps scoffed loudly. 'A Finnigan would never go over to the other side,' he said.

We had to get out of the hospital car park quickly before someone saw me and took me back into the isolation ward. In the distance I could see men in white coats searching. There was no time to lose. 'I'll do one quick whip round the grounds,' I said. 'And then we'll have to go without her.'

Gramps nodded. 'Watch out for sentries,' he said. 'And take these for the barbed wire.' He reached down under the seat and handed me a pair of pliers. Poor old Gramps. He thought he was back in the war again.

I slipped out of the car and started to run. *Crash.* I bumped into someone running just as fast in the other direction and we both sprawled onto the ground.

'Idiot,' said a familiar voice.

It was Dawn. She rubbed her big backside and grinned at me.

'Did you infect the snail?' I said hoarsely.

'The snail,' yelled Dawn. We both looked around. The lid had come off the box and the snail was heading across the car park at great speed. I had never seen a snail move so fast before. It was really travelling. I jumped up and ran after it with the box. I grabbed the snail by the shell and dropped it back inside the container and shoved the lid on.

'It must be infected,' said Dawn in amazement. 'A normal snail can't move that fast. You shouldn't have touched it.'

'It's okay,' I said. 'It's after Dad, not me. Let's go.'

I grabbed the front doorhandle of the Morris Minor with trembling fingers.

So did Dawn.

'I'm sitting in the front,' we both yelled at the same time.

I couldn't believe it. In the middle of all this excitement she was worrying about something as trivial as that. And I knew why. She was jealous of me and Gramps. We were becoming mates. And Dawn didn't like it.

Dawn shoved me aside and jumped into the front seat of the car with Gramps. Oh well, I still had my apple-man for company. And the snail for that matter.

I shrugged and scrambled into the back. Gramps crunched the gears and the car lurched forward. Blue smoke billowed out behind us.

'Which way is the snail headed?' Gramps yelled.

I stared down into the snail box. The snail was moving fast. 'That way,' I said.

Gramps threw a glance over his shoulder. 'North-west,' he said.

The snail reached the end of the box and stopped. I turned the whole thing around and the snail immediately turned and headed north-west again.

Gramps accelerated noisily down the hospital drive and stopped at the road. 'Now which way?' he said.

The snail was still headed north-west, which was lucky because the street ran in the same direction. 'Turn left,' I yelled.

Gramps followed my outstretched hand and the car lurched and swayed down the road. He was a terrible driver. He narrowly missed an old lady who was crossing the road. Then he stopped at a T-intersection.

This time we were not so lucky. The road ran from east to west.

'I don't know which way,' I yelled.

Gramps stared down at the snail. 'A strange compass,' he said. 'Must be captured from the enemy. It's not one of ours. But don't worry. They all work the same way. We just make every turn that takes us in the general direction. In the end we'll get there.'

Gramps lurched off to the right.

I looked at the snail. 'It's so creepy,' I said.

We both stared into the snail box. The snail looked normal but we knew it was intelligent now it was infected. It moved too fast. And those eyes. They were big. More like people's eyes. They swivelled on the end of their thin stalks. They looked back up at us. Filled with hate.

Dawn thought about it for a bit. 'All the infected creatures got smart,' she said. 'The sheep and the slobberers and the frogs. They all did clever things.'

'It's not the creatures,' I said. 'It's the germs. The germs take over their brains. This is not really a snail any more. It is only the body of a snail.'

I started to get scared. Very scared. 'Hey, Dawn?'

'What?'

'The frogs grew big.'

'Yeah?'

'So did the slobberers. And the sheep grew steel wool.'

'So?'

'So what's this snail going to do? Why is it just walking around inside the box? Why isn't it changing? Why doesn't it try to get out?'

'Because we are taking it to where it wants to go,' said Dawn. 'To your father. To the one next to you in the blood line. So it can infect him.'

She was right. Or was she? There was something that didn't make sense but I couldn't figure out what it was.

I had something else to worry about. The disease had infected me. And my mother. So what happened to the infected people? The virus fed on anger. We knew that. But in the end what became of the victims?

I tried not to think about it. But I couldn't help it.

'I'm going to die,' I blurted out.

Dawn reached over and put her hand on my arm. Even though I was panicking a little thrill ran through my body. She had a really soft hand for such a tough girl.

Gramps snatched a quick glance at me. 'Everybody dies sooner or later,' he said. 'It's just a matter of when.'

'That's okay if you're a hundred and fifty,' I said. 'But I'm only thirteen. There's still a few things I haven't done yet.'

'Like what?' said Gramps.

I stared at Dawn. She really did have a cute little turned-up nose. And very nice lips. I could feel my face starting to go red. 'Like nothing,' I said grumpily.

Gramps gave a smile. 'There's plenty of things I still want to do, too,' he said.

'Like what?' said Dawn.

'Like never you mind,' he said with a devilish grin.

'He's thinking about Mrs Mugavin at the bowls club,' said Dawn.

'I am not,' said Gramps hotly. Then he started to chuckle. 'Okay, you got me,' he said.

Gramps was great. He cheered us up without us noticing that he had done it. A little bit of the terror had gone out of the journey.

The snail crawled about in the box. And the Morris Minor crawled along the roads.

We followed that snail. Out into the country. Far, far, from home. The sun was just beginning to set as we reached the town of Mooraboolie.

Gramps stopped at a roundabout. 'This is a big town,' he said. 'What does the snail say?'

'Left,' I said. 'It's the only road running north-west.'

The more I thought about it, the more scared I became. At any moment I might see my dad. That was wonderful. I'd waited so long. But . . .

'What will the snail do when we get there?' I asked in a trembling voice. 'What if it bursts out of its box?'

Gramps changed the subject. 'We had snails in France,' he said. 'During the war. Do you know what we used to do with them? When we were short of rations . . .'

Gramps never got to tell us the rest. We passed under a sign which said AMBLE-BY COTTAGES. Gramps threw a glance at the sign and put his foot on the brake. I looked ahead and saw that the road came to a dead end. We were in a sort of crescent that ended in a circle.

I stared out of the window. There were lots of kids riding bikes and skateboards and mucking around on the footpath. More kids than you would normally see in a street like that. There was something different about them. What was it? Then I realised. They were all dressed alike. Not the same clothes. But the same *sort* of clothes. As if they had been bought in the one shop.

Gramps was looking at them too. With a horrified expression on his face. Suddenly he let out the clutch and did a u-turn. The Morris Minor bumped up over the kerb and started heading back the way we had come. Gramps had a wild, upset look in his eye.

'Hey,' I yelled. 'This isn't the way. The snail wants to go back there.'

The snail was going crazy. It was foaming with green bubbles and racing in circles inside the cake box. Its eyes blinked and winked angrily. It wanted to get out.

'I've just remembered something your mum . . .' said Gramps. 'I made a mistake. You don't use the enemy's compass.'

I reached over and turned off the ignition key. 'We're close to Dad,' I shouted. 'You're not stopping me now.' I jumped out of the car and checked the snail. It wanted me to go along the street. I ran, faster and faster. My heart was thumping. At any moment I would see Dad. My father. Who loved me.

Suddenly the snail stopped. Not a movement.

I was standing next to a large tree on the nature strip outside a house. I gave the box a shake. 'Which way,' I yelled. 'Which way?'

The snail started to climb up the side of the box. This was crazy. Was it trying to get out? Did it want to streak ahead and infect my father?

'Turn it on its side,' said a sad voice. It was Gramps. Dawn wasn't far behind him.

I turned the box on its side and the snail immediately started climbing.

'Up?' I said. 'It wants to go up?'

I looked into the tree. The leaves and branches were thick and I couldn't see into the top. I started to climb. It was difficult going. I had the slobberer's wound on one hand, a snail box in the other and the apple-man half hanging out of my pocket. But I climbed and climbed and climbed.

I was desperate. Branches scratched my face and sharp twigs clawed at my legs. But I ignored them. I didn't even notice my bleeding legs and fingers. All I wanted was to see my father again. Dad, Dad, Dad.

Finally, right at the top, I stopped. There was someone there. Sitting on a branch.

A head popped out between the leaves and looked my way.

My heart dropped. It wasn't Dad.

It was a boy. He was older than me. He stared at me with wide open eyes. For a moment he was frozen. Stunned. He looked at me wordlessly. He seemed to be choking with shock. He couldn't believe what he was seeing.

Neither could I.

The snail box slipped from my hand and tumbled down through the branches. I hardly noticed. I didn't even hear it hit the ground. And I didn't look down to see if the lid had come off the box.

I couldn't take my gaze off the boy. I had seen those big, brown eyes before. And that gap between the two front teeth. And the nose and the hair. And the ears. I had seen them all. In the mirror.

The boy in the branches. Staring into my eyes.

Was a dead ringer for me . . .

Book Four

DEAD RINGER

ONE

It was like looking into a mirror. The boy who stared at me through the tree branches had my eyes, and ears, and hair. Even my nose. There was a bit of fuzz on his top lip. And he was a bit taller and had a couple of pimples.

But apart from that, the boy was me. He blinked back – stunned – not believing what he was seeing.

I tell you this. I had been chased by slobberers. And I had looked into the jaws of a giant frog. I had seen Dawn's dead mother smile at me. And had followed a snail compass halfway across the state. But all that was nothing compared to this.

I knew this boy. And he knew me. But how can you know someone you have never seen before? And why was my stomach jumping? Why were my hands clammy?

RORY

I felt like you do on Christmas morning when you get an unexpected present. It was like witnessing a birth. Weird. Really weird.

'Aagh, the snail's out. The snail's escaped.' Dawn's shrieking voice came up from below.

I couldn't see the ground from where I was. But I realised with a shock that the infected snail must have escaped when I dropped the box. The snail that was seeking my next of kin. That wanted to kill my father.

'It's heading up the tree,' came Gramps' shaky shout. 'It's infiltrating our defences. Get the beggar.'

The boy was puzzled. But I was scared. Was my dad up there somewhere? I had to protect him. I scrambled out in the branches. 'Dad, Dad, Dad,' I yelled. 'Where are you? Look out. Jump. Get out of the tree. The snail's coming.'

No one answered. There was no one else up there.

I peered down and saw it. Coming up the trunk at a great rate of knots. The fastest snail in the world. I searched wildly for something to hit it with. I tried to snap off a small branch but it wouldn't break. There was only one thing to do. I pulled out my apple-man and started swatting wildly at the snail.

It was a bad idea. The snail vanished. Where was it? Where was the rotten thing? Where had it gone? Oh, shoot. It was crawling around on the head of the apple-man. It was sticking its face and horrible eyes into my apple-man's nostrils. Without thinking I grabbed the apple-man by the legs and started bashing its head against a branch. I didn't give a thought to the apple-man. I just had to get rid of the infected snail. It was clinging on like crazy.

I held the apple-man as steady as I could and bent back my finger. Flick. *Whap.* The snail spun off into the air and fell towards the ground.

'Look out, Dawn,' I shouted. 'It's back down there somewhere.'

'Got him,' came Gramps' excited voice. 'Got the bludger.'

'Put it in the box,' I yelled. 'Put it in the box.'

Then I forgot about the snail and turned to the older version of myself.

He was holding something out at me. At first I couldn't make sense of it. How did he get that? He had my apple-man. In his shaking hand he held out my apple-man, almost pushing him into my face.

Something was wrong. Something was very wrong. I looked down at my own shaking hand. I was still holding my apple-man. His head was a bit dented and there were sort of lumps under his shirt that I hadn't noticed before. I could feel them with the tips of my fingers. But he was still my apple-man. So how could the boy have it?

The answer was simple. He had one too – just like mine.

'Where did you get that?' I said in a shaking voice.

He came closer and examined me carefully. 'Where did *you* get my face?' he said.

I tried to stop myself from fainting. From falling out

of the tree. I tried desperately to fit all the pieces together. 'Concentrate,' I told myself. 'Work it out. Slowly, slowly. Bit at a time.'

The boy was a bit older than me – okay.

The boy looked just like me – right.

The boy had an apple-man – no doubt about that.

The snail was after someone related to me – Dawn had worked that out already.

My father wasn't up the tree – rats.

So the snail must be after the boy – that was the only answer.

So.

The boy must be related to me.

That's when it all clicked. The thought hit me like a train rushing out of a tunnel. Suddenly it all made sense.

'You,' I whispered to the boy. 'You . . . You must be my . . .' I could hardly get the word out. I seemed to choke on it. 'You're . . . my . . .'

'Brother,' he said softly. I could see tears forming in his eyes.

I had a brother. All these years he had been alive and I never knew. I was all mixed up inside. Why hadn't I been told?

I was confused. I was heartbroken that Dad wasn't there. But I had someone new. At that moment the world became a little more friendly. I didn't seem quite so alone.

My brother and I both started to sob. He reached out and grabbed my arm. He pulled me close. 'You're only a little squirt,' he said. 'But you're mine. A blood relative. I thought I was alone.'

A blood relative? That's right. The snail had been after him. Not Dad.

After a bit he managed to say, 'Your ... our ... my mother. And father. Are they still alive?'

I nodded. And hoped that I wasn't lying.

'What are they like?' he asked in a trembling voice.

I couldn't think what to say. 'Well,' I managed to get out. 'That gap between your teeth. That comes from Dad. And those pointy ears. They come from Mum.'

'Mum?' he said. 'Dad?' He seemed to have trouble getting the words out. 'I had a mum,' he said. 'And a dad. They were both killed.'

'But ...' I started to say.

'Wait,' he said. 'My real parents were only sixteen when I was born. I never met them. They gave me up for adoption. That's all I know about them. My new parents were wonderful. But they died in a car crash. And I ended up here. In the cottage homes.'

I didn't know what to say.

He looked so sad. 'Tell me about your parents,' he said. 'Because they are my parents too, you know.'

I knew what he said was true. But it still made me feel funny inside. Having a brother – a real brother – was good. But I wasn't sure that I wanted to share my parents ... again.

I started to tell him my story. It came tumbling out. Full of stuff about Dad and Mum and our step-family.

Halfway through the story a voice came floating up from below. 'Rory. What are you doing up there?' yelled Dawn. 'Hatching an egg?'

'That's the one I told you about,' I said to my brother. 'That's my step-sister. Big Bad Dawn. She's . . . She's . . . all right, I suppose.'

'Hang on to your britches,' I yelled at Dawn. 'I can't come down yet.'

There were more interruptions from below but Howard and I ignored them. We talked and talked and talked. Both learning what there was to know about the other. My new brother got upset when I told him about Mum being in hospital. And Dad being in danger of infection. I tried to explain about the germs but he didn't believe that part of it.

'That's bulldust,' he said. 'Are you weird or what?'

'Come down and see the snail,' I told him. 'It's after you. It wants to infect you. You'll see.'

'It'll be a long time, little brother,' he said, 'before I'm scared of a snail.'

We both climbed down the tree and jumped onto the grass.

'This is Dawn,' I said. 'My . . . your . . . our step-sister.' She was standing there with her mouth hanging open like one of those sideshow clowns.

'What?' said Dawn slowly. I could see that her mind was working overtime. She just couldn't figure it out. For once she didn't have a clue what was going on.

'This is my brother Howard,' I told her.

She was shocked. Totally gobsmacked. She just stood there looking from me to Howard and back again. She couldn't take it in. But there was one thing I noticed. Straight away.

She liked him.

'And this is Gramps,' I said.

Gramps had the engine running on the Morris Minor and the bonnet up. At first I thought that the car must have broken down. But it hadn't. Gramps was cooking something on the cylinder head of the engine. He grabbed the meal with his pliers and held it out towards my brother.

'Hello, Howard,' he said. 'Do you like escargots?'

Howard looked puzzled. Was he wondering why Gramps didn't seem surprised to see him? Or was he just trying to figure out if his new family really ate that sort of thing?

As if to answer his question, Gramps popped the hot snail into his mouth and began to munch. 'Delicious,' he said. 'Absolutely delicious.'

TWO

I was stunned. A step-brother I'd never heard of had just dropped out of a tree. I was gobsmacked. I was flabbergasted. But the shock hadn't affected me as badly as it had Gramps. He'd gone ga-ga.

'Gramps,' I screamed, 'spit that out at once.'

Gramps smacked his lips. 'Top tucker,' he said, swooshing the snail round in his mouth.

'Don't be a dope,' I yelled at him. 'Just because the infection wasn't after you before, doesn't mean it can't change its mind. Even microbes get angry when you eat them.'

I turned to Rory and Howard for support. Howard was staring at us all and slowly backing away. I could tell he thought we were mad. A gang of loonies. A few

billion brain cells short of a step-family.

I turned back to Gramps, who was still chewing happily. 'Do you want to turn into a walking monster?' I shouted at him, scared.

Everyone was looking at me now. Gramps as if I was

sadly misguided and Howard as if I was a mental case and Rory as if I was a thoughtless and hurtful step-sister.

Which I was.

Suddenly I realised it wasn't the microbes that were angry, it was me. Gramps was as bad as all the others. All the people I cared about ended up sick or hurt or dead. Dad in hospital with a damaged leg. Mum at the bottom of the river. When were people in this family going to start taking care of themselves?

Gramps swallowed the snail.

'Mmm-mmm,' he said, 'I could go another dozen of those.'

I held my breath and watched Gramps anxiously. Would the infection race through his body and turn his skin blotchy and make his memory even worse than it was now? I hoped desperately that Rory and I were right about the illness. That it only infected people who were related by blood. And that each new victim had to be related by blood to the person infected before them.

Gramps wasn't related to Eileen by blood, even though she'd squeezed a couple of his blackheads.

Gramps gave me a hug. 'It's okay, love,' he said. 'I used to eat snails by the barrow-load in France in the war. Scientists have proved that if you heat a snail above a hundred and six degrees Celsius, you kill any germs on it.' Gramps frowned. 'Or was that frogs' legs?'

I felt like shaking him, even though he was an old man and I loved him and his teeth weren't that secure.

But I didn't.

Because at that moment I realised how much danger we were in. A big group of kids had gathered round and were staring at us. Now that Gramps had finished his snack, they were staring at Rory.

'Gramps,' I whispered, 'we've got to get Rory out of here. Hospitals call the cops when people steal one of their patients. Rory's probably on the TV news. If he's recognised we'll be arrested.'

Gramps frowned. I hoped he was thinking about how we could get out of there without causing a disturbance. I know I was. Then Howard did something that saved us the trouble.

He touched Rory. Just put his fingertips gently on Rory's arm, the one that was purple and blotchy with the infection.

'Were you born like that?' he asked softly. His own skin looked pale and smooth next to Rory's.

Rory stared at Howard's arm. His eyes filled with tears. Suddenly he turned and pushed through the circle of gawking kids and broke into a lopsided run down the road.

'Quick,' I yelled at Gramps.

We struggled through the kids. I helped Gramps get the bonnet of the car down. Just as I was about to leap in, I saw Howard standing nearby, watching.

I'd never seen so much sadness on one kid's face.

Even as I opened my mouth, I knew it was a mistake. I knew I'd regret it. I didn't want another step-brother. I didn't want another kid living at my place sticking jammy knives in the margarine. I didn't want to have to share Dad with anyone else.

But he just looked so sad.

'If you want to find out about your parents,' I said, 'hop in.'

I got into the car. Gramps revved the engine and started doing a forty-nine-point turn. The other kids were staring at us and gabbling excitedly and yelling things.

Howard was standing very still. He looked scared and confused.

Gramps finally got the car pointing the right way. Just before we shuddered off down the road, Howard clambered in.

It was incredible. He was almost identical to Rory. Bigger, but a dead ringer. And he was holding an apple-man that was a dead ringer for Rory's apple-man.

'Welcome to the family,' I said.

'Thanks,' he said. He didn't sound too sure about it. 'You know,' he continued, 'people who suffer from crazy ideas about, say, killer snails and giant worms and steel sheep can get treatment. I can give Rory the name of a child psychiatrist.'

'I think,' I said, 'you'd better keep your head down.'

Howard ducked out of sight. I peered anxiously through the dusty windscreen. The street was empty. No sign of Rory.

I had a sick feeling in my stomach. What if he got lost? What if the infection wiped his memory and he forgot who he was and where he lived? The thought of

Rory ill and lonely made my eyes prick.

'Perhaps he's gone for a milkshake,' said Gramps. 'Can you see any milk bars?'

'I don't think he wanted a milkshake, Gramps,' I muttered.

'A burger?' asked Gramps hopefully

I sighed. The infection might be vicious and unstoppable, but at least it didn't seem to have made Gramps any worse.

Then I saw Rory ahead in the distance. He was turning down a side road. By the time we got there he was out of sight again. We skidded round the corner with Gramps flailing at the wheel and complaining about the stress on his suspension. After a few minutes I saw Rory again, heading out of town into the scrub.

When we caught up with him, he was crouched by the road, gasping for breath and rubbing his bad leg.

I gasped too. He looked worse than ever. The purple blotches were starting to come down his other arm. They must have spread right across his chest.

I leaped out of the car and went over to him. I put my face close to his. 'I'm sorry I said that stuff about the infection turning Gramps into a monster,' I said quietly. 'You're not a monster, okay?'

Rory didn't look up. 'Why did the infection get me first?' he whispered miserably. His eyes flicked towards Howard. 'Why not him?'

Howard was standing watching us. 'If that's an allergy,' he said, 'I've seen something a bit like it before. Similar but not as bad. There's a kid in the home who's allergic to food colouring and offal.'

I turned to him. 'Keep quiet,' I said, 'and you might learn something.'

'Whoo,' said Howard, amused. 'You're pretty young to be a school principal. Does your dad work for the Department of Education?'

I ignored him. This was exactly what I'd always feared having an older brother would be like.

The pits.

I turned back to Rory. Gramps was hugging him and promising him ridiculous numbers of milkshakes and burgers.

I took a deep breath. I didn't feel good about what I was going to say, but it had to be said.

'Rory,' I began, 'the snail wasn't going after your dad, it was going after your brother, right?'

'Give her a gold medal,' snorted Rory.

'Remember what we said,' I continued gently. 'We know your father's involved with the infection one way or the other. If he's not the next target, he must be the one who sent it in the first place.'

'*You* said, not we said,' hissed Rory angrily. '*You* were the one who said that.'

His face was starting to change. Whatever anger did to the infection, it was happening now. His face was shrivelling and twisting and distorting.

I glanced at Howard, whose own face was pretty distorted too. With amazement.

I pressed on. 'It *is* possible your dad's behind all this. Until we know for sure we've got to be careful, that's all. For your sake and your mum's sake and all our sakes.'

Rory's face was hardly recognisable.

I looked at Howard again. He was staring at Rory, stunned, and I could tell that all of a sudden giant worms and steel sheep didn't seem quite so dopey,

'You're just jealous,' spat Rory, glowering at me. 'You're just jealous that both my parents are still alive.'

I felt fury wrench my own face out of shape and I turned away before I did or said something I'd regret even more than bringing Howard along.

'My dad's not evil,' continued Rory. 'When we find him, you'll see.' Suddenly he was yelling at me. 'You'll see.'

I stared at him, my own step-brother who I wouldn't have recognised even if he had a name tag on. This stranger was the one person in the world who could help me find out the truth about my mum's death. I felt ill.

'Tomorrow,' Gramps was saying, furiously polishing his glasses and peering anxiously at Rory. 'We'll go and find your dad tomorrow.'

'No,' said Howard.

We all turned and stared at him. His eyes were shining and he looked different too. Kind of determined and almost grown-up in a bossy sort of way. I had to admit that the times I'd imagined having a big brother, he did have big brown eyes like Howard's.

'Tomorrow's too long to wait,' said Howard. 'I want to go and find my dad now.'

THREE

The approaching night had already begun to swallow the sun. Gramps, Big Bad Dawn, Howard and I scrambled into the Morris Minor. I sat next to Gramps. Dawn and Howard snuggled down in the back seat. We were so tired. A lot had happened in just one day.

There should have been a lot to say. But we just sat there wrapped in our own thoughts as Gramps drove us through the darkness. Each one of us was carrying a different sadness.

I wanted to find my father. I didn't believe that he had sent slobberers to get me. I thought the germs were after *him*. The snail had been going for Howard. Now that it was gone, Howard might be safe. But Dad could be in danger at this very moment.

I couldn't tell what Howard was thinking. He had just met me and found out that I was his brother. And I had told him that the mother he had never met was seriously ill in hospital. And his father was in peril. The poor kid. He must have been going through hell.

And Dawn. She wanted desperately to know what happened the day her mum died on the bus. I wished that I could remember. I would have told her if I could.

And Gramps. He just couldn't work out what was real and what wasn't. But his daughter had drowned in the bus. He must have wanted to know what happened to her as much as Dawn did.

Sometimes Gramps said a lot of silly things. And at other times, a lot of wise things. But mostly he just kept his thoughts to himself. I had the feeling that there was a lot more going on inside his head than he let on.

Finally Dawn spoke up. In a loud voice as usual. 'The snail was after Howard,' she said. 'It wasn't interested in Rory's dad at all.'

'Why not?' I said.

'Because he's not related to your mum.'

'They used to be married,' I yelped. 'In the good old days before step . . . families. You can't get much more related than that.'

Dawn shook her head in exasperation. 'Yes,' she said. 'But Eileen is not a blood relative. People are not even allowed to marry a blood relative. Your father is not related to your mother by blood.'

She was right. I hated to admit it but she was right.

'So,' said Dawn. 'There's no sense in rushing off looking for your dad, thinking you've got to save him. He doesn't need saving.'

'But we still want to find him,' I said.

'Why?'

Howard answered the question for me. 'Because he *is* our dad,' he said quietly.

That shut Dawn up for a bit. But only for a bit.

'He sent both apple-men,' said Dawn, looking at Howard's where it sat between them. 'Karl knows something about this disease. The slobberer spelt out his name. But how are we going to work out where he is?'

'Good point,' said Gramps. 'Where's the compass?'

'You ate it,' I reminded him.

Gramps shook his head. 'I'm old and tired,' he said. 'I don't know what I'm doing half the time. I must have been bloomin' hungry to eat a compass. I wonder if the magnet will pass straight through.'

We all lapsed back into silence. Dawn didn't really want to find our dad. She just wanted to stay with me till I remembered what happened on the bus the night her mum died. That's the only reason she was interested in me.

Gramps suddenly put his foot on the brake and pulled over next to a small clump of trees. It was completely dark outside. Night noises filled the air. Crickets chirped. Gum leaves rustled gently in the trees above. Somewhere nearby a wallaby bounded through the bush.

'No point wasting petrol,' said Gramps. 'We haven't got much so we'd better decide where we are going.'

Suddenly a splatter of liquid splashed across the windscreen and bonnet. Gramps jumped out and looked up into the branches above. 'A possum,' he yelled. 'A rotten possum is piddling on us.' He started wiping at the bonnet with his sleeve. 'Terrible stuff,' he yelled. 'Really eats into the paintwork.'

We all started to laugh like mad. Suddenly, for just a few minutes, we were not step-kids or adopted kids or jealous kids. We were just three friends laughing at something funny in the night.

'Wait a minute,' said Dawn. She stopped laughing and stared at Howard's apple-man. 'Let's have a look at your apple-man, Rory.'

I switched on the yellow roof light and took out my ugly little doll.

Both apple-men had been loved to bits. They were worn and flattened from being shoved inside our pockets.

'Mine came in the mail one day, years ago,' said Howard. 'The package was posted in the city.'

'So was mine,' I shouted. 'Maybe that's where Dad lives.'

Dawn examined the two shrivelled-up dolls closely. 'The clothes are home-made,' she said excitedly. 'There's no labels on them.'

She was right.

The stitching was crooked and loose. Not like the sort of thing done in a factory. Both apple-men had the same navy-blue jacket and pants. The clothes were exactly the same – except for one thing. Mine had the letters AMP sewn on to the pocket.

'AMP. That doesn't make sense,' I said.

Howard stared at his apple-man. It had the letters ACO sewn on to the pocket. He said it aloud and frowned. 'That doesn't mean anything either,' he said.

'Jeez,' said Dawn. 'You can tell you two are related. Can't you work anything out? Both uniforms were made from the same bit of material. Put the letters together.'

'ACOAMP,' I said. 'That doesn't mean anything, smartypants.'

Gramps was still outside picking something off the bonnet of the Morris Minor. He finally stopped and got back into the driver's seat.

'Try it the other way around,' said Dawn.

'AMPACO,' said Howard. 'What's that?'

'An oil refinery,' said Gramps. 'That's where Karl used to work.'

'What?' we all screamed at once. 'Why didn't you tell us?'

'There was a reason,' said Gramps. 'I know there was a reason why I didn't mention it. But I can't remember what it was. Oh, yes. When they shut down . . .'

'Hey,' shouted Dawn. 'Look at your apple-man, Rory. It's changing.' Everyone stared.

'It looks the same to me,' said Howard.

'No,' said Dawn. 'It's grown fingers.'

I hugged my apple-man close to my chest. Dawn tried to grab him but I held on tight.

'They're funny fingers,' said Dawn. 'No fingernails. She touched one of the little fingers and then pulled her hand away. 'Yuck,' she said. 'They feel like, like . . . a bit of worm or something.'

I peered inside the apple-man's blue uniform. The fingers were actually shoots growing out of the apple itself. They ran down inside the sleeves and out of the cuffs.

'Did it always have fingers?' asked Howard.

'No,' said Dawn. 'We'd better get rid of it. Fast.'

I hugged my apple-man even tighter to my chest. Those little apple-dolls were all we had to remind us of our Dad. There was no way I was going to throw mine out.

'Why does he have to get rid of it?' said Howard in a strained voice.

'Could be a spy,' said Gramps. 'Spies are always shot when they're caught.'

'There could be more slobberers in it,' said Dawn.

'There aren't,' I yelled. 'They've all gone. The apple's just started to grow a bit. So what? I've seen potatoes do it too. It's just an apple with a few suckers.'

'Listen, kids,' said Howard. 'I really can't believe all this stuff about slobberers. I'm not throwing my apple-man out and I don't think Rory should have to either.'

Dawn started to punch the seat. 'You two,' she shouted. 'Are so . . . so . . .'

We all knew that she was trying not to swear.

Gramps tried to calm her down. He passed over a grubby piece of newspaper. 'These'll cheer you up,' he said. 'Anyone like a chocolate-coated almond?'

Dawn glared at Gramps' little offerings of peace. Then she grabbed one and shoved it in her mouth.

I looked at the paper carefully. 'No thanks,' I said politely.

Dawn screamed and jumped out of the car. She started spitting and coughing as if she was choking.

'You knew,' she screamed at me. 'You rotten fink. You knew.'

'What's up with her?' said Howard.

This time I did laugh. I laughed like crazy.

'Possums,' I said. 'They don't just do pee, you know.'

FOUR

We decided to camp for the night. It was my idea. I wanted to show Worm Boy that it took more than a mouthful of possum poo to stop my brain working.

'I reckon,' I said, 'we should sleep here instead of driving on and getting even more tired and skidding off the road and rolling the car and being killed.'

Nobody argued with that.

Rory showed that he still had a working brain too, which was a relief. The way he'd cacked himself

over Gramps' chocolate almond mix-up, I'd started to worry that the infection and lack of sleep was turning his brain into that stuff they use for kitchen sponges.

Suddenly he went serious. 'I reckon,' he said. 'Howard should sleep in the car.'

Nobody argued with that either. Including Howard, even though he was the tallest so the car was going to be more uncomfortable for him than anyone else. We all knew leg cramps were better than sleeping under the stars and being exposed to possible attacks by relentless and vicious microbes.

As Rory and Gramps were getting out of the car, Howard cleared his throat. 'Thanks for bringing me along,' he said. 'I'd rather meet my real parents and risk snuffing it than be stuck in that home.'

Rory's eyes shone. He looked more like himself than he had for hours. 'In this family,' he said, 'we don't leave brothers behind.'

It was a nice thing to say, even though up until that afternoon it hadn't exactly been true.

'Tosh,' said Gramps to Howard. 'A healthy young bloke like you shouldn't be talking about death. You'll probably be getting married soon.'

Howard's cheeks went pink. 'I'm only fifteen,' he said.

It made me feel funny inside seeing Howard blush. Sort of warm.

Then I had an awful thought. Did they put fifteen year olds in jail? Kids who ran off from homes probably got into big trouble. I asked Howard what would happen if the police or social workers caught him.

'It wouldn't be pretty,' said Howard. 'I'd probably be history.'

'Don't worry, Howard,' I said, 'we'll look after you.' It felt strange saying that to an older kid, but Howard gave me a grateful smile.

'I'm starving,' said Rory to Gramps. 'It's okay for you and Dawn, you've eaten, but me and Howard haven't had anything.'

'Very funny,' I said.

'I did have a chocolate cake in the boot,' said Gramps thoughtfully. 'But that was a couple of years ago.' He had an idea. 'We could catch that possum and roast it.'

Rory said he wasn't that hungry after all.

'Oh well,' said Gramps, 'at least we've got some water.' We all perked up. 'In the car radiator,' he said. We all groaned.

Gramps promised us he hadn't bunged in any anti-rust chemicals, so we had a couple of mouthfuls each. It was better than nothing.

We built a camp fire. Then we dragged Gramps' old tarpaulin and blankets out of the boot and made up beds on the ground and one in the car.

'G'night,' said Howard with another grateful smile as we shut him in.

After shifting some rocks from under my blanket and staring into the camp fire for a bit and thinking about curried-egg sandwiches with chips, I tried to go to sleep.

Even though I was exhausted, it wasn't easy. The

blanket smelled of car oil and the hot rusty water had only taken away about one-quarter of the taste of the possum poo.

Plus I was worried about Gramps. What if the snail was stronger than Gramps' digestive juices? What if it was swimming around inside him spreading the disease? An old person might not be able to survive an infection like that.

The bush was alive with strange noises. I listened fearfully. Then I told myself to calm down. The slobberers and the sheep and the frogs were all dead. The only way another creature could get infected and come after us was if the hospital people didn't keep Eileen in quarantine properly.

I hoped the sheets of plastic across the hospital corridor didn't have as many holes in them as Gramps' blanket.

Thinking about Eileen made me think of Dad. Was he still in hospital with his bung leg? Or was he out in the night somewhere, worried and angry, searching for us with the police and State Emergency Service? I rolled over, scraped my pelvis on a rock I'd missed and wished remote bush camping spots had phone boxes.

Then things got worse. Thinking about Dad made me think of Mum. I had a silent cry. I often thought about her at night, wondering if she really had been the wonderful loving Mum I remembered, or whether she'd just been faking it and had actually been a miserable suicidal drinker like some people said.

I could hear Gramps snoring softly on one side of me.

On the other Rory's shape was still and silent.

'Rory,' I whispered, 'are you asleep?'

'I would be,' he hissed, 'if you weren't yakking.'

'I was just wondering,' I said, 'if you'll be seeing any visions of Mum tonight.'

'How do I know?' he replied crossly. 'I'm not a telly. These things aren't scheduled. I can't look at a listing in the paper and see "9.30: Rory's infection gives him more hallucinations and he discovers why Dawn's mum crashed the school bus and died."'

'Sorry,' I said. Even though I felt very disappointed, I felt a bit guilty as well. It was amazing how quickly you could forget that another person was suffering an awful infection when you weren't.

I must have gone to sleep soon after that because the next thing I knew I'd snapped awake.

There was movement nearby. Twigs crunching.

I froze.

In the faint moonlight I could just make out two large figures. They were bigger than sheep. They were even bigger than slobberers.

A horrible thought hit me. What if the frogs weren't all dead? What if they'd come back for a second attack? Rory and Gramps had defeated one giant frog. Maybe this time the frogs had sent two.

Trembling, I groped around in the darkness for a weapon. A stick, Rory's smelly socks, anything. I'd have given all the curried-egg sandwiches in the world for my steel fence post.

Nothing.

Then one of the figures spoke. 'Sorry,' it muttered. 'When your bladder's as old as mine it needs a regular empty.'

'That's okay, Gramps,' mumbled the other figure. 'I could do with one too.'

My body went limp with relief as I watched Rory lead Gramps into the bushes for a pee.

Three seconds later I was tense again. What if Eileen had infected something else? What if the hospital had cockroaches? They could get in and out of Eileen's room even if the door was sealed with silicon grouting. I shuddered as I thought of giant cockroaches scuttling towards us through the bush, huge eyes bloodshot with hatred.

Or bedbugs. The hospital could have bedbugs, which would escape when the sheets were changed. I didn't even know what a bedbug looked like, but my blood still ran cold when I thought of one twenty metres tall with Howard in its mouth.

Or spiders. Or snakes. Or the hospital caretaker's cat.

Suddenly I realised the bush noises had got much louder. What was that? It sounded like something doing horrible things with its own saliva. I couldn't hear properly because my heartbeat was thudding in my ears. I peered frantically into the darkness. All I could see were the black shapes of trees.

Then I realised something else. Rory and Gramps hadn't come back. I opened my mouth to call to them, then closed it. Better keep quiet. I couldn't remember if cockroaches had ears or not.

Trembling, I stood up and fought off a powerful urge to go to the car and wake Howard. It wouldn't be fair, he was more at risk than any of us. Instead I started taking terrified steps in the direction Rory and Gramps had gone. Soon I was among the trees.

I heard the saliva sound again and remembered Rory's description of the giant frog's long slimy tongue.

'Oh no,' I sobbed under my breath, 'the frogs are back.'

Things rustled. Shrill noises rang out and I couldn't tell if they came from tiny throats or huge hungry ones. Wet things brushed against my face and I didn't know if they were dewy creepers or strings of frog saliva.

I panicked and ran. Struggling through tangled under-growth and branches that clawed at me. Then I burst out of a clump of bushes and froze. Silhouetted against the moonlit sky were several massive shapes. I prayed they were trees. Almost fainting, I waited for the sound of a huge tongue moving at speed.

Suddenly something long and dark shot out in front of me. I stifled a scream.

'That's the Southern Cross,' said Gramps' voice. 'My favourite.'

It was an arm. Gramps' arm, pointing.

'Wow,' said Rory's voice.

I couldn't believe it. They were star-gazing. While I was losing years off my life with fear and stress, they were star-gazing.

Anger cleared my vision. I saw that the massive shapes were trees, not frogs. Trembling, I leant against one.

Stifling the scream had been hard, but it took even more effort to stifle the urge to strangle Rory. I didn't know what made me angrier, that he thought star-gazing was more important than finding out the truth about my mum's death, or that he was doing it with my Gramps.

I was about to inform him of the ancient belief that stars are actually the souls of selfish and thoughtless step-brothers glowing with embarrassment. Then something happened which completely distracted me.

Frantic, fearful shouts came from the direction of the car.

'Howard,' I yelled. Rory and Gramps stared, startled to see me. Then we tore back to the car.

I pulled open the rear door. Howard was clutching his blanket around him, white-faced even in the yellow car light. He was sweaty and panting.

'My parents . . .' he sobbed. 'They're all dead.'

I held his hand. 'It was just a dream,' I said, hoping desperately I was right.

'Nightmare,' said Gramps. 'I often get 'em if I have a warm drink just before I go to bed.'

I told Rory and Gramps to go back to sleep. No point in us all being awake.

'Come on, Gramps,' said Rory sulkily, 'I think they want some privacy.'

Howard squeezed himself across the back seat and I sat in the front and talked to him. I told him about his mum and what a good person she was despite her temper and messy bathroom habits. Then I surprised myself and asked him if he had a girlfriend. He said there was a girl at the home he'd quite liked but he didn't think he'd ever see her again.

'What about you?' he asked sleepily. 'Have you got a boyfriend?'

I was glad it was dark and he couldn't see me blush. 'No,' I said, 'I haven't really had time.'

Howard didn't say anything, but I sensed he knew I wasn't telling him the whole story. So I told him the whole story. I don't know why. Stuff I'd never told anyone, not even Dad. How I was waiting desperately to grow out of being an ugly tomboy. How I feared that I was doomed to be one forever. How if what people said about Mum was true, I was probably being punished in some way for having an evil mother.

When I finally shut up I saw that Howard was asleep. I didn't mind. I hadn't meant to blab so much anyway.

With his eyes closed and his face scrunched up he looked almost as young as Rory. I wondered if we'd be able to save him from being infected. I hoped we would. He looked so hurt and he'd had such a tragic life that I wished I could make myself the target of the infection instead of him.

At least that would give me a better chance of finding out the truth about my mother's death.

FIVE

Camping out is all well and good. But when all you have is an old blanket on the ground and no pillow it's the pits.

The sound of kookaburras told me that dawn was approaching. I stood up and shivered and tried to shake the pain out of my stiff neck. Gramps was snoring softly and sleeping just as if he was at home in his own warm bed.

Mist crept through the gum trees and joined a long, soft cloud that floated just above the ground. Nearby my apple-man stood to attention and seemed to watch silently like a small, stiff sentry at the end of his night shift.

Peace. Absolute perfect peace. 'Wouldn't it be nice,' I thought to myself, 'if we could just stay here and live.

Catch rabbits and listen to the birds. No germs. No slobberers. No worry.'

Then my heart felt heavy. No Mum – and no Dad either.

The peaceful thoughts drained away. We had to get going. We had to see this through. We had to move Howard to a safe place before some creature infected him. And we had to find Dad – if he was still alive. We had to discover what it was all about. I walked over to the Morris Minor and looked inside.

Dawn was sleeping softly. Her face seemed gentle and happy. She was even prettier when she was asleep than when she was awake.

A painful thought made me frown. I felt the germs stirring and coming to life inside me. My arm ached and throbbed. The world seemed a dark and unhappy place.

What was happening to me?

Jealousy. That's what. Dawn had spent the *whole* night in the car with Howard.

She had fallen asleep with one arm draped over the seat. Her hand was resting on Howard's knee. And I didn't like it. Not one little bit. She was *my* step-sister first. She should have been resting her hand on me. Not him. She probably thought he was more mature than me. I grew more and more angry.

'Hey, you two,' I yelled. 'Wake up. We have to get going.' I banged on the roof of the car so hard that it shook. Dawn and Howard sat up and stared around in fright.

'What is it?' yelled Howard.

'Time to go,' I said grumpily.

'Keep your shirt on,' said Dawn. 'It's only just got light. It's still early.'

I stared around the clearing and tried to control my jealous thoughts. After all, Howard was my brother. And who cared about Dawn anyway? She was just a bossy step-sister with a cute turned-up nose.

'What's for breakfast?' said Dawn, smiling at Howard.

'What about snails?' he said.

Dawn shook her head and laughed as if it was the funniest joke in the world.

'How about chocolate-coated almonds?' I asked.

'Very funny,' said Dawn.

No one laughed.

I walked away in embarrassment. My little apple-man was still standing to attention. But he was different.

His fingers had grown. In fact they were so long that they touched the ground.

'Hey,' I yelled.

'What?' said Dawn.

I opened my mouth to say something but nothing came out. I *couldn't* tell them. I couldn't bring myself to say the words. It was as if a battle was going on inside my head. I wanted to scream out and say, 'The apple-man's fingers are growing. The snail must have infected him when I was in the tree. The germs can infect plants too.'

But instead I said nothing.

I could almost feel the disease inside my head. Trying to take over my brain. Trying to make me do its will. Feeding on my jealousy and anger.

Terrible thoughts filled my head. Dawn and Howard were ganging up on me. All she wanted was for me to remember what happened to her mother on the bus. After that she would probably try to get rid of me. Dawn hated my apple-man. If I told her about his fingers she would make me destroy him so she could be alone with Howard. And she didn't like my dad. She didn't care that he could get infected.

Dad gave me that apple-man. He was my friend. Standing there in his blue refinery uniform. So what if he *was* growing fingers? It was probably going to help us.

That's the way my mind was working. The stupid thoughts rushing around inside my head seemed perfectly normal.

So I didn't say anything. I just watched as the index finger on the apple-man's right hand grew out like a moving piece of rope.

I said nothing as it slowly and steadily wormed across the ground towards the sleeping figure of Gramps.

Closer, closer, closer.

Still I kept quiet. Still the words of warning that I wanted to shout would not form in my mouth.

The finger – no, it wasn't a finger. It was a sucker. Or a creeper. Something like that. Whatever it was it had almost reached Gramps. It wormed its way up to the little cup that he had put his false teeth into. It climbed up the cup and crept inside. It was drinking the water.

Gramps snored. Dawn and Howard looked at each other with big smiles. They hadn't seen it.

I struggled. Oh, I really struggled with the terrible germs that were fighting a battle for my mind.

The root crept towards Gramps. Was it going to put

its terrible finger into his ear? Or his mouth? Was it going to drink him?

I tried to say something but I couldn't. The words just wouldn't come out. In the end I managed to point. 'Aagh,' was all I could get out. A sort of strangled cry. 'Aagh.'

Dawn and Howard stared. And stared. And stared. Not at the apple-man. But at me. What was wrong? Suddenly I realised. My face must be twisted and ugly. Changing with the black thoughts that were swirling inside my skull.

I forced my feet forward. I staggered towards Gramps like a drunken man. 'Aagh,' I gurgled. 'Aagh . . .'

Suddenly Gramps sat up. He reached into his pocket and took out the little silver pocket knife that he used to peel apples and pears. He flicked open the blade and with one swift slash, cut off the end of the creeping root.

'Gotcha,' he shouted. 'A Finnigan doesn't sleep on guard duty. I've been watching you for a while.'

Dawn screamed as the cut root started to whip and curl around like a worm that had been chopped in half.

'Into the car,' yelled Gramps.

I threw a look at the apple-man. Some of his other fingers had reached the ground by now. They disappeared into the soil. They were sucking up moisture. One of the fingers of the other hand was writhing its way towards the car. Faster and faster.

Dawn grabbed Gramps by the shoulder and started to pull him towards the car. But he broke away and hurried back to the cup. 'I'm not going anywhere without my teeth,' he yelled. He grabbed his teeth and shoved them into his wrinkled mouth. Then he tottered to the car and fell into the driver's seat.

I just stood there watching it all. I wanted to help Dawn and Howard and Gramps. And I also wanted to help my apple-man tear them to pieces. Oh, terrible, horrible thoughts. What could I do?

Think. Think peace. Think beauty. Think love.

I stared at the whispering trees and the morning's blanket of mist. I heard the happy call of the waking kookaburras. I thought of my mother's smile as she read me a story in bed. I thought of Dawn and her funny laugh and her soft hands.

Then I turned my back on my old companion the apple-man and ran to the car and jumped inside with my friends. It was a huge wrench but panic drove the sadness from me.

'Go,' I screamed to Gramps. 'Go, go, go.'

Gramps started the engine and put the car into gear. He let out the clutch and the back wheels spun.

'Faster,' yelled Dawn. 'Faster.'

Faster? Didn't Dawn know anything? It wouldn't be hard to go faster. We weren't moving at all.

I threw a glance out of the back window. Thick smoke filled the air. A sharp smell of burning rubber stung my nostrils.

'What's up? said Howard. 'Is the engine on fire?'

'No,' I screamed. 'The wheels are spinning. The tyres are burning. Stop, Gramps. Stop.'

It was just as if the back of the car had been tied to a tree with a rope. Except the rope wasn't a rope. It was a finger. A root. A horrible curling creeper sent out by the apple-man. It was wrapped around the back bumper.

There was no way that the Morris Minor was going anywhere.

Howard was in the front with Gramps. And I was in the back with Dawn. I could feel that my face was going back to normal. What was happening? Was it because I'd done the right thing and sacrificed my apple-man? Was that like having calm thoughts?

I took Dawn's hand and gave it a squeeze but she didn't seem to notice. Maybe she was just too occupied with the plant tendril that was hanging on to the back bumper.

'This car's got holes in it,' she shrieked.

'Like this one,' said Howard calmly. He sure was a cool customer. He was pointing at a green tendril snaking its way through a rusty gap in the door. He took Dawn's mother's shoe and started hitting at the horrible root. No panic. Just calm action. The tendril took no notice. It kept on coming. A bit like a cobra rearing its head out of a basket when a snake charmer plays his flute.

'Give me that,' yelled Dawn.

She grabbed the shoe and shoved it at the tendril. Straight away the writhing finger started to retreat. It squirmed back out of the hole as if it had been stung.

My mouth just fell open. In Dawn's hand the shoe seemed to have a power all of its own.

The shoe had scared the tendril. But my apple-man was busy in other directions. One long shoot was wriggling down into the ground. Plants need water. And it wanted some. Badly.

'Right,' said Gramps. 'We're getting out of here.'

He put the car into reverse and backed up towards the place where my apple-man was growing. The tendril that had attached itself to the car fell slack. Gramps shoved the Morris into first gear and let her rip.

'Racing start,' I screamed.

The Morris Minor leapt foward like a Ferrari off the starting line.

'Way to go,' I yelled as the Morris rocketed forward in a shower of stones and smoke.

The tendril suddenly tightened as the car took up the slack.

Twang. The bumper bar was ripped straight off the car. It bounced up into the air with the tendril still grabbing on to it.

We sped on to the road and raced away like a bat out of hell. Gramps grinned. 'Yahoo,' he shouted.

But he was too early. I looked back in disbelief. There was only one word to say and I said it.

'Shoot.'

Out of the back window I could see the tendril following. It was growing in fast-time. Streaking along behind us like a skinny piece of living rope.

'Faster,' I yelled. 'Faster.'

The car rocked and bumped and lurched along the

road. The landscape was growing lonelier. And drier. All night we had camped without one car passing. I hoped and prayed that another car would come. But I knew it was unlikely. We were in this on our own. On the edge of the desert.

The speedo was showing fifty-five miles an hour. Gramps read my thoughts. 'About ninety kilometres an hour,' he said. 'We can't keep this up.'

He was right. The tendril was coming up fast behind, growing and stretching at enormous speed. 'It's catching us,' I shouted.

The tendril suddenly started tapping at the back window like the finger of death beckoning. It sent a shiver down my spine. Dawn screamed.

'It's after me, isn't it?' said Howard.

I didn't have time to answer. The tendril suddenly curled down and grabbed the Morris' towbar.

The car stopped with a bang, just as if it had hit a brick wall.

SIX

The jolt was so violent that my head snapped forward and my chin banged onto my chest. Then my head flew back and smacked against the rear parcel shelf.

My brains turned to curried egg.

Something was holding me tight around the middle and for a moment I thought it was Mum's strong arms. Thanks, Mum, I thought. Without you I'd have gone over those front seats and through the windscreen.

My eyes cleared. I looked down. It was only the seat belt. Same difference, but. Mum had made Gramps put those seat belts in.

'What did we hit?' mumbled Gramps.

'Nothing,' said Rory. 'The root grabbed the towbar.'

'Flamin' towbar,' growled Gramps. 'I should have listened to Louise. She told me it was a dopey idea putting a towbar on a Morris Minor.'

'Start the engine,' said Rory. 'Quick.'

'No point,' said Howard. 'Even if we can snap the root again, it's faster than us.'

'He's right,' said Gramps.

207

From under the car came a scratching, slithering sound. The root was wriggling around the chassis, looking for a way in. I gripped Mum's shoe but it was no good. There were too many ways in for one shoe.

'Block up all the holes,' I yelled.

We tore off our windcheaters and socks and clambered over each other, stuffing them into rust holes and the gaps around the clutch and brake and accelerator pedals.

Then we held our breaths and listened.

Scratch, scratch.

Slither, slither.

Suddenly the root shot across the windscreen. Halfway up it stopped, pulled back from the glass and swivelled from side to side, white hairy tip pointing towards us like a blind snake sensing the movements of its lunch.

I tried not to tremble.

'Flamin' mongrel,' muttered Gramps. 'If I had my rotary mulcher in here, you'd be history.'

The root ignored him. It slithered across the bonnet and into the front of the engine.

'Oh no,' said Rory. 'It's going to try and come in through the dash.'

We stuffed more socks into the air vents. I'd been wearing the same pair for two days and two nights, so I hoped the infection had given the root a strong sense of smell.

Then we heard another sound. The squeak of metal turning against metal.

'What's it doing?' breathed Howard.

I had a horrible vision of the root slowly undoing all the nuts and bolts until the car fell to pieces and we were left sitting in the middle of a pile of spare parts.

But it wasn't doing that. 'It's unscrewing the radiator cap,' said Gramps.

The squeak was replaced by a slurping sound, like liquid being sucked thirstily up a straw.

'It's drinking the water in the radiator,' said Rory.

Gramps rummaged under his seat. He pulled out a metal tyre lever.

'No mongrel drinks my radiator water,' he yelled, opening his door.

'Gramps, don't,' I shouted. I pointed out the window at the flat dusty plain all around us. 'There's hardly anything growing out there. That means no water. Once the root's finished the radiator it'll want to drink you.'

To a thirsty root Gramps would have looked like one of those dried goatskin water bags from Greece only more wrinkly.

I pulled Gramps' door shut and locked it.

The slurping sound stopped.

'What now?' said Rory.

'I think I should go out there,' said Howard quietly.

We stared at him.

'It's here because it wants to infect me,' he went on. 'I really appreciate you protecting me, but let's get it over with and then perhaps the root'll leave us alone and we can go and find Dad.'

'No,' said Rory.

'Why not?' said Howard.

I opened my mouth to give Howard a couple of million reasons, but Rory got in first.

'Because,' he said quietly, 'there might not be a cure.'

He looked so scared and lost when he said that, and so brave, that I wanted to put my arms around him. I didn't. Kids got really embarrassed if you hugged them in front of their older brothers.

'You and Mum are infected,' said Howard. 'If there's no cure, I don't want to be left ...' He couldn't finish the sentence. His voice choked and his eyes filled with tears.

Rory leant over and hugged him. 'Dad'll have a cure,' he said. 'He's got to.'

I had a strong urge to ask Rory how Karl would have a cure if he was just the next innocent victim, but I didn't.

Rory stopped hugging Howard. 'You're not going out there,' he said fiercely.

'Okay,' said Howard.

'You're a brave lad for volunteering,' said Gramps. 'When we get out of this I'm going to recommend you for a medal and a job in the bank.'

Howard gave a little smile. I could tell he was starting to like his new step-grandfather.

Then I saw a movement outside the car. A thin hairy root tendril was wriggling through the dust towards Howard's door. We heard it scrabbling its way up the duco. We waited for it to appear at Howard's window. It didn't.

'Where's it gone?' said Howard after a couple of minutes.

I was trying to see it through my window but I couldn't.

'Perhaps it's given up,' I said.

No such luck. A faint rattling sound came from inside Howard's door. What was it doing? We strained our ears.

Suddenly I noticed something that sent a chill through my guts. The handle on the inside of Howard's door was vibrating slightly. Howard had decided not to open his door, so the root was going to open it for him.

'It's inside the lock,' I yelled. 'It's trying to pick it.'

Anger surged through me. How dare that slimy, sneaky apple-man root threaten a kid who was prepared to sacrifice himself for us?

I grabbed Mum's shoe and pressed it against the inside of the door as close as I could to the lock.

'Cop that,' I hissed.

'Hear hear,' said Gramps. 'I wish I had my spray gun.'

But this time the shoe didn't have any effect on the root at all. I didn't understand it. The rattling continued. Then Howard's door unlocked with a snap. I threw myself forward and pushed the handle into the locked position and held it there. Howard put his hands on mine and we pushed till our knuckles were white and we were dripping with sweat.

Rory and Gramps leaned over the other side of Howard and pressed their hands against ours. We stayed that way for what seemed like hours. It was hot and cramped and painful and every second I expected the root to burst in through the base of the handle and rip the skin off our hands.

But something made me stay there. Something apart from fear and desperation and the fact that Howard and Rory and Gramps were pressing so hard I couldn't have got my hands off the handle even if I'd wanted to.

Crouched there shoulder to shoulder with my two step-brothers I felt something unexpected. I felt like I was in a family. It was a good feeling and I didn't want to lose it.

The root had other ideas.

Suddenly it changed tactics. We saw it shoot up the outside of Howard's window. It slithered across the roof, shot down the outside of Gramps' window and scrabbled under the floor before climbing up my window.

We fell back into our seats and watched in horror as the root wound itself round and round the car. It didn't stop until it had wrapped itself around us about twenty times.

'Why's it doing that?' whispered Rory.

I didn't know.

I didn't want to imagine.

SEVEN

My apple-man had started off okay. But germ-carrying slobberers had grown in him. And now he had become infected himself. He had put down roots and turned into a wicked plant. It wanted to get Howard. And it would kill anyone who tried to stop it.

My apple-man had been my friend for so long.

Now it was our enemy. My heart was aching at the thought. Dad's gift was trying to kill us. I couldn't bear to think about it. But I had to.

One thing I had was a good imagination. I could let my mind wander and take me into all sorts of places. And I could see what that crawling, writhing finger was capable of.

If I tried to protect Howard the tendril could wrap itself around my neck and squeeze until my eyeballs bugged out. It could choke off my windpipe so that I couldn't breathe.

It could get Gramps and drag him out of the car by his legs. It could send little suckers into every hole in his body. I shuddered at the thought.

Then it would go for Dawn. She was strong. She was tough. She would put up a good fight. But in the end it would get her. Wrap itself around her lovely hair. And pull her down into the earth. Suck her into a rabbit burrow. Bury her forever.

It was strong was that tendril. As strong as steel rope. And it was growing stronger by the minute. Little apple leaves were sprouting along its length. Taking in energy from the sun. Giving it strength. And it was putting down more roots. Suckers pushed down into the ground looking for moisture. It was building itself up for the final attack.

On Howard.

What would it do to him? It would leave him alive. To infect another plant or animal. Which could then infect Dad.

First it would put a tiny sucker into Howard's mouth. And infect him. Or drop a little seed into his ear. Then roots would grow. Eating into his brain. Tracking through his veins and nerves. Feeding on the anger and fear inside him. Spreading the germs into every cell.

Just like the infection was doing to me.

I stared outside at the bleak landscape. Nothing. Not a person to help. The sun beat down fiercely on the Morris Minor. Heating it up. Heating us up. We had no water. No food. Nothing to look forward to. Except death.

Death in the form of a vine that was slowly tightening its grip on our metal prison.

An hour ticked by. And another. We couldn't get out. And we couldn't stay.

'We need water,' said Howard. 'Or we'll die of thirst. I'm going to get out and fight the rotten thing. It's only a plant.'

'No,' I said in a dry, rasping voice. 'Look.'

Something was moving on the horizon. Far in the distance I could see smooth shapes moving. Yes, yes, yes. Help was coming. Just in time. I strained my eyes, trying to see.

'Look,' I said. 'Dune buggies.'

'Panzers,' said Gramps.

'No,' said Dawn. 'They're not machines. And they're not people either.'

'Oh no, not frogs,' I croaked. 'Please don't let it be frogs.'

The brown shapes grew larger. Running on four legs. Not frogs. They looked like running rocks. Smooth animals. Moving towards us at a fast pace. About ten of them.

'Pigs,' yelled Howard. 'Feral pigs.'

We slumped down into the seat. If only it had been dune buggies. Pigs were no use.

Or were they?

The pigs trotted furiously in a straight line towards us. What did they want?

The tendril, that's what. The pigs started scratching and chewing at the plant and its roots. They worried at the earth with their slimy snouts and dripping green teeth. They dug and pawed with their claws. They began munching and chewing. Ripping and tearing. There wasn't much food in this dry country. The pigs were starving hungry.

'Hooray,' shouted Gramps. 'Reinforcements.'

We all smiled and cheered. And patted each other on the back. The feral pigs were attacking the terrible tendril.

But the plant was not so easily defeated. A thin, whip-like sucker shot out and wrapped itself around the biggest pig's tail. The plant lifted the whole pig up by the tail and started swinging it in a circle. Faster and faster like a propeller on a plane. The pig squealed and grunted in terror. It was nothing but a blur. Its squeal became a high-pitched whine.

The other pigs suffered the same fate. Suckers grabbed them all by the tail and swung the terrified animals around in the air at a furious speed.

Suddenly the plant let go. The pigs arced up into the air. Higher and higher as if they had been shot out of the barrel of a cannon.

Then they began to fall. Down, down, down. Twisting and turning. Squeaking in terror. Each pig hit the ground with a soft, sickening thud. One or two of the poor creatures twitched and then lay still. The others didn't even move.

They were all dead meat.

Like we would be if we didn't do something.

The vine began to squeeze the car. It creaked and groaned under the strain. The roof began to buckle and collapse.

We all ducked our heads and slid down in the seats.

There was no one to help. We were on our own. My whole body was wracked with fearful shaking. My head felt like it was filled with a million bees. I hated this plant. I hated the germs.

I was only a kid. I didn't want to die in the desert.

'Let's get out of here,' I shrieked.

My head seemed to spin and twirl. The floor underneath me bumped and shook. I felt the wheels turning. I heard the engine groaning. The exhaust backfired loudly. I looked along the row of seats and stared at all the kids from school. Laughing and joking and shoving each other.

I winced as the gears crunched and groaned. Morris Minors didn't have synchro on first gear.

Neither did 1975 Leyland buses.

EIGHT

Rory's eyes opened wide. He sat up staring. For a second I thought he'd seen something on the back of Gramps' neck. A root tip wriggling out of Gramps' collar or something.

My heart thumped.

But Gramps' neck was okay. Rory's eyes weren't even focussed on Gramps.

'Waylan,' he shouted excitedly.

I didn't understand. The only Waylan we knew was Waylan Hicks who used to be in our class in first year. I peered through the windscreen into the heat haze. Had Rory seen Waylan Hicks coming towards us across the scorched plain with a really big pair of gardening shears?

It seemed unlikely, though when you're suffocating in a car surrounded by dead pigs and an evil tree root, anything's possible.

'Waylan,' yelled Rory. 'Sit over here.'

My heart went from sheep-dip pump to fence-post excavator. Suddenly I realised what was happening. The thing I'd been praying for since yesterday.

Gramps and Howard had turned round and were looking at Rory anxiously.

I put my finger to my lips. 'He's back on the bus,' I whispered.

Suddenly I didn't care about the root or the pigs or the heat. I wanted to grab Rory and beg him to tell me everything he was seeing and hearing of my mother's last hour of life. But I didn't. Even though I'd never actually seen a person having an hallucination before, something told me I should keep quiet.

I waited, sweat pouring off me, for Rory to give more clues.

Rory started swaying from side to side in his seat as if he was being driven along a bumpy road. That made sense. The road out of town to Rory's old place was bumpy all right.

Suddenly he gave a jolt and stopped swaying. 'See ya, Lochie,' he shouted. 'See ya, Ellen.'

Kids I hadn't thought of for years suddenly tumbled into my memory. Lochie Dunbar who moved to Adelaide. Ellen McIntyre whose mum made her change schools after the accident because she reckoned our school bus was too dangerous. Which was a slander on Mum.

I blinked back tears.

A thought hit me. I glanced anxiously at the root wrapped around the car to see if Rory's shouting was affecting it. Enraging it and making it more determined to get us.

It wasn't moving. Its strands were still stretched tightly across the windows. Except they didn't seem to be quite as tight as before.

I didn't look for long because Rory was swaying again. Then he stopped with another jolt. 'Bye, Kylie,' he yelled.

Gramps and Howard were staring at him, open-mouthed. 'He thinks he's on the bus,' Gramps whispered to Howard. 'With Alan Fosdyke and Des Kyle. The German bus we nicked from Rommel.'

I didn't try and explain to Howard. There wasn't time. My brain was working feverishly.

Rory's place had been the last drop-off on Mum's afternoon school-bus run. He used to live way out of town, over the river. The drop-off before that had been ... had been ...

'See ya, George,' called Rory.

Of course. George Dale.

Rory started swaying again. George must have just got off. That meant the bus was on the last leg of its journey. The ten-minute drive from the Dales' place to Rory's place across the bridge. With Rory the last person on the bus.

Except for Mum at the wheel.

I felt dizzy with heat and thirst and excitement. In ten minutes I'd know the truth. The truth I'd been waiting five years for.

Then something happened that almost made me faint.

Rory spoke again. 'Pretty good, thanks, Mrs Enright,' he said. 'Though my dad's a bit sick.'

Mrs Enright. That was Mum. Rory was speaking to Mum.

I heard myself give a cry. I couldn't stop it and I couldn't stop the tears filling my eyes.

Mum was alive.

In Rory's terrible, sick, wonderful vision Mum was alive.

I wanted to be there so much. Just to throw my arms round her. Just to say goodbye and tell her I'd always love her.

No. More than that. To try and save her.

Something was slithering. A scratching, sliding noise next to my ear. 'The root,' yelled Howard. 'Look at the root.'

I tore my eyes off Rory. The strands of root were sliding down the window and hanging loosely off the car. I didn't care. I turned back to Rory. Who was looking at me.

'I'm parched,' he croaked.

I saw instantly he wasn't on the bus any more. 'No,' I screamed. 'Go back. Please.'

His lips were cracked and dry. 'I need a drink,' he whispered.

I bent forward and started rummaging on the floor of the car, desperately hoping that Gramps had left an old soft-drink bottle there with some dregs in it. Or a plastic bag with a damp window-wiping cloth inside. Anything to moisten Rory's mouth so he could go back on the bus and tell me about Mum.

Nothing.

Just the metal tyre lever and Gramps' little pocket knife and one of the curried-egg sandwiches from wedding.

No fluid of any description. I was losing Mum for the sake of a mouthful of liquid.

Suddenly a rage bigger than anything I'd ever felt exploded inside me. I nearly crammed the sandwich into Rory's mouth, even though it was two days old and the bread was hard and dry and it was super-hot because Mrs Conti didn't understand the strength of curry powder.

I just managed to stop myself.

It wasn't Rory's fault that his dad had sent him a slobberer-riddled, infection-spreading apple-man. And it wasn't Rory's fault that thirst had interrupted his vision.

It was the root's fault. The stinking apple-man root that had drunk all our water.

I grabbed Gramps' pocket knife and wound down my window and started slashing at the poxy root.

'No,' yelled Howard.

'Put the window up,' croaked Rory.

'Scumbag,' I screamed at the root. I hacked and sawed wildly. The root was like steel cable and the little knife wouldn't go through. But I did manage to scrape off some of the brown hairy skin. The wound I made was wet and purple. The root quivered angrily.

'Suck on this,' I yelled. I scooped the lumpy curried egg out of the sandwich and rubbed it into the purple wound. The root flailed against the side of the car as it tried to uncoil itself.

I grabbed the tyre lever and forced my door open and squeezed out.

'No,' yelled Howard and Rory and Gramps.

Too late. I was on my face in the dust. I scrambled up and turned round and started pounding the root with the tyre lever. I was pounding Gramps' car too, but I didn't care.

'You're compost,' I screamed at the root.

I could feel it crunching under my blows. The last couple of loops slithered from around the car.

'That's it,' I yelled. 'Rack off.'

Instead of snaking away across the dusty plain, the root reared high above me. I gripped my weapon. 'You want more, mulch-breath?' I screamed.

It wanted much more.

Before my eyes it grew twice as thick, from a finger to a hairy, knobbly hosepipe. Then in a blur it cracked itself like a giant whip.

The noise it made was painful. But not as painful as when it flew at me and flayed me across my back. And even that searing white-hot pain wasn't as bad as the agony and despair and fear I felt when it coiled around and around my body like a rough-skinned steel snake and started to squeeze . . .

Book Five

THE CREEPER

ONE

I was history.

The longest root in the world was wrapped around me. Squeezing me. Crushing me. I'd hurt it and now it wanted revenge.

Kilometres away, back where we'd camped the night before, Rory's evil infected apple-man was sending a message along its root ducts to the ends of its strangling tendrils.

Kill Dawn.

I started to send one back.

Get st –

Pain seared through my chest. My ribs felt like they were cracking. I struggled to suck air into my squashed lungs. I tried to force my thumbs down inside the rough steely strands to tear them away from my body.

I couldn't.

Even as it was killing me, the root was bursting with new life.

DAWN

I could feel shoots running down my back and coiling round my legs. Suckers sliding along my neck and slithering into my hair.

I tried to claw them off but new coils pinned my arms. The hairy tendrils cut into my skin and my hands started to go numb.

I realised I was screaming.

I stopped.

I fought to get more air. It was hopeless. My brain was running out of oxygen. My eyes started to go funny. Everything around me started to shimmer and wobble. The narrow dusty road, which I knew ran dead straight through the flat scrub, suddenly looked as twisted and snaky as the root that stretched along it to the horizon.

Gramps' car looked all out of shape. I knew I hadn't hit it that many times with the tyre lever. And Howard and Rory and Gramps, who were scrambling frantically out of the car, looked blurred and wavy as if they were underwater.

Their voices seemed slow and distorted.

'Hang on, Dawn,' warbled Rory.

'We're coming,' growled Howard.

'Howard, no,' boomed Gramps.

In slow motion, Gramps grabbed Howard and pushed him back inside the car. Somehow through the pain I felt glad. Even though the stinking vicious root was killing me, it wouldn't have won if it didn't get to infect Howard.

Rory was lifting his arm. It seemed to take an age.

He was throwing something at me.

As the tendrils round my throat tightened, I watched the object spin slowly towards me through the air. It landed in the dust at my feet.

Mum's shoe.

Suddenly my fear and anger went. All I felt was sadness. My knees gave way and I fell forward onto the ground, dragging the root with me. My face slammed into the dust.

Poor old Rory. He'd done his best. But he'd forgotten that Mum's shoe had lost its power.

I tried to get a hand to it, to touch something of Mum's for the last time. My hands were still pinned. With my last whisper of breath I squirmed forward and touched the shoe with my cheek.

Oh Mum, I thought. Was this what it was like for you, trapped under the surface of the river, your life ending? Was your windpipe on fire? Were your lungs exploding with pain?

I squeezed my eyes shut and saw her smiling at me with her soft brown eyes just like she used to.

In my imagination I held her tight and waited to die.

But I didn't.

I heard a noise. Loud sobs. They were coming from my chest. And shuddering into me were painful gulps of air.

I could breathe again.

The pain was going.

The root had stopped squeezing.

For a few seconds I thought I was going to faint with relief. I forced myself to concentrate. I kicked and squirmed and twisted and clawed and wriggled out from between the hairy coils.

Then I scrambled to my feet and looked around in a daze for the tyre lever so I could pulp that stinking root into mulch.

'Dawn, don't,' yelled Rory. 'Don't get angry.'

I stared at him. My eyesight was wobbly and his face was blotchy and swollen but I could still make out his intense expression. He wasn't taking his eyes off the root. It had moved a short distance away and was tracing slow patterns in the dust with its tip.

I knew the root didn't have eyes, but I could have sworn it was warily watching Mum's shoe.

'Don't get angry,' said Rory again. 'If you get angry, we're history.'

I didn't understand.

Gramps appeared behind Rory, wide-eyed and waving a street directory. 'Run for it,' he yelled. 'I'll distract it with this.'

'It's okay, Gramps,' said Rory. 'Dawn and me have got things under control.'

I stared at Rory again. Under control? I hoped desperately the infection wasn't turning his brain into roof insulation.

'Dawn,' said Rory quietly, 'stay as calm as you can and pick up the shoe.'

I didn't know what else to do, so I took a deep breath

and picked up the shoe. Rory came and stood next to me.

'Stay close,' he said.

Before I could ask him what he was doing, he darted over to the root and grabbed the tip in both hands.

'Don't be an idiot,' I yelled.

My body tried to make me run for it but he was my step-brother so I went with him.

'Stay close,' he said, 'and whatever you do, don't get mad.'

The root started writhing and shuddering in Rory's hands. I pressed Mum's shoe against the root tip. The root went limp.

Suddenly I understood why Rory was so worried about me getting angry. In the car I'd grabbed Mum's shoe in anger and attacked the root, and the root hadn't even noticed. Anger must be the thing that somehow made Mum's shoe lose its power. Just as anger also made the infection stronger.

'Okay,' said Rory, 'stay calm and let's go.'

Normally I'd have got really mad with him for that. Expecting me to keep up with him without explaining what he was doing.

This time, as he dragged the root towards the car, I kept the shoe touching the tip and tried to think of good things about him. His knees. How funny he looked in old ladies' clothes. How brave he was for a puny kid.

'Gramps,' yelled Rory, 'take the petrol cap off.'

Gramps looked confused.

'Quick, Gramps,' I yelled without having a clue why it was so important.

Gramps unscrewed the petrol cap with shaking hands. I could see Howard staring anxiously out the car window at us. I felt pretty anxious too. What if Rory was having another hallucination? What if he thought he was with his dad filling the car up at Kellett's Service Station?

Rory jammed the end of the root into the petrol tank.

Oh no, I thought, he does.

From inside the tank came a loud sucking noise. I stared in amazement. 'It's drinking the petrol,' I said.

Rory nodded as though this had been his plan all along.

Gramps was staring in amazement too. 'Jeepers,' he said. 'We didn't do this in the war.'

The sucking noise went on for several minutes. Then it changed to a slurping noise. The root was devouring the last drops of petrol in the tank.

'Okay,' said Rory. 'Stand back.'

'Lead poisoning,' cried Gramps excitedly. 'You've given the blighter lead poisoning.'

But that wasn't what Rory had in mind. From his pocket he took the box of matches Gramps had given him to light our camp fire.

We stood back.

Rory pulled the end of the root out of the tank, flung it to the ground, struck a match, dropped it onto the root and stepped well back himself.

There was an explosion of flame and a loud whoosh.

A blue and yellow fireball hurtled away from us along the road. We stood and watched it, open-mouthed, until it had disappeared over the horizon.

Even when the fireball had gone we still stood staring because what it had left behind was so incredible. The entire root, kilometres of it, was writhing and twisting in flames.

'Unreal,' yelled Howard, clambering out of the car. He gave a loud whoop. 'My brother,' he yelled. 'My brother did that.'

Rory glowed, and not just because the explosion had almost taken his eyebrows off.

I didn't blame Howard for being a bit hysterical. In less than twenty-four hours he'd met a brother he didn't know he had, discovered his real mother was still alive, plus learned that both of them were sick with a vicious disease that wanted to infect Howard and all their blood relatives. To top it all, the infection had come after him via fifteen kilometres of killer root. It was a wonder he wasn't totally ga-ga.

We watched the root burn until the flames died out and there was just a ribbon of ash along the road.

I turned to thank Rory for saving my life.

That's when I saw it. Something moving through the dust. Smouldering at one end. A length of green shoot that had somehow escaped the flames. It was snaking towards Howard's feet.

'Howard, look out,' I screamed.

Howard saw the shoot just as it was rearing up and

about to strike at his ankle. He tried to jump back, slipped in the dust and fell heavily. The root clamped itself around his sock.

'More petrol,' yelled Gramps.

'The shoe,' shouted Rory.

Howard and I moved at the same time. I hurled myself at him, clutching Mum's shoe. Howard flung something at the root. It was his apple-man. It hit the root with a crunch and bounced away.

The root stayed clamped.

Breathing steadily, I held Mum's shoe against it. The effect was instant. The root gave a spasm and went slack. I tore it off Howard's sock and flung it on the ground, all the time keeping the shoe pointing at it.

We watched wide-eyed as the fleshy green root shrivelled and turned brown. The breeze made its smouldering tip glow red. Then it burst into flames.

'Are you okay?' I asked Howard anxiously. What I meant was, did the root infect you?

Howard jumped up and waggled his toes. 'Thick socks,' he said, grinning.

We watched the breeze scatter the ash through the scrub. Howard gave another loud whoop. 'My step-sister,' he yelled. 'My step-sister did that.'

My skin was scraped and my bones were bruised and my lungs were aching, but I still felt pretty good when he said it. And I stayed feeling good right up to the moment I remembered we were miles from anywhere without any petrol, food or water.

TWO

Okay, so I saved Dawn from the killer root. I felt good about that. And my big brother Howard had actually patted me on the back. Unreal.

It was a hairy experience. Wild. And scary. I was really packing.

After it was all over I sort of freaked out.

I had blown up the root or whatever it was. But what about my apple-man? Was it still growing, back at the camp site? With greedy roots running into the ground?

Or was it dead?

The thought of that just ripped into my guts. Dad's apple-man gone. Killed by me. When we found Dad I'd have to tell him. What would he say? I couldn't bear to think about it. I felt as if I had murdered my closest friend.

But then I *had* to save Dawn. She was my step-sister. I felt really close to her now. Not like a sister actually. More like a . . . girl-friend.

I wondered how she felt about me. That's what I really wanted to know. I saved her life. So she must

235

be starting to think that I wasn't too bad.

Dawn took a deep breath. She was going to say something really nice to me.

'Listen, Worm Boy,' she said. 'We have to face facts. Your dad sent you an apple-man that has nearly killed us twice. First the slobberers came out of it. And now it's grown into a deadly apple tree. The tendril might even have passed on the infection to Howard's apple-man.'

Dawn stopped for a second to let it all sink in. We all looked at Howard and he shoved his apple-man down deeper into his pocket. He didn't like that suggestion one bit.

And neither did I. Dawn wasn't even grateful. Just practical as usual. Always thinking about the next thing. Not even one word about me saving her life.

Dawn still had more to say. 'If apple-man number two is infected,' she said gently to Howard, 'guess who he will be going for next. Guess who will be getting the next little gift from your dad.'

Boy, she made me mad. 'Dad didn't send the germs,' I yelled. 'Why do you keep putting dirt on him?'

'Listen, Rory,' she said. 'The facts speak for themselves. We have to get rid of Howard's apple-man. If it's infected, anything might happen. It could start to grow like the first one. When we're asleep. Think about the infected frog. It turned into a giant. What if the apple-man grew that big? What if it started walking around like a human being?'

Howard took out his apple-man and held it up. 'My parents let me keep this,' he said. 'They knew that it was special – from my real dad. Nothing has happened to it. And nothing is going to. I haven't even seen my father. I've never talked to him. Never even seen a photo of him. This is all I have. I can't get rid of it. I just can't.'

I knew exactly how he felt.

Dawn stamped her foot. Now *she* was really angry. 'You two are so dumb,' she shouted. 'You're never going to find your father if we all get murdered in the night by a giant apple-man.'

'Shut up,' I yelled. 'Aren't you ever happy? I burnt *my* apple-man to save you. I nearly got myself killed for you. And what do I get back? You hate my father. And my mother. And me. We're not going to get rid of Howard's apple-man. Never. I'm sick of you being such a bossy-boots. If you really want to know – '

Another voice interrupted me. A kind, soft, wise voice. 'Rory,' said Gramps. 'She's right. We can't have the enemy in the camp. If that apple-man attacks us, who is going to save your mum? She's dangerously ill. No one knows what's wrong with her. Except us. We have to find . . . what's his name? Montgomery . . . no, no . . . you know . . . your dad, Karl. We have to find out where these germs came from. The apple-man has to face the firing squad. There's no way out of it.'

Howard started to nod his head sadly. 'Okay,' was all he said.

'See,' said Dawn.

She was so childish. All she wanted was to win the argument. My arm and chest ached terribly. I could feel anger growing inside me again. The slobberer's germs were spreading through my body. I was growing weaker. I was sick. And there was no cure. All I could do was to try and slow the spread of the disease by controlling my anger.

'Okay,' I said. 'We'll get rid of it. Come on, Howard.'

Howard and I started walking slowly into the parched scrub. Dawn followed. 'Not you,' I spat at her. 'This is a funeral. And you're not welcome.'

Gramps grabbed her arm and pulled her back. 'Leave them alone,' he said gently. 'After the battle there's always a truce. Let them bury their dead in peace. We'll wait in the car.'

Howard and I kept walking. 'How would we destroy my apple-man?' said Howard. 'Even if we wanted to.'

I pointed to a small mound I'd noticed a bit earlier. 'An old mine shaft,' I said. 'We could throw it down there.'

We walked over to the mine shaft. It was a very deep, black hole that disappeared straight into the earth. Howard picked up a small stone and threw it down. Seconds passed. And more seconds. Then ... *clunk*. The stone had hit the bottom.

'Let's drop the apple-man down there. That'll kill it,' I said sadly.

'But it's not alive,' said Howard. 'Not at the moment anyway.' He turned the apple-man over in his hands.

'It *could* come to life down there,' he said. 'It could infect a rat. Or a toadstool. Or another frog. Or a bit of fungus might grow on it. Or mould. It might come to life and climb out. And come after us. And we wouldn't know. I think we should keep it.'

I was tempted. But what if Dawn and Gramps were right? We couldn't risk it. I tenderly took the apple-man from Howard's hands and prepared to drop it into the black hole.

An angry look swept across Howard's face. He grabbed the apple-man's head and pulled. His fingers dug into the brown, wrinkled skin and for a second I thought he was going to rip the head right off. I let go. I understood. He was just like me. He didn't want to go through with it. He didn't want to destroy Dad's last gift.

Howard stuffed the apple-man into the front of his jeans.

'What are you doing?' I whispered.

I could see Dawn watching us from inside the car. Howard bent down and pretended to be peering into the mine shaft. He picked up a rock. Then he stood up and quickly threw the rock into the shaft. There was a long silence. Then we heard a distant *thunk*.

'Goodbye, apple-man,' he said in a fake loud voice. Howard winked at me. I grinned and winked back.

'It's better if the apple-man goes with us,' he said softly. 'Then if it starts to change or grow we'll know. And we can deal with it. And if it doesn't – then we're no worse off.'

'Good thinking,' I said.

We walked slowly back to the Morris Minor. The boot was still open. And the snail box was where Gramps had put it after he'd eaten the snail compass back at the children's home. Howard placed the apple-man in the snail box and put the lid on. Then he hid it under the spare wheel.

'He won't get out of there,' Howard whispered.

'You hope,' I said.

I closed the lid of the boot and gave it a couple of thumps. The boot lock had never worked properly. It was a real old car. But still and all, it had stood up to the creeper so I couldn't complain.

When we got back into the car Dawn patted me on the hand and smiled kindly. 'You did the right thing,' she said. 'I know it was hard. But we didn't have any choice.'

I started to feel guilty. I almost told her what we'd done. That the apple-man was hidden in the boot. Dawn turned to Howard and patted him too. She gave him the biggest brightest smile ever.

I knew it. It was Howard she was interested in. She didn't give a stuff about me. Anger and jealousy burned inside my guts. I gritted my teeth and said nothing about the apple-man. What Dawn didn't know wouldn't hurt her.

That's what I thought anyway.

THREE

Howard saw it first.

'Look.'

The rest of us turned and peered out the back window. A cloud of dust was travelling towards us along the road. Coming from the same direction as the root.

'It's a car,' yelled Gramps excitedly.

Rory and I didn't join in the excitement. We knew Gramps was just being hopeful. There was no way poor old Gramps could spot a car a kilometre away. He found it hard enough telling Rice Bubbles from All Bran across a kitchen table.

We couldn't see what was coming towards us either. We squinted for a clue.

I felt my bruised stomach tighten. What if Rory's apple-man hadn't been burnt to bits? What if the flames hadn't travelled all the way back along the root to it? What if it had survived and infected something else that was hurtling towards us?

'Howard,' I said, 'you'd better keep out of sight.'

Howard looked alarmed. 'Why?' he said.

I didn't want to panic him. No point in saying scary stuff about the infection coming after him again until we knew for sure.

'You've run away from a kids' home,' I said. 'The authorities'll be looking for you. Keep your head down.'

'You're right,' said Howard, huddling low on the back seat.

'What about me?' said Rory indignantly. 'I've run away from a hospital. They'll be looking for me too.'

I sighed. Rory could be so childish sometimes. Then I saw his blotchy infected face and remembered it probably wasn't his fault.

'You too,' I said to him. 'You keep your head down too.'

'And your bottom,' said Gramps. 'Des Kyle didn't keep his bottom down at the Battle of El Ahid and a German camel bit him.'

I wanted to scream at Gramps to start the car and get us out of there, but I remembered we didn't have any petrol. Instead I gripped Mum's shoe.

Gramps and I got out of the car and turned to face the approaching dust cloud. It was about half a kilometre away. Images from Road Runner cartoons kept flashing through my mind. Except it wasn't Road Runner and Wily Coyote I was seeing, it was horrible bloated nameless creatures.

My chest hurt and I realised I'd stopped breathing.

'Shoulders back,' said Gramps. 'Chest out. We might be in a pickle but we're still Australians.'

I couldn't help grinning. There were times when a potty Gramps was better than a bullet-proof vest or a rocket-launcher.

Something glinted in the dust cloud. Sunlight on glass. I strained my ears and caught the distant whine of an engine. Through the dust I saw glimpses of white duco.

'It *is* a car,' I gasped. 'You ripper.'

'Told you,' said Gramps.

It was a battered four-wheel drive. We waved wildly as it got closer, and it veered off the road and skidded to a stop in front of us.

A tough-looking woman with leathery skin climbed out from behind the wheel.

'Had a prang?' she said.

'We've run out of petrol,' I said.

'And water,' said Gramps.

'Jeez,' said the woman. 'You prepared well for your trip.'

'If you must know . . .' said Gramps indignantly. I gave his hand a hard squeeze and he pretended to be having technical problems with his teeth.

The woman grabbed a jerry can and a funnel from the back of her four-wheel drive. She went over to the car and jammed the funnel into the petrol tank.

I hurried after her, positive she'd spot Howard and Rory. But when I peeked through the window, all I could see were two mounds on the back seat covered in blankets.

'Quite a load you've got there,' said the woman, glugging the petrol in.

'Chocolate cakes,' said Gramps before I could stop him. 'We're on our way to a wedding.'

The woman gave him a strange look.

'I've put enough in there to get you back to town,' she said.

'You're an angel,' said Gramps.

'Too right,' I said warmly, but my insides weren't smiling. Going back to Howard's town meant risking him being captured by social workers. Plus it meant passing our camping spot. What if Rory's apple-man was waiting there for us?

The woman grabbed another can, let us both gulp some water, then filled our radiator.

'How far to the next town?' I asked.

'Hundred and eighty clicks,' said the woman. 'I'm not giving you that much petrol.'

'This has been more than kind,' said Gramps, holding out one of his hub caps. 'Could I have a drop of water in this? For the trip back?'

The woman gave him another strange look and filled the hub cap. Gramps put it down carefully, then rummaged in his pocket.

'Please,' he said, holding out money. 'I insist.'

'Don't worry about it,' said the woman. 'Buy me a beer some time.'

She tossed the cans into the back of her four-wheel drive and climbed into the driver's seat. An awful thought struck me. What if she was some sort of official who was suspicious but hiding it? Who was going to report us as soon as she could?

'Excuse me,' I said as casually as I could. 'Are you in the State Emergency Service?'

'No,' laughed the woman, gunning her engine and pointing to the boxes of books on her back seat. 'I'm a librarian.'

She roared off in a cloud of dust.

Rory and Howard drank the hub cap dry in about three seconds.

Then we drove back towards town in silence. Nobody said much. Rory was probably thinking about his dad. Howard was probably thinking about what happened to people who ran away from kids' homes and got caught. I was thinking about Rory's apple-man.

Suddenly, after about ten minutes, there it was at the side of the road. Our camping spot. Gramps slowed down. I could see the ashes of our camp fire. And near it, flat on its back, arms and legs clearly visible against the orange dust, the remains of Rory's apple-man.

Ashes.

I gave a big whistle of relief. In the rear-vision mirror I saw Rory look away and the blotches on his face squirm a bit. I felt sorry for him, but I also felt safer than I had for the last two days.

A bit further down the road I heard some knocking sounds from the back of the car.

'What's that?' I asked.

Gramps was on another planet humming to himself.

I saw Rory and Howard look at each other. 'Sounds like the rear suspension,' said Howard. 'Nothing serious. The rear shockers get a bit clunky on these old cars.'

It sounded possible.

After about an hour we reached the outskirts of town. Howard and Rory ducked under the blanket. Gramps and I found a petrol station on the other side of town to the kids' home, but we still made Howard and Rory stay in the car.

While Gramps filled up with petrol, I bought us all food and drink. I had enough coins left for a long-distance call, so I tried to ring Dad.

There was no answer at our place. I got the number of the hospital from directory enquiries.

'This is a relative of Jack Enright and Eileen Singer,' I said, hoping my mouthful of burger would disguise my voice.

I was put through to a matron who explained that Eileen's condition had been too rare for them to diagnose, and she'd been transferred that morning to the infectious diseases unit at the Royal Prince Edward Hospital in the city, and Dad had gone with her.

I felt a bit shocked that Dad would go that far away with Eileen when I was missing. Then I remembered they were newlyweds. Anyway, Dad knew I could look after myself.

'Guess what,' I said when I got back to the car. 'Our parents are all in the city.' I explained about Eileen and Jack.

'Ace,' said Howard. 'Hope Mum's hospital's near Dad's refinery.'

Rory didn't say anything.

As we turned onto the main highway and set off for the city, I watched Rory in the rear-view mirror. He was slumped in the back seat, both arms and most of his face covered in blotches. He looked so unhappy I had to stop myself clambering back and giving him a hug. He didn't want an ugly great lump like me all over him. Not when he was feeling so bad.

I knew exactly how Rory was feeling. Soon we'd be coming face to face with Karl. Who was the reason the infection had come into our lives and put us all in terrible danger.

Or was he?

It was a crook thing for a kid. To want more than anything in the world to know the truth about your parent. And to fear more than anything in the world what that truth might be.

I tried to get those thoughts out of my mind.

'Gramps,' I said. 'Are you sure you're okay to drive all the way to the city? It's about five hours.'

'Course I am,' said Gramps. 'I've always been good at driving long distances. On my honeymoon I drove sixteen hundred miles to Rockhampton. Seventeen hundred because we had to go back for the beer.'

I wondered if I should try to persuade Gramps to take the long route to the city through our town. At least then we could call in at home and shower and change and freshen up. But that would mean a three-hour detour. I glanced back at Rory, who was looking sicker by the minute, and decided against it.

Nobody said much for the next couple of hours. We were all lost in our own thoughts. Gramps hummed a bit and they weren't military tunes so perhaps he was thinking about his honeymoon.

I stared at the road and thought of the distance ahead and hoped the car body could stand the strain. I hoped Gramps' body could too.

I thought about Mum and felt a sick aching inside and wondered if I'd ever find out the truth about her death. I knew I couldn't do it on my own. My only hope was if Rory survived long enough to help me find out. I prayed he would. Then I felt awful because I wanted him to survive for his sake too.

I must have fallen asleep because the next thing I knew Gramps was yelling.

'There it is. There it is.'

I blinked my eyes open. It was night, but there were thousands of lights all around us. On every side rows of lights stretched away into the distance. It was like another planet.

But it wasn't, it was the city.

We were streaming forward in a river of cars. Ahead of us hundreds of brake lights glowed on and off. Even though they were red not green, they reminded me of another river at night and the evil eyes of the slobberers.

Gramps was balancing his battered old street directory

on his knees and juggling a torch and chortling to himself. 'I've still got it,' he was saying. 'The old navigator's still got it. Look.'

I wasn't sure what I was meant to be looking at. Gramps was pointing through my window. I wound it down so I could see better. The traffic noise was worse than the unrestricted event at our local speedway. The fumes were worse too. But mixed in with them I could taste something I'd never tasted away from the dinner table before.

Salt.

We were near the coast.

Then I saw it. In the distance. A giant forest of dark shapes silhouetted against the electric glow of a far-off part of the city.

The refinery.

My insides went tight. In that dark jungle lay the future of our family. If we were lucky.

We turned off the main road. As we got closer to the refinery the street lights got dimmer, then vanished. The only lights ahead of us were the two beams of our car.

Already I was having a bad feeling.

I could hear Rory and Howard stretching and grunting in the back. And I could hear something else. A banging sound coming from the rear of the car.

'That's not the rear shockers, is it?' I said.

Rory and Howard didn't say anything.

'What?' said Gramps. 'Sorry, I was miles away.'

Suddenly he braked sharply. The car shuddered to a

stop. The road had run out. In front of us stood tall wire gates. On them I could see big rusty letters.

AMPACO. Just like on the apple-man uniforms.

'Dad's refinery,' yelled Rory. He flung the car door open and leapt out.

'Wait,' I shouted, going after him.

I'd already seen what he was about to see.

In the mountainous jumble of giant tanks, pipes, ladders, buildings and walkways looming over us, there wasn't a single light. The rusted wire gates were chained shut.

The refinery was abandoned.

'No,' screamed Rory. 'Dad.'

He hurled himself at the gates and tried to tear them open. Then he started climbing them.

'Don't,' I shouted. 'It's too dangerous.'

'We'll find another way in,' shouted Howard.

'Tunnels are good,' croaked Gramps.

'Rory,' I yelled. 'There's no point. He's not here. You'll hurt yourself.'

It was too late. Rory's foot slipped. He hung for a moment, scrabbling at the wire, then fell.

Thankfully it had been raining and the ground was muddy. When we got to him he was lying on his back in a puddle, eyes open.

They were moving. His pupils were huge in the glare from the headlights. At first I thought he had concussion. Then he spoke.

'How's Dawn, Mrs Enright?'

My heart leapt into my throat.

'Is he hurt?' asked Gramps anxiously.

Rory wasn't hurt. He wasn't even lying on his back in a mud puddle. He was six hundred kilometres and five years away, enjoying the ride home from school on the day my mother died.

On the bus.

FOUR

For some reason it felt strange being the last one on the bus. Just me and Mrs Enright. She was a really nice person and a good bus driver. The only thing I didn't like about her was her daughter.

Dawn Enright.

Talk about bossy. Just because she was the fastest runner in the school she thought she could tell you what to do.

And talk. Boy, could she talk. Always raving on about sheep and dags and fly-blown lamb bottoms.

And always eating curried-egg sandwiches.

But Mrs Enright was always nice to me. I think she felt sorry for me because I didn't know where my dad was.

'Come and sit up the front with me, Rory,' she said. 'It's warm near the heater.'

I scrambled into the little seat up the front next to the driver and watched as we bumped over the winding country road. Mrs Enright started to sing a little song to herself. It's funny, I thought, how adults sing the same song over and over. It can drive you bonkers.

'Marie, the dawn is breaking,
Marie, you'll soon be waking,
To find, your heart is breaking.
Marie.'

Dawn is breaking. That was a good one. Actually it would soon be dusk and growing dark. It had been a long day since we'd visited the historic homestead and gone back to school. The weather had turned bad and the river was swirling savagely below us as we crossed the bridge. It had started to rain and a miserable mist was settling into the valley.

I peered out of the window at the darkening forest. 'Look out,' I screamed.

Mrs Enright jammed her foot on the brakes and the bus skidded and swerved wildly on the wet gravel road. I was thrown forward and my head banged painfully on the windscreen. What was going on? What was that out there? A creature had darted out of the forest. An animal. I blinked and tried to see what it was. A stupid goat. Just in front of us. Running along the road right in front of the bus.

We were going to hit it. There was nowhere for the bus to go. The road was narrow with trees on one side and the cliff dropping to the river on the other. 'Shoot,' I shrieked.

Mrs Enright gritted her teeth and pushed the brakes with all her might. Stones and gravel spat up from under the wheels. The goat fled in front of us. As stupid as a sheep.

Wham. The bus hit the goat with a bang and it disappeared between the front wheels.

Mrs Enright stopped the bus and took a deep breath. She was terribly upset, I could tell that. But she didn't panic. She switched off the engine and turned on the warning lights. 'You stay here, Rory,' she said. 'This might not be a pretty sight.'

She stepped out into the misty shadows. All was silent. Then I heard her voice. 'Oh the poor thing, it's still alive,' she called. 'Give me a hand, Rory.'

I hurried out of the bus and gently touched the goat. It was wedged under the sump. It was definitely alive, because it was breathing. But it was unconscious. It didn't make a sound.

We grabbed the goat's back legs and pulled. 'It won't come,' I gasped.

'Harder,' panted Mrs Enright. 'Pull harder.' She was strong was Mrs Enright. It was probably where Dawn got her big muscles from. It was in the blood.

Slowly, slowly, we began to move the goat. We dragged it out in front of the bus and examined it in the beam of the headlights.

There was no blood or signs of injury but the goat was still unconscious. 'You're going to be late home tonight, Rory,' she said. 'We have to take this goat to the vet.'

I nodded and we started to pull the limp animal around to the side of the bus. I held back the door and we dragged the goat up the first step with great difficulty. It was hard work because the goat was so heavy. We puffed and panted with the effort. 'I don't think we're going to be able to get it up there, Rory,' said Mrs Enright.

Suddenly something happened. The goat opened its eyes and stared at us.

For some reason it gave us both a terrible fright and we jumped back. The goat struggled to its feet and scampered up the steps into the bus with a loud *baa*.

'Stupid thing,' I yelled.

We both laughed. The goat had got inside without our help. 'Maybe it's not so stupid after all,' said Mrs Enright.

The goat scrambled into the gloom at the back of the bus.

'We'll still have to take it to the vet,' said Mrs Enright. 'It might have internal injuries. I'll have to go back into town. There's just enough room here for me to turn.'

She began to back the bus across the road. It was a tight squeeze on such a narrow road. Back. Forward. Back. Forward. Back. Forward. The engine groaned and moaned and the gears growled in protest. Bit by bit Mrs Enright turned the bus until it was halfway around. It completely blocked off the road. The front faced the river and the back was pushed right into the trees.

'Rory,' said Mrs Enright. 'Look out of the back window and tell me when to stop.'

I ran down to the back of the bus. But I didn't look out of the window.

The goat was sitting up on one of the seats. It made me jump. For a second I thought it was a person. The goat sat there with its back legs crossed and its front legs folded like arms. It reminded me of an old man sitting there patiently waiting for the next bus-stop.

'Aaagh,' I screamed. 'Aaagh.' I belted down to the front of the bus. Mrs Enright didn't even notice me. She had just put her foot on the clutch and selected first gear. The bus was pointing straight at the river.

She was staring out through the side window.

There was someone outside. A man. He was running down the road towards us. He started to beat on the door with his fist. He banged so hard that the whole bus rattled.

'Open up, Louise,' he yelled in a desperate voice. 'Quick. Open up.'

I knew that voice. My heart jumped with joy.

I rushed to the door and looked at the figure outside.

DAWN

It was him. I pulled frantically at the door but it didn't want to open.

'Dad,' I screamed.

FIVE

My heart nearly stopped when Rory sat up in the mud and screamed 'Dad'.

For a second I thought his father was there, behind me, crouched over Rory with the rest of us outside the refinery gates.

I spun round. Nothing. Just Gramps' and Howard's anxious faces.

I realised the 'Dad' had been part of Rory's hallucination. The memory dream I so much wanted to share. The one I'd been struggling to piece together in my mind from the few words Rory had mumbled in the mud.

While he'd been on the bus.

It couldn't have been great for

Rory, lying there in a puddle, but it had been torture for me. When he'd jolted and cried out in pain, I'd nearly fainted. Was this the moment Mum had died? Then he'd used her name again and I'd realised it wasn't.

'Rory,' I'd whispered, not wanting to wake him but desperate to know more, 'what's happening?'

He hadn't heard me. His eyes darted around. Sometimes his legs and arms moved and twitched. Now and then, much too rarely, he muttered a word or two. Goat. Vet. Seat.

'What about Mum,' I wanted to yell. 'What's happening to my mum?' But I kept quiet. I knew the only way I'd find out the truth about how she died, and whether it was her fault or someone else's, was for Rory to stay in the dream.

Then he'd sat up and screamed 'Dad'. And tears of frustration had burned my eyes.

Now Gramps was cradling Rory in his arms and patting his cheek. 'Rory,' he said, 'can you hear me? How many fingers am I holding up?'

'One,' said Rory. 'Don't give me the finger, give it to that poxy no-good abandoned refinery. Why did they have to close it down? Why couldn't they have let Dad work there at least until today?'

Gramps started gently trying to explain to Rory. Something about multi-national companies and capital investment and how fuel pipes rusted if you didn't give them a regular spray with WD40.

'We should get him to hospital,' said Howard. 'In his

condition concussion could be really serious. If we take him to the Royal Prince Edward I can visit Mum.'

Suddenly I wanted to strangle Howard. His mum. His mum. What about *my* mum? I wanted to make Rory lie back down in the mud and go back on the bus and tell me about my mum.

But I knew I couldn't.

'Can you feel your legs?' Gramps asked Rory. 'Squeeze there with your hand. Can you feel that?'

'That's *your* leg, Gramps,' said Rory.

'Sorry,' said Gramps. 'My circulation goes bung when I've been crouching.'

'I don't need a hospital,' said Rory, struggling to his feet. 'I just need to get out of the wet.'

It had started to rain. We helped Rory into a sagging wooden gatehouse that stood just outside the barbed wire fence and sat him on a rusty old office chair.

'Tell me what you saw,' I whispered. 'Please.'

Rory told me. The accident. The goat. Mum turning the bus halfway around. The appearance of his dad. His eyes filled with tears as he told me that bit.

'Nothing else?' I pleaded. 'No other clues?'

I was as bad as Howard.

Rory shook his head. Poor kid. There was hardly a patch of normal skin on his face. It was nearly all blotched and swollen. 'We'll find out,' he said, 'next time I go back.'

I turned away. What if there wasn't a next time? What if Rory couldn't go back again because he got too sick or because he – because he –

Rory screamed.

'Aaghhh.'

He pointed, terrified, at the little gatehouse window.

'There,' he yelled. 'He was looking in. The apple-man.'

I rushed outside. And caught a glimpse of something that froze my blood. A figure, running away along the refinery fence into the darkness.

A figure dressed in the same blue overalls as the apple-men.

But there was something worse. I glimpsed it just before the figure moved out of the glare of the car headlights. Something much worse. The skin on the figure's face didn't look like human skin. It was more like wrinkly, dried-out apple skin.

And it was covered in furry white mould.

'Dawn,' yelled Gramps, 'stay here.'

I wasn't going anywhere.

Rory and Gramps staggered out of the gatehouse. We peered into the darkness, but we couldn't see anything.

'Probably just a tramp,' said Gramps. 'Or a spy. They're everywhere, you know, spies. Even in supermarkets.'

I shook my head. I still couldn't speak. But I knew it wasn't a spy.

Rory still looked terrified. And he was shuffling in an agitated sort of way. I thought it was just because he had wet undies.

Suddenly I realised Howard wasn't there. 'Where's Howard?' I said, alarmed.

Gramps and Rory looked around. 'Perhaps he's in the car,' said Gramps.

We hurried over to the car. Howard wasn't there either. Then I saw the note on the driver's seat.

Gone to see Mum at the hospital, it said. *I've waited fifteen years. Hope you understand. Sorry. Howard.*

I realised it must have been Howard I'd seen running along the fence. Stress and the rain in my eyes must have made me imagine the overalls and the mould.

For a second I felt relieved. Then I thought of Howard going to the hospital and felt sick.

'Doesn't he realise?' I said. 'Eileen's infected. It'll only take one tiny living thing to go from her to him and he'll be infected too.'

I noticed something scribbled on the bottom of the note. *P.S. Rory, check the boot. It's gone.*

When Rory saw this he scurried to the boot and threw open the lid and rummaged around inside.

'What does he mean?' I asked. 'It's gone?'

Rory looked at me as though I was an idiot. 'Howard's letting us know that the boot lock's broken,' he snapped.

I didn't get it. Why had Howard bothered mentioning that? And why was Rory so jumpy about a dopey broken boot lock? Then Rory dropped the lid with a bang and I understood.

'That's the noise I heard as we arrived,' I said. 'The boot lid must have been flapping open then.' I banged it a few times to show them.

'Lock's been a bit dicky,' said Gramps, 'ever since I

tried to squeeze a hedge-mulcher in there.'

Rory was staring at the boot, pale and concerned. I thought it was just delayed shock. And I had other things to worry about.

'We've got to go after Howard,' I said.

Gramps was already behind the wheel trying to start the car.

'No,' said Rory. 'I'm staying. I've got some business to finish here.'

I pointed to the dark refinery looming over us. 'Your dad's not here,' I yelled. 'It's abandoned. The gates are chained. The windows are boarded up. The power's turned off. They haven't done that just while they're having a tea-break.'

Gramps was cursing and pumping the accelerator. The car wasn't starting.

'I don't care,' said Rory. 'I'm staying. Anyway, there might be a clue to where Dad's gone.'

The starter motor in the car was chugging more and more slowly. 'That's the one drawback with this model,' said Gramps. 'Won't start in the wet when it's been parked with the headlights on.'

'I'm going after Howard,' I said.

'I'm staying,' said Rory.

Gramps emerged from the car and straightened up painfully. 'Flamin' back,' he said. 'When the supply trucks get here remind me to requisition some painkillers.'

I wished I had a fistful of the strongest painkillers in the world. Painkillers so strong they'd obliterate the lousy infection that was trying to kill people I cared about.

I looked at Rory's poor sick distorted face. Desperate to see his father for what could be the last time.

Then I thought about Howard. Desperate to see his mother for the first time.

If I stayed and helped Rory he might just tell me the truth about Mum. If I went after Howard I might just save him from being infected and possibly killed.

I stood there, torn. I couldn't be with them both.

I turned and went after Howard.

SIX

Dawn had gone off with Howard.

Jeez, my blood was boiling. After all the things Dawn and I had gone through together – fleeing from slobberers, burying our pets, escaping from the hospital, beating a killer creeper, surviving step-parents – after all that you'd think she would have stuck by me. But no. The rotten good-for-nothing girl had shot through with Howard.

Probably in love with him. She wouldn't look at me.

A diseased sick kid who was growing uglier by the minute. To her I was just a dying bag of festering germs. She must have thought I was revolting.

Well, she could get nicked. I had other things to worry about.

'Dawn's gone,' I said to Gramps. 'Raced off with Howard. Gone to the hospital with him.'

Gramps was worried. 'They'll get lost,' he said. 'Or run over by a tank. The big city is dangerous. There are panzers everywhere.'

'There's something else,' I said. I hung my head in shame. 'Gramps,' I whispered. 'We didn't throw Howard's apple-man down the well. We put it in the boot of the car.'

'The spy,' yelped Gramps. 'It's still alive? But the boot is empty. Where's the spy gone?'

'It's disappeared,' I said. 'Either someone's taken it or . . .'

'Or what?' said Gramps.

'Or it's climbed out itself. It might be after Howard. He's the next in the bloodline.'

'We'll have to go after it,' yelled Gramps. 'The spy will kill him. And it will kill Dawn too. She's my little sweetheart – my only grandchild. We have to save her, Rory.' A tear started to trickle down his face.

His only grandchild. Wasn't I a

grandchild? No, I was a step-grandchild. I didn't count.
I wasn't the real thing. Oh, it made me mad. It was only
blood relatives that mattered. Dawn and all of them could
get stuffed.

Like slobberers, when it really came down to it, adults
only wanted blood relatives.

I turned towards the refinery. All was dark. Rain
drizzled down. Huge steel chimneys pointed at the sky.
Rusting tanks sat silently like the bodies of dead elephants
in their final resting place. 'My dad used to work in
there,' I said. 'He's my real relative. My real father. And
I'm going to find him.'

Gramps was terribly upset. 'Karl was . . . is . . . a man.
Dawn and Howard . . . they're kids,' he said. 'The spy
will kill them. Let's get the spy first. Then we can come
back here and look for Karl.'

'It's only an apple, Gramps,' I said. 'My dad is a person.'

'It's a spy,' said Gramps. 'Spies are killers.'

'Gramps,' I said bitterly. 'I can't go after the apple-
man. Not when I'm this close to Dad. Let's face it, Dawn
is big and smart and tough. She can handle anything.
She doesn't need us. She can look after herself.'

'She's only a kid,' said Gramps.

He was right. She *was* only a kid. I remembered the
frog general. And how he had eaten all his little soldiers.
And grown as big as a truck. Could the apple-man grow
that big? I shuddered at the thought of what might
happen to Dawn and Howard if it caught them.

I was sure that the refinery held a clue about Dad and

where he was. This might be my only chance to find him. But Gramps was right. We had to try and save Dawn and Howard first.

Nearby was a large round pipe. Foul water was running swiftly out of it and splashing into a large open stream. I looked nervously at its black mouth and shivered. There was something awful about it.

Suddenly Gramps sprang to his feet. 'There he is,' he shrieked. 'The spy. The scumbag spy.'

I looked up and saw a monstrous white face disappear into the drain. I had never seen such a frightening sight. White wet furry stuff covered the horrible creature's entire head. I couldn't even see any of its skin. There was only mould.

Gramps bolted over to the drain. It was amazing how fast he could go on those tottery legs. In a flash he had disappeared inside.

I put aside all thoughts of Dad. This was serious. I realised that I loved Gramps too. Suddenly it didn't matter that he was a step-Gramps. I had to help him. If I survived I would come back and look for Dad.

I turned and took one last look at the refinery. 'Oh Dad, I love you,' I said to myself. 'I'll find you one day.' Then I turned away and went after Gramps.

'We know how to treat spies,' came his echoing voice. 'Mister Apple-head, I'm coming to get you. You won't kill my Dawn. You won't kill my . . .'

I couldn't quite hear the last word. But I think it was *Rory*.

RORY

I tried to follow Gramps but my feet just wouldn't go properly. My bad leg ached and my whole body seemed to be wracked with pain. 'Wait on, Gramps,' I screamed.

There was no reply from Gramps. The only sound was his splashing footsteps as he waded further and further into the drain.

I took a deep breath and forced my weary body into the drain after Gramps. I had to save him.

The water was cold and slimy and came up to my knees. My jeans flapped against my sodden skin like rotten garbage bags. I shivered and stared into the darkness. I could see nothing. Nothing at all. I turned around and looked back towards the entrance where the dull glow of the night sky crept faintly into the tunnel.

A little group of flat furry things was floating along with the current. They looked like slippers that had been run over by a steamroller.

I gave a shudder and turned back into the drain. Somewhere up ahead was Gramps.

I hoped.

I stood still and listened. Only the gurgling swirl of the foul water around my knees met my straining ears. I stumbled on blindly. Stretching my hands out in front of my face to protect myself. I touched the slimy concrete wall and followed it. On and on I went. The tunnel twisted and turned. I had no idea where it was going. No idea where I was.

Suddenly I heard a new sound. The scamper of small feet. Squeaking and squealing. Rats. Somewhere above me, rats were rustling in the darkness.

I felt so alone. So small. Just a kid who wanted his father. And his Gramps. I wanted to call out for Gramps. But what if Apple-head was nearby? He would know where I was. I couldn't see a thing in the pitch-black drain.

Finally I gathered courage. Enough to call into the evil night. 'Gramps. Gramps. Where are you? It's me. Rory.'

There was no answer. Only more squealing from above.

I staggered on. And on. And on. The water seemed to be flowing faster and faster. Had the rain outside turned into a downpour? The current swirled higher above my knees making it difficult to walk. Trying to push me backwards.

I don't know how long I forced my way against the current. An hour? Two? Fear made every second stretch into a year.

Finally I stopped. Unable to go on. But wait. What was that? I strained my eyes. Yes. There was something ahead. Further along the tunnel. A dim glow. Hope?

No.

A furry figure in flittering shadows. On a small platform. Was it Gramps? Oh, please be Gramps.

It wasn't. It was Apple-head. He was carrying something heavy. Dragging it towards the edge of an underground jetty.

Splash.

Apple-head had thrown something or someone into the water.

My heart froze. Gramps. Oh Gramps. Apple-head had killed him – I was sure of it.

'Murderer,' I screamed.

I braced my legs in the water. His body would be coming my way. I had to catch it. I had to get poor old Gramps' corpse out of there.

I gritted my teeth and waited. And waited.

Kerthump. Bang. A dead weight hit my legs and I felt my knees buckle underneath me.

SEVEN

All the way to the hospital my mind kept leaping back and foward. Back to the refinery and the pain waiting

for Rory when he finally accepted his dad wasn't there. I knew what that felt like, discovering a parent was gone.

Then my mind would jump forward to the hospital and the pain waiting for Howard if he found his mum and got infected. I knew what that felt like too, having a parent hurt you without meaning to. Dad had never actually passed on an infection to me, but he'd still hurt me when he'd married Eileen.

I wanted to help Rory as well as Howard. Guilt chewed at my insides. A couple of times I stopped on dark deserted street corners and wondered if I should turn back.

I didn't. I remembered what Dad always said. Better to do one thing properly than stuff up twice.

I needed directions to the hospital. I decided I'd ask the first people I saw. I hoped the first people I saw would be Salvation Army women looking for lost people to give lifts to.

They weren't. They were rough-looking men drinking in a dimly lit pub. As a rule Dad didn't like me talking to strangers in pubs, but this was an emergency.

I took a deep breath and went in.

'Excuse me,' I said in a loud voice.

Everyone stared. At first I thought it was because I was under-age. Then I remembered I hadn't had a shower or changed my clothes for three days and I'd been sleeping rough and wrestling in the dust with a giant root.

I smoothed my hair down.

'Can you direct me to the Royal Prince Edward Hospital, please?' I said.

A couple of the men smirked. They reminded me of the steel sheep. 'Why?' said one.

'Because,' I said, 'my dad's out in the car and he's really sick.'

The men stopped smirking. My neck started cramping. I hoped lying was okay if you had a really good excuse.

A couple of other men stood up and peered out the door.

'He's got scarlet fever,' I said hastily.

The men sat down.

After they'd given me directions I ran out of the pub and kept on running for about ten minutes in case they realised there was no car.

Then I bush-hopped the rest of the way. Five minutes walking and five minutes running and five minutes walking and so on. I wanted to save my energy in case I had to wrestle Howard to the ground to stop him getting too dangerously close to his mum.

It wasn't easy. The footpath went over freeways with about a million steps involved and through dark tunnels where you had to run whether your five minutes walking was up or not.

Plus there was the energy drain of getting lost eight times.

It took me more than an hour to find the hospital. Once I was there, though, I couldn't miss it.

The Royal Prince Edward was huge. It had huge car parks and a huge number of floors. I stared up at it and my stomach sank.

It wasn't a laid-back country hospital you could sneak into with an op-shop disguise and an obliging pensioner.

This hospital had boom gates. The only way you got into this hospital was if they invited you.

I decided to get myself an invitation.

One of the good things about a big city hospital, I discovered, was that it had toilets on the ground floor with soap and hand-dryers. I snuck in and tidied myself up.

Another good thing was that the hospital chemist and newsagent stayed open at night, probably so bored patients could pick up some aspirin and another Joan Collins novel.

I spent the last of my money on chocolate and textas and conditioner for permed or coloured hair.

Back in the toilets I locked myself in a cubicle and gobbled most of the chocolate. I felt guilty because I knew Rory and Gramps must be starving too, but there was nothing I could do so I gobbled the last two squares. Then I smeared the conditioner all over my face and arms.

When I was three I smeared Mum's conditioner for permed or coloured hair all over myself and discovered I was allergic to it. My skin went all bumpy and blotchy.

As I sat on the toilet in the Royal Prince Edward, I felt the same thing happening again.

When my skin was really hurting, I went over to the mirror and coloured in my blotches with purple and yellow textas. Then I rubbed some more conditioner on to blend the colours.

It didn't look exactly like Rory and Eileen's infection, but it was close enough.

The nurse at the admissions desk was fooled.

'Excuse me,' I said. 'My step-mother Eileen Singer is

in here with a mystery infection and I'd like to see her, please.' I tried to sway and sound a bit brain-affected.

The nurse stared. Then she grabbed her phone.

Everything happened very quickly. In a couple of minutes I was on a trolley with a clear plastic lid over me. Medical people were wheeling me fast and saying urgent things to each other.

We had to wait a few minutes for a lift. While we were waiting I tried to tell my heart to calm down. It was all okay. Eileen would be in a stable condition. I'd be able to stop Howard from being infected. Dad would be pleased to see me and willing to come back to the refinery to find Rory's dad and a cure for the infection.

That's what I hoped.

Suddenly we were in the lift. Going up. Everything was happening fast again. I was wheeled into a quarantine area just like the one I'd seen on telly. Double sliding doors with a microwave oven for handbags.

Then I was wheeled into a room and put in a bed. 'Rest quietly,' said the nurse, 'and we'll be back shortly for tests and admission.'

I rested quietly for about nine seconds. Just long enough to remember the last time I'd been in a hospital. Infecting a snail had been easy compared to what I was trying to do here. Stopping a kid from getting close to the mother he'd never seen.

As soon as the nurse had gone I got up and snuck out of the room. Just in time to see something that made me feel sick enough to be in the gastric ward. Howard, climbing out from under the sheet-draped trolley I'd been brought up on. He'd been lying on the base of the trolley all that time. Instead of stopping him I'd helped bring him to his doom.

I should have stopped him there in the quarantine area. But I didn't. Because I could tell from his face that he'd already seen her.

His mother.

His face was shining with so much love and sadness. It looked like mine felt when I thought of my mum. My brain was screaming 'stop him' but my heart just glowed.

Howard walked into the room opposite mine, and there was Eileen. I gasped when I saw how bad she looked. Her face was almost unrecognisable. I'd have needed a dozen textas and three bottles of conditioner to get close.

When she saw Howard she stared, trembling. Only when he sobbed 'Mum' did she struggle to sit up and hold her arms out.

Suddenly my brain started working again.

'Howard,' I yelled. 'Stay back.'

Howard spun round, glaring, and when he saw me a terrible thing happened to his face. It twisted and distorted into an ugly mask of hatred.

Just like Rory's after he got infected.

I stared at Howard, sick with shock.

No, it couldn't be. We'd protected him. We'd kept him in the car. I looked around wildly for a doctor so I could prove it was a mistake. Howard couldn't be infected.

Then I remembered.

That last smouldering length of root. The one that had clamped onto his ankle. His sock mustn't have been thick enough after all.

I crouched down and pulled his jeans leg up. His ankle was swollen and purple. Gently pulsing blotches were already spreading up his leg.

'Oh, Howard,' I whispered, close to tears.

He stared down at me, not ugly any more, just a very sad big brother.

'Thanks for trying,' he said, touching my shoulder. Then he turned and sank into his mother's arms.

I was still crouched there, dazed, when Dad walked in. At first I couldn't understand why he was staring in horror at me instead of Howard. Howard was the one who was infected. Then I remembered my skin.

'It's okay, Dad,' I said, standing up. 'It's just texta.'

Dad grabbed my arms, tearful and furious. 'How can you,' he said. 'How can you carry on with your stupid games when I've been worried sick about you and Eileen is dying and the doctors say there's no cure.'

He went over to Eileen, barely glancing at Howard who was kneeling by the bed stroking her hand. Eileen was slumped back on her pillow. She did look like she was dying.

That's when I knew Rory and me were their only hope. And we had to move quickly before Rory got as bad as Eileen. We had to find Rory's dad and pray he had the secret to the infection.

First I had to get out. I ran out of the room and down the corridor and round the corner.

In front of me was a sheet-draped trolley like the one I'd come up on. As I climbed under the sheet and lay on the trolley base, I prayed I'd be as lucky getting out of the hospital as Howard had been getting in.

Three lives depended on it.

EIGHT

I tried not to breathe. I closed my mouth and eyes as I was pushed under the foul water. I felt something bump overhead. Something hard. It wasn't a body. Fantastic. I was so happy. Gramps could still be alive.

But what was it that had banged into my legs and knocked me into the flow of the rushing drain?

As it passed over me I reached up and grabbed it. A railway sleeper. Hurtling along at a terrific speed. Just what I needed – a raft.

I dragged myself onto the slippery wood and felt a surge of relief. It was carrying me back along the tunnel to safety. Away from the terrible smells. Away from the fearful furry figure that had thrown the sleeper into the stream. Away from danger and darkness.

Away from Gramps. Wherever he was. Just what Apple-head wanted. To knock me over and get rid of me.

Without another thought I rolled off the sleeper. It bumped ahead of me into the darkness. The gurgling water washed me along after it on my backside. Desperately I grabbed at the concrete wall with my fingers. It was like running my hand across sandpaper. I could feel the skin on my fingertips breaking. The pain was terrible.

Suddenly I felt something hard and smooth. A handle embedded in the wall. I grabbed it with one hand and stopped my rush down the tunnel with a jolt that nearly pulled my arm out of its socket. Slowly I pulled myself to my feet.

I had to save Gramps. I couldn't leave him to the revolting creature that I had glimpsed up ahead.

But first I had to save myself. What if that furry apple-head sent another sleeper down the stream? In the pitch dark I wouldn't see it. All I could do was listen. Listen for bumping. Knocking. The sound of wood on walls. I strained my ears trying to sort out the sounds. Water bubbling and splashing. Nothing else.

Except . . .

'Eeeeyow.' A long drawn-out cry. A wailing yell of

fury. Coming towards me. Borne down with the current. Oh, no. There was nowhere to run. Nowhere to hide. No escape from the moaning monstrosity.

'Eeeyow,' came the cry. 'Eeeyow, Apple-spy. I'll be back. I'll get you. You don't get rid of a Finnigan that easy. Aaagh . . .'

'Gramps,' I yelled. 'Gramps.' It was him. Coming down the stream. Out of control. I couldn't see anything. There was nothing I could do except brace my legs again and wait.

I took a firm hold on one of the safety handles that seemed to line the edge of the tunnel.

Thump. For a second time in a couple of minutes I was whacked in the legs. Gramps slammed into me and almost took me with him.

'Gotcha, Gramps,' I yelled. 'You're safe now.'

Gramps hung on to my legs desperately as I slowly pulled him to an upright position.

'Rory, boy,' he said. 'Is that you?'

'Yes, Gramps,' I spluttered. 'It's me. Let's get out of here.'

Gramps fought for breath. Finally he managed to get a few words out. 'We have to kill the apple-spy. It's turned into a, a . . . terrible mould-head. A foul, mouldy fiend. Strong like a snake. Sneaky. Rotten. Rotting. Urgh . . .'

'Shoot,' I yelled. 'Let's go. We have to get back to the car.'

'No,' said Gramps. 'It's too far. I can't make it. Go

forward. There's a light further on. And a landing. It's our only hope.'

'But what about the . . .' I didn't finish. If we couldn't go back to the entrance we had to go forward. But the thought of what we might meet up ahead was just too horrible. I tried and tried but I couldn't push it out of my mind.

'Hang on to my belt,' I yelled. 'And don't let go.'

I began to trudge on against the flow of the water. Deeper and deeper into the drain. I was getting weak myself. My bad leg was throbbing. My lungs were raw and my breath wheezed from my throat. The germs were attacking my muscles. I grew weaker with every step. Fear and anger swirled through my veins.

I wouldn't have been able to make it, not pulling Gramps after me, if it wasn't for one thing. The thought of the people I loved. That thought kept me going. Gave me strength. I thought about them all. Gramps. And my father. And mother. And Big Bad . . . No, not her. Nuts to her.

Thank goodness for the safety handles on the side of the tunnel. I couldn't see them but they were evenly spaced in the wall. I grabbed each one and hauled us slowly forward.

Every few paces we stopped for a rest.

Gramps was too puffed to speak. And I wasn't much better.

I was scared of what was ahead. It was unknown. This was all too big for us. We needed the police. We needed the army. The mouldy apple-man needed to be flushed out with gas. Like a rat in a sewer. But first we had to get out of there.

Then I felt a little ray of hope. Maybe Dawn and Howard had gone to the police. Maybe at this very moment they were bringing top scientists to our aid. But how would they know where we were? Dawn would think I had gone into the refinery to look for Dad.

No one was going to come and help us.

We trudged on and on and on. Against the stream in the darkness. Pulling our way further into danger. Forward. Rest. Forward. Rest.

'Gramps,' I finally managed to say. 'What did you see down there?'

'The apple-spy has grown and changed,' he said. 'It has mould all over its hands and face. It's definitely one of Rommel's men. I could have shot it. But I lost my .303. I was helpless.'

Gramps was remembering the war again.

'It's horrible beyond belief, Rory. I shook so much I fell into the water.'

'Gramps, I think you're getting mixed up again,' I said.

'No, I saw its clothes,' said Gramps. 'It's wearing the same uniform. AMPACO panzers.'

We trudged on further. I couldn't go on much longer. My legs were freezing. I was shivering and shaking with the cold. And I was tired. And I knew that if *I* felt like that, then Gramps must be even worse. His tottery old legs must just about be collapsing.

RORY

'Look,' yelled Gramps.

I peered ahead. Yes, there it was. The flickering yellow light. Hope. A small, distant hope.

On, on and on we went. Slipping and sliding. Resting and striding.

I didn't know how we did it. But in the end we reached the yellow light. It hung above a small platform where a ladder stretched down into the water. I hauled myself up and then grabbed Gramps' hand and pulled him after me.

We both lay there panting and shivering in the yellow light. A fatal fever was tearing at my guts. I was terribly weak. And I wasn't the only one. I stared at Gramps' feeble frame and wondered if he could go on.

Gramps stared at me.

And started to scream . . .

Book Six

TILL DEATH US DO PART

Gramps stared at my face and screamed. He looked terrified. I staggered backwards on the little underground jetty.

What was going on? I looked around wildly and tried to make sense of it. Water gurgled along the underground drain. Rats scampered in dark corners. We were alone and helpless, but I couldn't see anything to scream about. There was no sign of the terrible apple-man. There was no mouldy-faced horror glaring out of the darkness.

Or was there? Gramps was looking at me as if *I* was the enemy.

'What's the matter, Gramps?' I gasped. 'I won't hurt you.'

'Get away. Get away, spy,' yelled Gramps. His spindly legs began to shake and for a moment I thought he was going to fall back into the dark water below.

'Gramps, it's me – Rory,' I

shouted. 'You're just seeing things again.'

'Rory?' he said. 'Rory? You can't be Rory. You're, you're . . . ugly.'

I held my hands up to my face and touched the skin. My flesh was all loose and wrinkled. It was horrid to touch.

But there was something else. Something terribly wrong. I couldn't feel the pressure of my fingers on my cheeks. I pinched my nose. Nothing. My fingers could feel my face. But my face couldn't feel my fingers.

I frantically touched my chin and lips and explored the curve of my mouth. Everything was still there but nothing seemed the same. My own face felt as if it belonged to someone else.

Invaders.

Cold fear washed over me. I had been invaded. Evil germs were taking hold. It all flashed through my mind. Everything that had happened. The slobberers infecting me back in the wrecker's yard. Me passing the disease on to the sheep. And then my mum catching it from the lamb. The frogs looking for Mum. The snail and the vine that wanted to infect Howard. The apple-man. The horrible germs that were following my bloodline. Trying to kill me and my relatives.

From animal to human being. From human being to animal. And plants. It used them too. Frogs, apple-men, snails, vines. All wanting me and mine.

The germs were changing my appearance. Feeding on my fear of the mouldy apple-man. The fearsome foe who had grown to human size and was trying to kill us. Now the wicked illness had changed me so much that Gramps couldn't even recognise me.

'It *is* me,' I shouted. 'It *is*. It's me — Rory.'

Gramps moved forward carefully. He was still scared of me. He peered at my face. 'Okay,' he said nervously, 'I'll test you out. If you're Rory you'll be able to answer a few questions.' He bent down and picked up a rusty iron bar which lay on the jetty. 'If you get them wrong you cop this, Apple-spy.'

I took a few steps backwards and stood precariously on the edge of our little refuge. One more step and I would fall back into the rushing stream. 'Anything,' I said. 'Anything.' I nodded my head furiously.

Gramps began to quiz me. 'What did I eat that I shouldn't have?'

'A snail,' I yelled.

'Wrong,' shouted Gramps. 'You're not Rory at all.' He started to walk towards me with the iron bar held above his head. I didn't know what to do. Gramps was old and tottery. I could have knocked him over but I didn't want to hurt him. I didn't want to get clobbered with the iron bar either. He came towards me. He was going to let me have it.

I tried to think. What was the answer? What could it be? 'A compass,' I shouted. 'You ate the compass.'

Gramps lowered the iron bar. But he still wasn't sure that the ugly person facing him was really me.

'What did I throw in the mouth of the frog?' he demanded.

'Salt.'

'Who put the apple-man spy in the car boot?'

'Howard. And . . . me.'

'What is your father's name?'

'Karl.'

'Who is the best Gramps in the world?'

'You are,' I shouted. I threw myself into his arms. He was smiling. He believed me. He knew it was really me. He hugged me tight.

'Rory,' said Gramps. 'You're in a bad way, mate. We have to get help.'

I passed my hand over my rotting face. 'I'm terribly sick,' I said faintly. 'And no one can help me. But I've got one thing to do while I still can. I'm going to find my dad. I have to see his smile just one more time.'

Gramps gave my hand a squeeze. 'This is only a battle,' he said. 'The war's not over yet. We'll find the answer. You wait and see.'

I walked around the small jetty looking for a way out of the drain. We could go back the way we had come but I wasn't sure that we could make it in the strong current. Neither of us was strong enough. Or we could head upstream, further into the tunnel. But where did it go and how far was it?

Then I noticed a steel ladder on the wall across the water. It stretched up above our heads into another huge chimney-like tunnel. The ladder had at least a hundred rungs and it led up to a steel door. It was a long way to the top.

Suddenly a rusty squeal filled the air. The door opened and light filtered into the shadows above. Someone or something was standing in the doorway.

'The apple-spy,' whispered Gramps.

'The mouldy apple-man,' I said hoarsely.

It was him. It was him. Our deadly enemy was looking down at us. He was high above and I couldn't make out the details. But there was one thing for sure. He had something white and hairy and foul where his head should have been. Just the thought of that terrible being made my stomach churn. I felt as if maggots were eating my last store of courage.

But I still had a little bit left. I snatched the iron bar from Gramps' hand and hurled it up at the mouldy apple-man. 'Take that,' I screamed.

The bar hurtled upwards, turning and twisting through the air. Then it clanked harmlessly into the wall halfway up the ladder and began to fall. It fell with a splash into the water below.

The mouldy apple-man quickly ducked back and slammed the door.

Once more we were alone.

I could feel defeat and despair gnawing away inside me. I looked at my hands and arms. The flesh was loose and sagging. The germs were spreading, spreading, spreading. I couldn't bear to think what might be ahead.

Suddenly the despair turned to anger. My mother was infected. And maybe my father. And now that mouldy spectre wanted to spread the disease and kill my brother.

And anyone else who got in its way. Even poor old Gramps. How dare it. I didn't care about myself any more. I was filled with rage.

'Okay, Apple-head,' I yelled into the shadows above. 'So you want a fight, do you? Okay, here I come.'

'You can't go up there,' shouted Gramps. 'It's a trap.'

'Just watch me,' I said.

Gramps tried to hold me back but I pulled away. I lowered myself into the water and waded into the stream. I felt my foot touch something hard. The iron bar. I bent down and picked it up. Then I splashed my way across to the steel ladder on the other side.

'Don't, Rory boy, don't,' pleaded Gramps.

I ignored him and started to climb. One, two, three, four rungs. Suddenly my fingers touched something hanging on a rung above my head. I stopped and tried to work out what it was.

'What's up?' yelled Gramps.

'I've found something,' I said. Then I began to scream. And scream and scream.

'Hands,' I shrieked. 'There's a pair of hands hanging on to the rungs.'

'Don't touch them,' yelled Gramps. 'I'm coming.'

Touch them? I couldn't touch them, not in a million years. They weren't just hands. They were sucked-out hands. With no bones or muscles. Flat, empty skins. Some poor person had had their innards sucked out. Only the dried-out hands were left, still gripping the ladder. Suddenly I realised what the furry slippers were that I had seen at the entrance to the drain. Sucked-out rat skins.

Something terrible was in the water below. 'Hurry,' I yelled at Gramps. 'Hurry.'

Gramps struggled slowly across the stream and pulled himself up onto the ladder. He stared at the hands which gripped the rung like a pair of frozen . . .

'Gloves,' said Gramps.

'What?' I yelled. 'They look like hands to me.'

'Can't be,' said Gramps.

'Why not?' I shouted.

'They've got no fingernails.'

I suddenly felt stupid. Thinking that gloves were hands. A wave of relief washed over me. But it didn't last for long.

'What about the rat skins?' I yelled. 'What about those? There are slobberers here, Gramps.' I threw the gloves into the stream below and continued to climb. Gramps followed, grasping each rung weakly with his knobbly fingers.

Up, up, up. I stared down. The dimly lit jetty looked like a child's toy in the water way below. On I went until at last I reached the door at the top. There was no handle. I knew that on the other side – somewhere – was the mouldy apple-man.

I tried to stop a terrible thought entering my mind. A thought that had been trying to surface ever since my appearance started to change. I didn't want it out in the open. I didn't want to know what this disease was going to do to me.

DAWN

I had to stop myself thinking about it. Action was better than thoughts. Anything but face the truth. I clung on to the top rung with one shaking hand and desperately beat on the door with the iron bar.

'Come on, mouldy Mister Apple-head,' I yelled crazily. 'Come on, slobberers. Come and see what I've got for you.'

TWO

I lay as still as a corpse on the hospital trolley. The sheets draped over it hid me from view, but I was still taking a huge risk.

I gripped Mum's shoe. It had saved me from killer sheep and evil strangling apple-man roots. Would it save me from two nurses and a doctor?

They were wheeling me along a corridor in the huge city hospital. 'Heard the news?' I heard the doctor say. 'This morning's triplets. Two of them were two kilos but the third was only one kilo and a bit.'

The nurses made sympathetic noises. 'Is the littlie okay?' one of them asked. 'Fine,' said the doctor. 'Mum and dad are over the moon.'

I gritted my teeth and forced myself to stay hidden on the base of the trolley. I wanted to leap out and give the doctor and nurses a good shake. I wanted to tell them that Eileen and Howard's ward was where their attention was desperately needed, not the maternity ward.

'Families aren't only loving parents and two-point-five children,' I wanted to yell at them. 'Families are also step-families struggling with jealousy and sadness and evil diseases.'

But I didn't because my family was one of those and the only way I could save them was to get out of the hospital without being caught.

I spent the rest of the trip down the corridor planning the details of how I'd save them. I knew I didn't have much time. The infection was killing Eileen and that meant it was doing the same to Rory, with Howard not far behind. They might only have a few hours.

I made a list in my head of everything I had to do in that time.

1. Find Rory's dad.
2. Get him to say where the infected slobberers came from.
3. Tell the doctors so they could find out more about the infection and discover a cure for it.
4. Wait for the results.

It seemed a lot. And what if we couldn't find Rory's dad? I prayed Rory and Gramps had found some

clues at the refinery. But then what if Rory's dad didn't know where the slobberers had come from? I didn't want to think about that.

I didn't get a chance to.

The trolley stopped suddenly. I heard the doctor and nurses walk away. I decided to risk lifting a sheet to see where I was. Before I could, the trolley swung round and a male voice started humming.

There was a bump and a jolt and I heard lift doors closing. We were going down. I had a horrible thought. What if we were going to the hospital laundry? What if they just chucked their sheets in the washing machine on hot without checking for stray bedsocks or children?

The lift jolted and we clattered out. Then the trolley stopped.

Silence.

It wasn't the laundry. I couldn't smell steam or detergent or stain remover or fabric softener.

The humming started again. It was getting fainter. The man must be moving away from the trolley. Should I run for it now?

I decided to wait, just to be safe. Time was tight but another couple of minutes wouldn't make any difference. It wasn't as if Rory and Gramps were facing immediate danger.

That's when it hit me.

I should have thought of it before. In the quarantine ward. When I realised Howard was infected.

TILL DEATH US DO PART

Howard's apple-man. If the root infected Howard, it probably infected his apple-man too. I remembered the crunch when Howard hurled his apple-man at the tendril clamped round his ankle. Okay, he and Rory dropped the apple-man down a mine shaft, but so what? Infected worms could turn into slobberers. Infected sheep could turn into steel killers. An infected apple-man could easily turn into something horrible and climb out of a hole and come after us.

The figure I'd seen at the refinery. The evil figure running along the fence. I hadn't imagined its mouldy wrinkled apple-skin after all.

I had to warn Rory and Gramps.

Now.

I flung the sheet aside and scrambled off the trolley. Bright lights. Trolleys everywhere. In the far wall, an open roller-door. A cloud of insects and a black square of night.

'Hey.'

A man in a white smock. Turning from a bench. Holding a spanner.

'Please,' I begged, backing away, banging into trolleys. 'My step-brother and my Gramps. They're in terrible danger.'

The man ran at me, then his eyes widened and he stopped. He was staring at me, horrified. What was wrong? Did he know Gramps? Perhaps they'd been in the war together.

Then I realised. He was staring at my skin. At the

purple and yellow blotches I'd drawn on to get into the quarantine ward.

'It's okay,' I shouted as I sprinted for the door. 'It's only texta.'

I dashed through a car park full of ambulances, up a ramp and into the street. It was a street I hadn't seen before. I didn't care. There was a bus in it, waiting at traffic lights. I hammered on the door. The driver let me in. He must have sensed I was related to someone in the bus-driving business.

'I'm never going back,' I said to him as I dug in my pocket for money. 'That face-painting class was a joke.'

He looked at me for a long time. Then he hit the accelerator and we jolted into the night.

The other passengers were all staring at me. I considered asking if any of them was an ex-commando with a couple of hours to spare, but decided against it.

We were hurtling down dark streets and I realised I didn't have a clue where we were going. I also realised I didn't have any money for my fare.

I turned to the driver again. 'I shouldn't have been going to face-painting classes anyway,' I said. 'Not with the homework I've got. I'm doing a huge project on why the oil refinery closed down. You know, that one over there.'

I pointed through his window.

'You mean over there,' he said, pointing in the opposite direction.

Luckily someone wanted to get off at the next stop.

I dashed down the steps after them. 'Hey,' yelled the driver. 'That's seventy cents.'

I felt bad, jumping off without paying, specially as he'd pointed me in the right direction. I made a mental note to post seventy cents to the bus company if I was still alive next pocket-money day.

I ran until my lungs were on fire and I kept on running.

In the distance I heard a siren. Were the ambulances out looking for me? I told myself not to be dopey, then ran across a park to throw them off the scent.

I shouldn't have done that. The park had twisty paths and by the time I came out the other side I'd lost my direction. I kept running. Every dark street looked the same. I sprinted round a corner, praying the refinery road would appear.

It didn't.

I gasped air and sobbed desperate tears. The same desperate tears as Rory was probably sobbing as the evil mould-dripping apple-man lurched towards him.

I pressed Mum's shoe to my forehead. 'Help me, Mum,' I whispered. 'I need you. Even if you were the bad person people say you were, I still need you.'

That's when I heard it. The hum of fast traffic in the distance. The freeway.

I reached it in a few minutes. There was a pedestrian bridge. As I staggered to the top, my mind was racing. Gramps had turned left off the freeway to get us to the refinery. We'd been heading towards the city centre.

DAWN

I scanned the horizon and saw the city skyscrapers lit up against the night sky. I turned to my left and peered into the darkness. And just made out, faint and distant, a familiar forest of dark shapes silhouetted against the electric haze.

The refinery.

It took me another half-hour to find the refinery road. The pub where I'd asked directions was closing up. I slipped past it in the shadows and stumbled along the road, beyond where the streetlights stopped, through the darkness to the towering, rusty, chained refinery gates.

Gramps' car was parked where we'd left it. I threw myself on the back seat and sobbed tears of exhaustion and relief and fear.

Then I pulled myself together. I let Gramps' handbrake off and pushed the car slowly and painfully over to the gates. I climbed on to Gramps' roof trying not to scratch his duco and flung the tarpaulin and blankets from the boot over the barbed wire at the top of the gates.

No sound came from the hulking darkness of the refinery. No rattle and clatter as Rory opened old filing cabinets looking for his dad's forwarding address. No swearing as Gramps banged his head on cranes. No evil rasping breaths as the apple-man crept up on them.

I wouldn't have made it over the gate without the thought of Rory and Gramps to keep me going. Finally I dropped into the mud on the other side.

I crouched and listened. Nothing.

I gripped Mum's shoe in one hand and Gramps' tyre

lever in the other and wondered if I should call out to warn Rory and Gramps. I decided not to. No point in letting the apple-man know they were there.

As I picked my way between the huge storage tanks, I peered desperately into the darkness. I didn't want to miss seeing Rory and Gramps. If the apple-man had already found them, they might be somewhere nearby.

Unconscious.

Or dead.

I felt panic in my throat and tried to force those horrible thoughts out of my mind.

They were replaced by another horrible thought.

What if I came face to mouldy face with the apple-man?

I could run. I could try to save myself. But I knew I wouldn't do that. There was no point. I'd never get back over the fence.

Plus there was another reason.

I'd had enough. I'd already lost my mother. I wasn't losing anyone else. Not without a fight.

I peered through the tangle of pipes and ladders ahead of me. Suddenly I almost wanted to see that ugly, white, mould-covered face gleaming in the moonlight.

'You evil slimebag,' I whispered. 'If you've killed my step-brother and my Gramps, you're dead meat.'

I stuffed Mum's shoe inside my shirt, gripped Gramps' tyre lever and stepped into the darkness.

THREE

I clung desperately to the top of the ladder and beat on the door until I was exhausted. But it was no use. There was no way of opening it from my side. I looked down and groaned.

Gramps was still climbing slowly up the ladder. 'Hang on, Rory boy,' he called in a faint voice. 'I'm coming.'

'Go back,' I screamed. 'I can't get in.'

Gramps didn't take any notice. He just kept coming.

I kept banging the door with the iron bar but it was shut tight. The filthy stinking apple-man was on the other side. I just knew he was. I was filled with rage. 'Apple-head,' I screamed. 'I'm going to rip your ears off.'

Without warning the door above me swung inwards and a dim glow of light filtered into the air above us. A shadowy figure stood there. 'Got yooooooo ... ' it screamed in a savage voice. It stepped out. Onto

nothing. The sound choked off as the figure began to fall. A hand grabbed my jeans and almost tore me away from the ladder.

'Let go,' I shouted. 'Let go, you scumbag.'

My fingers began to slip. The

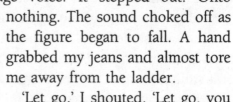

298

weight was terrible. In any second we would fall down onto Gramps and the three of us would plummet to certain death. I started to kick at the head beneath me.

The figure below screamed in fury. 'Where's my step-brother, you overgrown apple?'

'Dawn?' I gasped. It was her. It really was. My step-sister. Big Bad Dawn. I was so happy. Help had arrived.

Dawn grabbed the ladder with one hand and managed to get a foothold. Then she started to pull at my feet, trying to dislodge me from the ladder. She was trying to kill me. She didn't recognise me.

'Stop it,' I screamed. 'It's me. Rory.'

Dawn stared up through the shadows at my twisted ugly face.

'Bulldust,' was all she said.

'It *is* him, sweetheart,' came a weak voice from below.

Dawn looked down and stared in amazement.

'Gramps?'

'The one and only,' he chuckled.

Yes – chuckled. I couldn't believe it. With all this danger. With all this trouble. The three of us stuck up a ladder in deadly peril. In the middle of all this he could still chuckle. Good old Gramps.

'Rory,' shouted Dawn. 'Where's the apple-man? I heard someone scream. I thought he was killing you. I rushed here to save – ' She was interrupted by a loud squealing noise.

'Quick,' I said. 'Go down.'

But I was too late. With a tortured howl of grinding

metal the top of the ladder came away from the wall. Bolts and chunks of concrete fell into the darkness then splashed into the water below.

'Aaghhh,' we all screamed together.

The ladder bent backwards and yawed away from the wall. We were stranded in mid-air as if we were at the top of a flagpole. A flagpole that at any moment was going to topple.

'Don't move,' yelled Gramps. 'Don't move, whatever you do. The rest of the bolts will give way.'

We couldn't go up. And we couldn't go down. And there was no way we could hang on for much longer.

Suddenly I saw something – a long piece of thin timber was making its way towards us out of the door. Was it trying to push us over? Or was it the hand of help? I couldn't see who was holding the other end. Could it be Dawn's dad, Jack, come to save us? Maybe it was the police or a caretaker.

Was it a friend?

Or was it the evil, stinking mouldy apple-man?

I grabbed the end of the waving strip of timber with one hand and hung on. Slowly the ladder began to move back towards the door. Someone – something, was pulling us in. We were nearly there. Closer, closer.

Yes, yes. A cold damp hand reached out for me. I grabbed it and was heaved into a room. I lay gasping on my stomach and heard Dawn and Gramps scramble to safety. I sensed that it was Apple-head that had reeled us in. But I didn't want to look at him. Like a little kid who thinks that they can't be seen when they have their eyes closed, I refused to look.

But I had to. I rolled over and stared. My heart missed a beat. The blood froze in my veins. We all gasped and shrank back in fear at the horrible sight.

The wicked eyes of the appalling apple-man stared at us through a coating of wet, horrible mould. He held out his long crooked fingers and began to stagger towards us.

I was paralysed. I couldn't move. Couldn't think. Like a timid mouse before a snake I just lay there and quivered in terror.

Dawn sprang to her feet. She bent down and picked up a length of chain and threw it at his rotting face.

'Take that, you putrefied pile of poop,' she screamed.

The chain tore a track through the white mould on its head and revealed folds of sagging flesh. In an instant the mould spread across the track and reclaimed the skin for itself.

The rotting figure staggered forward. It ignored Gramps who was feebly trying to regain his breath. It ignored Dawn as she searched desperately for something else to throw. It was me that it wanted. The iron bar fell from my trembling fingers as the mouldy creature staggered forward with outstretched hands. I fell back helplessly and pushed myself away. Trying to force myself into the wall – through the wall – to safety.

Suddenly it leapt and pinned me to the floor. It reached into the blue refinery uniform and tore something from a hidden pocket. It waved it in my face.

I blinked and tried to see what the monster was holding. It was, it was. It couldn't be. Howard's little apple-man. The horrible creature was clutching Howard's apple-man. Even in my terror I could see that.

The little apple-man's head was split open. And was covered with worm tracks.

This rancid, mouldy figure that was pinning me down was not Howard's apple-man grown huge and come to life.

So who was it? What was it?

'Rory,' it croaked. 'Oh, Rory.'

I looked into that decaying face – and for the second time in one week saw myself in another's eyes.

I let out one terrible, wonderful word. One wailing, despairing question.

'Dad?'

FOUR

Even when Rory said the word, I couldn't believe it. Rory's father was the apple-man? This horrible pathetic stomach-turning walking fungus was Rory's dad? I didn't want to believe it.

Yes, I was in shock. Yes, I was dazed and trembling. But I still had a mind of my own.

I wouldn't believe it.

Then I saw the tears. Running down that awful face. Making little rivers through the white mould. And I knew they were a dad's tears.

Rory knew it too. He threw himself into Karl's arms. 'Dad,' he sobbed. They held each other for a long time. It was a dad's hug all right. I blinked back my own tears.

Poor Rory. He'd waited so long to see his dad again. He must have imagined this moment a million times. But not even after eating pickled onions at midnight could he have dreamed it would be like this.

I wished I could do something to make it better for them both. 'I'm sorry, Mr Singer,' I said. 'I'm sorry I called you a putrefied pile of poop.'

Gramps struggled to speak. He was in shock too. 'She – she's sorry she chucked the chain at you too,' he stammered. 'Childish high spirits, you know.'

Karl didn't even hear us. He was staring at Rory. At Rory's own sagging face which now had its own patches of mould.

'Oh, son,' croaked Karl. 'I tried to keep you away. To scare you off. But all the time it was too late.'

He put his face in his hands and

puffs of white powder floated off him as his shoulders shook with grief.

'It's okay, Dad,' sobbed Rory. 'You didn't know my apple-man was infected when you sent it.' He paused, then added in a tiny voice. 'Did you?'

Karl took a painful breath. He shook his head and held up the remains of the apple-man. 'I only discovered it was infected tonight,' he said. 'When I took it from your car.'

'Point of order,' said Gramps. 'It's actually Howard's.'

Karl stared at Gramps with narrow bloodshot eyes. Gramps shifted uncomfortably. 'Sorry,' he said, 'Shouldn't have interrupted. Sorry.'

Karl swayed and for a second I thought he was going to faint. Rory grabbed him. Karl gave an anguished moan. 'Not my other son too,' he croaked. 'Don't tell me Howard's infected too.'

I didn't want to tell him. Karl looked so sick and weak I was worried he wouldn't survive any more bad news. But a father had a right to know. So did a brother and a step-Gramps.

'I'm afraid so,' I said quietly. 'I've just come from the hospital.'

Rory and Gramps both groaned. Karl put his face in his hands again.

'He's not very far gone,' I said. 'Nowhere near as bad as . . .' I stopped.

Rory put his arm round his father's shoulders. 'Mum's infected too,' he said softly. They held each other for a long time. My eyes filled with tears.

After a bit I pulled myself together. We needed information. Something was nagging at me. 'Mr Singer,' I said, 'how did you know the apple-man in the car was infected?'

'I didn't at first,' said Karl. 'I went to your car to scare you away. I looked in the boot for some brake fluid to burn a message in the duco.'

Karl paused for breath. Gramps gestured for him to continue. 'It's okay,' said Gramps. 'It's an old car.'

'I found the apple-man in the boot,' continued Karl. 'I saw the worm holes in it. And when I got back, there were creatures here.'

I stiffened. Creatures?

'Slobberers,' said Rory.

My insides froze. Suddenly I was aware of every tiny noise as I strained to hear something I'd hoped I'd never hear again.

The slurping, sliming sound of slobberers.

I looked at Rory and he looked away. I wanted to yell at him. He and Howard hadn't ditched the apple-man after all. They'd hidden it in the car. And now the slobberers were back.

I made myself control my anger. Blame wasn't going to save our family. Anyway, I sort of understood. There was no way I'd have ditched Mum's shoe under any circumstances. I gave Rory's hand an understanding squeeze and turned to Karl.

'Mr Singer,' I said urgently. 'We need to know everything

you can tell us about the infection.'

'I'll explain everything,' said Karl, 'but not here. It's too dangerous with the creatures about.'

He didn't need to persuade us. We helped him along a dripping metal tunnel that stank of diesel fumes. As I gripped his arm to take his weight I was shocked by how cold and saggy his skin was.

I didn't let him see me flinch. I wouldn't if it had been my dad, and Karl was Rory's dad which was almost the same.

As we made our way down the tunnel, moving through faint patches of electric light and pools of darkness, Rory told him about our run-ins with the first slobberers and the steel sheep and the frogs and the snail and the root. Karl didn't say much, just groaned sometimes. He might have said some other stuff, but I wasn't paying that much attention.

I was listening for other sounds. Sucking, slobbering sounds.

The tunnel suddenly ended. In front of us was a metal wall with a round door in it. The door was studded with rivets and had what looked like a steering wheel in its middle.

Karl tried to turn the wheel. Rory and Gramps helped him. 'Air lock,' wheezed Karl. 'I chose it because nothing can get out. Luckily for us nothing can get in either.'

The door swung open. We stepped through.

We were in a room shaped like the inside of a giant baked-bean can. Loose planks of wood made a sort of floor. Standing on it were a few bits of office furniture.

Gramps swung the door shut and turned a wheel on the inside.

'Dad,' said Rory, close to tears. 'You can't live in here. It's too unhealthy.'

'No, son,' said Karl quietly. 'You've got it wrong. I'm too unhealthy to live anywhere except in here.'

Rory started to protest, but Karl held up a big spongy hand. 'I'll explain,' he said.

He sat down slowly on a narrow bed made from two filing cabinets and a padded insulation jacket like the one on our school water heater. He tried to continue but his head dropped and he slumped against the wall.

'He's unconscious,' said Gramps. 'Medics on the double.'

We laid him gently on his bed. Rory and I squeezed his hands. It was like squeezing cold cooked cauliflower.

'Don't die, Dad,' begged Rory.

'Rations,' said Gramps.

The only food I could find was in tins. I opened a can of sliced peaches and moistened where I thought Karl's lips would be with the juice.

After a few seconds Karl opened his eyes.

'Sorry,' he said weakly. 'I must have blacked out. I've been doing that a bit lately.'

'Mr Singer,' I said gently, 'we need to know how the infection started.'

Karl sighed and I could see he was making his mind go back to a place it didn't really want to go. I hoped the infection would help his memory like it had Rory's and not damage it like Eileen's.

'About six years ago,' Karl began slowly, 'we were stripping the refinery before it closed down. I was the safety officer. It was my job to make sure nobody got hurt or infected. Pretty funny, eh?'

I hoped he wouldn't try to laugh. He didn't. He just took a wheezy breath and carried on.

'I had to inspect an old tanker before a demolition team went in to pull out the pumps and stuff. That's where I found it. In one of the bulkheads. White mould.'

He stopped to catch his breath.

Rory gave him a sip of peach juice.

'I'd never seen anything like it,' continued Karl. 'Did some tests. Didn't seem to be toxic, so I cleaned it out and didn't think any more about it.'

'Mr Singer,' I said quietly, 'were any of the other workers infected?'

Karl shook his head. 'None. I checked later. Dunno why they weren't. I was probably the only one who touched the mould.'

My brain was racing. Something clicked. 'Were you very angry in those days?' I asked.

Karl looked at me for a long time. 'Yes,' he wheezed finally. 'I reckoned it was my wife's fault our marriage had ended. Eileen blamed me for having Howard adopted, even though we'd both made the decision. I was very angry with her.'

I looked at Rory. He was upset at what he was hearing,

but he knew why I'd asked the question.

'When the refinery closed five years ago,' continued Karl, 'I went back to be near Rory. I didn't know I was infected. When I started to get sick, I tried to get treatment. The doctors told me it was a virus but they didn't know how to cure it. I knew it was the mould. Bits would sometimes grow between my toes. I tried to cure myself with health food. Organic vegies. Goat's milk. One day my goat Ginger ate one of my thongs and went crazy. Chewed her way into the drawer where I kept some of Rory and Howard's old baby clothes. Ripped them to shreds and didn't touch anything else. Then she ran off after the school bus.'

I stared at Karl. My head was spinning as I digested this.

Karl looked up at Rory. 'I realised then that the virus was after you and Howard,' he said. 'I had to leave, for your sakes. I came back here to the refinery to try and find a cure. I couldn't tell you in case you followed. That's why I sent you both the apple-men. So you wouldn't forget me. Stupid. It was stupid ...'

Tears made new irrigation channels through the mould on Karl's cheeks. He struggled for each rasping breath.

Rory gripped his hand. 'It wasn't stupid, Dad,' he sobbed. 'It wasn't.'

They were both so sad I wanted to stop the questions and hug them. But I had to press on. I could see Karl wouldn't be able to talk for much longer.

'Mr Singer,' I said urgently. 'You've been infected for

five years. Rory's been infected for only three days. Yet he's almost as sick as you. Can you think of anything that has slowed down your infection?'

For what seemed like an hour Karl just struggled for breath. Then at last he spoke.

'Blue mould,' he whispered.

We all leant forward.

'Blue mould?' I said.

'In the tanker,' he croaked. 'In the sick bay. I've been growing it. Only small amounts, though. Kills the white mould.'

Gramps and I looked at each other excitedly.

'Then the white mould kills it,' continued Karl.

Gramp's face fell.

'Doesn't matter,' I said. 'It's better than nothing. I'll go and find it.'

'Me too,' said Rory.

'No,' gasped Karl. 'Too dangerous. Creatures.'

I pretended I hadn't heard that. To myself as well.

'Before we go,' I said to Karl, 'one last question.' I couldn't go without asking it. 'The goat and the bus,' I said. 'When my mother died. Tell me what happened, please.'

I held my breath. Karl sat up. Then he muttered something and slumped against Gramps.

'He's unconscious again,' said Gramps. He listened to Karl's chest. 'I don't think he's going to come out of this one for a while. I'd better stay with him, I was in the tank corps. You infantrymen get the mould at the double.'

'But what did he say?' I yelled as Rory and I headed for the door.

'He said "Watch out for the queen",' said Gramps. He gave Rory a sympathetic look. 'I'm sorry, Rory, but I think he might be going a bit senile.'

FIVE

I left Dad's room with an aching heart. I was in the grip of hopeless grief and despair.

Dad was dying. I kept remembering the old Dad. The one with the kind, handsome face. The one with white teeth and smooth skin. Now he was a germ-riddled wreck, hardly alive. Unconscious. Helpless, and covered in a greedy invading mould.

And me. What about me? I was getting weaker all the time. My face and skin were sagging and collapsing more with every passing minute. The virus was eating away at me. I couldn't see myself but I knew that I must be incredibly ugly. Normally a person's face just looked unhappy if they were angry or sulky or whatever. But those feelings were like fertiliser to the virus. All the bad thoughts I had ever had. All the wicked things I had ever done were like food for the germs. My hateful thoughts were written on my face.

But maybe there was hope. Just a tiny hope. Maybe we could find the blue mould. And maybe it could save me and the others.

Maybe.

Dawn kept her distance. And I knew why. She could hardly bring herself to look at me, let alone touch me.

We made our way down a steep ramp and found ourselves in the middle of a group of oil storage tanks. Tiny-looking ladders spiralled around each one leading up to giddying heights above.

'Which way to the dry dock?' asked Dawn.

'Why?' I asked.

'Your dad said the mould is in the hulk of a ship. An old tanker. It will have to be in dry dock.'

'How would I know?' I snapped. I'm just an ugly, infected step-brother. You're only coming with me for one reason.'

'Not that again,' said Dawn.

She made me so angry. 'You want to be there at the death knock. Just in case I hallucinate. Just in case I see what happened to your mother. You even had to go and worry my dying father with it. You are so selfish.'

'I do want to know, Rory,' said Dawn. 'But I want something else too.'

'What?' I said scornfully.

'I want to help you. I want to find the blue mould. If there is such a thing. I want you to go back to normal.'

'Don't you like the way I look?' I spat out. 'Don't you want to come close to your worst nightmare?'

'It doesn't matter what you look like,' said Dawn. 'Even if you have got a face like a dag on a sheep's bum, it doesn't mean that you're not still the same person.'

'Thanks,' I said sarcastically. 'That makes me feel a lot better.'

We stared into the dark night. A cold drizzle soaked through our clothes.

Twisted ladders and huge chimneys filled the spaces between the oil tanks. At their feet tangles of pipes fought for space. The whole refinery was like a dead rusting monument to wickedness.

In the distance I heard a bird squawk. 'A seagull,' said Dawn. 'The dry dock must be that way.'

We trudged forward through the darkness. Two lonely figures. Frightened, small and hopeless.

'What did your dad mean by the – '

'Queen?' I broke in. 'Probably just some other bossy female.'

Dawn said nothing. We threaded our way through the dead refinery peering into every shadow. Hoping, hoping, hoping that slobberers were not waiting for two juicy kids.

'There it is,' said Dawn. We both stared at the deserted oil tanker. Huge and rusting in the dry dock. Propped up by hundreds of wooden beams, it stood alone, abandoned like Noah's ark after the Flood. We perched there on the edge of the dock at deck level and looked down at the silent propeller and the useless rudder.

'How will we ever find a bit of mould in a monster like that?' I said in a defeated voice.

'Listen,' said Dawn quietly. 'What's that?'

We looked up to where the noise was coming from. 'Rats,' I whispered.

Hundreds of rats were running up a rope on to a crane high above our heads. They were squeaking and squealing in terror. They wanted to get off the ship. A terrible smell filled the air. My knees shook as I watched the wretched rodents. 'I can't take much more,' I choked. 'I just can't.'

Dawn tried to cheer me up with a joke. 'Rats always desert a stinking ship,' she said.

I peered down into the dry dock beneath the hull and saw something else. It looked like thousands of pairs of old slippers had been thrown out of one of the portholes. I knew straight away what they were.

'More rat skins,' I gasped. 'Sucked-out rat skins. There are slobberers around here somewhere.'

We both stared up at the rickety gangplank that led on to the ship and shivered. Neither of us wanted to go.

'Come on,' said Dawn. 'Don't think about it.'

I couldn't figure out if she was incredibly brave or just

stupid. 'Think of the rats,' I said. 'How would you like to end up like that? Sucked out.'

'Think of your mum,' said Dawn. 'Think of your father dying of a terrible disease. Think of Howard. Think of – '

'Okay, okay, okay,' I said. I hung my head in shame. We had to find the blue mould. If there was any such thing. Otherwise everyone I loved was going to die. I pushed past her and headed up the gangplank. At the top was a roughly painted sign saying:

I laughed wildly.

'Rory,' said Dawn. 'You're hysterical. Pull yourself together.'

'I'm already contaminated,' I said. 'I'm the danger.' I cackled away like a crazy chook.

The ship seemed dead. All the useful parts had been stripped away and it was only a hulk. There would have been no way that we could have gone into the black insides of that ship. Except for one thing.

A long electrical lead with dim lights glowing from it led down a steep ladder.

I had a hunch. 'Dad did that,' I said.

Dawn didn't ask me how I knew. She was listening to something. 'I thought I heard a slurp,' she said. 'Maybe we should get help.' I couldn't see her knees but I knew that they must have been knocking. Like mine.

Suddenly she started climbing down the ladder. 'Come on,' she said.

I hobbled towards the ladder and followed her. I felt as if my body was a heavy load. I was dragging my infected flesh around. Taking it where it didn't want to go. It was almost as if the germs inside my body were trying to control me. And stop me going.

At the bottom of the ladder was a corridor. A battered sign pointed to the dining room in one direction. The lights led the other way. Dawn took a curious step into the darkness. 'Aagh,' she screamed. 'What's that?'

'Yuck,' I said. 'That's the worst stink in the world.' I was so scared. Something awful. Something evil was down that passage. Dawn swallowed her own fear and tried to cheer me up. She was gutsy. Trying to pretend that she wasn't scared.

'Reminds me of Lester Green's halitosis,' she said. 'Only a million times worse.'

'Huh?' I said.

'Bad breath,' explained Dawn. 'There wasn't a girl in the school who would kiss him.'

I was just going to say something rude when we both froze on the spot.

Hhhhccchhhssshh. A horrible deep breath. Like a monster

snake about to strike. And then a worse sound. One I had heard somewhere before. A terrible, gobbling, sucking noise came from the direction of the dining room.

We both fled in the other direction, following the lights without any idea of where they might take us. We scrambled down stairs and around corners. I lost track of how far we ran following those lights. But there was one thing I did know. We had not passed one other door or passage. We had only two ways to go. Back. Or forwards. We could go back and try to sneak past the dreadful slobbering noise. Or forwards into the silent unknown depths of the hulk.

'What *was* that thing?' I yelled when we finally stopped.

'From the smell,' said Dawn, 'and the hissing and sucking, it could be – '

'Look,' I shouted.

It was the sick bay. The door had a round handle on it like a safe. And just above that was a small glass window with a light above it. We had found what we had come for. Dad's experimental laboratory. Maybe we could find something that would save Dad and Mum and Howard and . . . me. The answer to all our prayers.

We hoped.

I stood on tiptoes and stared into the window. Then I screamed. The most ugly, rotten, decayed face in the world was looking back at me. A face with hateful watering eyes. With sagging skin and patches of white mould and twisted dirty hair. With rotting teeth and bleeding gums.

The face screamed back. It was scared of me.

It *was* me.

I was looking at my own reflection in the glass.

I sagged down like a sack of jelly. Even if we found the blue mould, my life wasn't worth living. I could never leave that ship. I could never face another person. I had the ugliest face in the universe. The virus was ripping into me. Turning me into a monster.

I was too ashamed to look at Dawn. No wonder she was keeping her distance. I sank down on to the metal floor and pulled my windcheater over my head. I wanted to crawl into a hole and never see another person as long as I lived. I wanted to stick my head into a dunny and flush it away.

How could Dawn even bear to look at me?

At that very moment an awful wet spattering sound filled the air. It reminded me of the time the Year 7 boys had a competition to see who could spit the furthest. Only this was worse. *Spit, spit, suck, spit.* Wet and bubbling. Horrible. Horrible. Somewhere back along the corridor.

SIX

I tried to ignore the distant slobberer sounds as I gripped Mum's shoe and pulled the sick-bay door open. An avalanche of washing powder knocked me over.

I floundered around on my knees in the torrent of white granules. I tried to crawl away, but they poured out with such force I ended up sprawled on my stomach.

'Rory,' I screamed. 'Help.'

Finally the torrent stopped. The stuff was everywhere. In my hair. In my mouth. I was half buried in it.

'Good one, Worm Boy,' I spluttered. 'This isn't the sick bay, it's the ship's laundry supply store.'

Rory didn't reply. Once I'd got the washing powder out of my eyes, I looked over to where I'd last seen him.

He was huddled on the passageway floor, his wind-cheater pulled over his head. Laughing at me, probably.

I felt like going over and giving him a good shake. Instead I made myself remember that he was sick. And that the virus must have infected the part of his brain that knew about good manners.

Something was weird. I smacked my lips. The washing powder didn't taste like washing powder. It didn't smell like washing powder either.

That's because, I realised with a sudden jolt of panic, it wasn't washing powder.

It was white mould.

'Aagh,' I screamed. I staggered to my feet and shook my hair and frantically brushed myself down.

A shower. I needed a shower. A big ship like this must have heaps of showers. Then I remembered what Karl had said. The ship had been stripped for demolition. What good was a shower without taps and water?

Anyway, it was hopeless. Even if I scrubbed every grain off myself, it had still been in my mouth.

The horrible truth sank in. This wasn't Karl mould that fed only on him. Or Rory mould that fed only on Rory. This was the original mould that had started the whole nightmare.

And now the virus was inside me. The virus that had infected Karl, that had created the slobberers, was inside me. Now the cycle would start again. I'd infect something and it would infect Gramps. And he'd infect something and it would go after Dad.

And soon our whole family would be dead.

I sank to my knees. Oh, Mum, I thought. Perhaps you were the lucky one, dying first. At least you didn't have to see faces you loved going mouldy in front of your eyes.

I glanced over at Rory. He was still huddled against the wall with his head in his windcheater. I was glad.

I didn't want him to see me blubbing.

I wanted Mum. I wanted to be on her bus kneeling with my head in her lap so she could stroke my hair between gear changes. I wanted to be there when she drove off the cliff into the river so I could see why.

Why she'd died.

Then a thought hit me. The virus that was inside me was the same virus that had given Rory his hallucinations. That had helped him remember what happened on the bus up until just before Mum died.

Now I was infected, perhaps I'd have an hallucination. Perhaps at last I'd be able to find out why.

Heart thumping, I screwed up my eyes. 'Come on,' I said to the virus. 'Show me.'

Then another thought hit me. The only reason the virus had been able to bring back Rory's memories of the bus was that he'd been on the bus in the first place. He'd seen Mum's death.

I hadn't. The virus couldn't give me memories of something I hadn't seen.

I grabbed a handful of mould and flung it angrily away. 'Stinking, scumbag virus,' I screamed.

There must have been quite a draught on that half-demolished ship because the tiny grains of mould seemed to float in the air. In the faint gleam of Karl's makeshift lighting system they seemed to glow. And some of them glowed blue.

I grabbed another handful of granules and studied them. No wonder I'd thought it was washing powder. In amongst the white grains were blue ones.

'Blue mould,' I yelled. 'Rory, I've found the blue mould.'

If the blue mould had slowed Karl's sickness from three days to five years, perhaps it could also cure it. Perhaps it could save us all.

Frantically I started trying to collect it. Only about one in every hundred grains was blue. I lifted one up between my fingertips. Before my horrified eyes it turned white.

I picked up another one. It turned white too. Was I doing that, by touching it? Rubber gloves. I needed rubber gloves. Even sailors must have done washing-up.

Then I saw the horrible truth. The blue grains were dying without me touching them. They were appearing from nowhere, bursting into life, then almost immediately turning white. The white mould was killing them.

'Stop it,' I screamed at the white mould. 'Stop it.'

Desperately I tried to pick out several blue grains so I could put them together and they could draw strength from each other away from the white predators.

My fingers wouldn't move fast enough. Big, clumsy fingers. I wanted to chop them off. Why did I have big clumsy fingers when Mum's had been so slim?

I smashed my fists down into the white powder, causing a mini-avalanche. When the grains had stopped tumbling, something familiar was left poking out.

Mum's shoe.

I stared at it. The colour looked different. Instead of scuffed, watermarked brown, it looked almost blue.

I saw why. All the grains sitting on it were blue. And they were staying blue.

Excitedly I picked a blue grain out of the white heap and tried to add it to the ones on the shoe. Before I could let go of it, it had turned white. I tried to flick a blue grain on to the shoe with my fingernail. No good. I tried to scoop blue grains up with the shoe. Hopeless.

My neck ached with frustration. I felt like giving up and going back to punching the white mould. But something Dad always said popped into my head. 'If at first you don't succeed, stop and think.'

Then I remembered what Karl had said. About trying to grow blue mould. That must be where the blue grains were coming from. His experiments in the sick bay.

I waded through the mould into the sick bay. The small room was waist-deep in white powder. There were bunks on one side and shelves on the other. The shelves were piled high with jars and soft-drink bottles. All full of white mould. Karl's failed experiments.

I swore at the jars and bottles. Until I realised what I was doing. My anger was turning the blue grains on Mum's shoe white. I shook them off and took deep breaths and remembered what Dad said about not giving up till you'd searched the back paddock.

I examined the shelves again. And there, high on the top shelf, I found them. Three small Vegemite jars. One containing a dried-up piece of cheese. One half-full of water. One stuffed with leaves and twigs. And each one with a lump of blue mould in it about the size of a Smartie.

DAWN

Hands shaking with excitement, I carefully lifted the jars down. Would this be enough to cure us all? Even as I asked myself the question, I knew it wouldn't. It probably wasn't even enough to cure one infected person, or Karl would have used it on himself.

I knew what I had to do. It was a risk, but my family was dying and I didn't have time to be cautious. I unscrewed each jar and tipped each tiny lump of blue mould into Mum's shoe.

Then I waited.

In less than a minute the blue lumps started to grow. 'Yes,' I screamed. 'Yes.'

The lumps were already the size of Maltesers and still growing. 'Good on you, Mum,' I yelled happily.

I stopped yelling. Something strange was happening. The blue mould was creeping over the entire surface of the shoe, inside and out. The shoe was completely blue.

And getting lighter. Not in colour, in weight.

The blue mould was eating Mum's shoe.

'No,' I screamed. 'No.'

Cupping the crumbling shoe in both hands, I waded frantically out of the sick bay.

'Rory,' I yelled, staggering over to him. 'Stop fooling around. I need your help.' With my foot I dragged the windcheater off his head. And gasped.

His face was terrible. I'd almost got used to what the virus had done to it before, but this was worse. Much worse.

Even worse than Karl.

Rory's tiny breaths sounded like milkshake fighting its way up a very thin straw. His eyes were closed.

I crouched close to him and as I did I saw that in my hands was just a pile of blue powder. Mum's shoe was gone. I felt grief surging up, but I locked it down with my throat.

'Rory,' I said, 'don't die. I've got some blue mould. Don't die.'

His eyes fell open. They flicked wildly around.

'The goat,' he shouted.

I didn't bother looking behind me. I knew there was no goat on the ship. And I knew Rory wasn't dying, not yet.

He was on the bus.

SEVEN

The bus was facing the river.

The goat was pawing with its front hooves and stamping. Ready to charge down the aisle.

Mrs Enright had selected first gear and had the clutch pressed to the floor.

RORY

My father was banging desperately on the door trying to get into the bus.

And I was screaming. 'Dad, Dad, Dad. It's really you.'

He was yelling something and trying furiously to open the door. What was he saying? Something about a boat? No it wasn't that.

'Watch out for the goat,' he shouted. 'Don't touch the goat.'

I threw a quick glance down the bus. The goat was charging. Its eyes glowed horribly. Its face was almost human. As if it knew who we were. It thundered down the aisle with its horns lowered. What was it up to? Was it attacking Mrs Enright?

Crack. I felt the bone break under my jeans. My leg twisted sideways at the knee. The pain was terrible. I screamed in agony and fell to the floor. The goat half jumped, half fell over me and skidded on into the back of Mrs Enright's seat and jolted it forwards so that her legs were crushed up under the steering wheel. It had enormous strength.

'Get out, Rory,' Mrs Enright screamed. 'Get out. I can't reach the gear lever. I can't hold the clutch. Get out. Now.'

The goat backed up over me and positioned itself for another charge. Its horns were aimed right at me.

'I can't move,' I screamed. 'I can't move. My leg is broken.'

With a sudden crash Dad burst into the bus.

'Get him out,' screamed Mrs Enright. 'Get Rory out. I can't hold the clutch much longer. We're going into the river.'

Dad threw a horrified glance at the goat, which was thundering back down the aisle towards us. Then he snatched a look at Mrs Enright trapped under the steering wheel trying desperately to keep the pedal pressed in. Finally he turned to me. I groaned in agony. My leg was killing me.

Dad didn't know what to do. I could see it in his face. He had to decide. Help Mrs Enright get the bus out of gear. Stop the goat. Or pull me to safety. Dad groaned in agony. And made his choice.

EIGHT

Rory opened his eyes. I knew immediately that he was back with me in the passageway of the abandoned ship. Back in his poor twisted infected body.

The bus trip was over.

I knew because his eyes were full of tears.

He didn't speak. He just lay there panting with shallow rasping breaths. He didn't need to speak. I could see the horrible truth in his brimming eyes.

So it was true. All the things people had whispered about Mum. All the things I'd kept locked away in my nightmares. She had been mad. Or drunk. Or criminally careless. She'd hit a goat and tried to turn the bus around on an impossibly narrow road and had killed herself doing it.

Perhaps it was just as well that her shoe was gone. Now I didn't have anything to make me think about her.

I stayed kneeling next to Rory for a long time, rigid with misery. I knew I should have been trying to make him better with the blue mould, but suddenly it all seemed hopeless.

Tears ran down my face and dripped onto Rory's hand. They seemed to stir him into action. Wheezing, he dragged himself up onto his elbows.

'I know what happened to your mum,' he said.

'No,' I said. 'Please, I don't want to hear the details.'

He told me anyway.

He described how the goat charged into his leg and broke it and rammed Mum's seat so she was trapped behind the wheel.

'Bull,' I said. 'Goats don't bend steel seat supports. Not unless they're ...' I trailed off, remembering how strong the infected sheep had been. Then I remembered that the goat had eaten Karl's mouldy thong.

'Don't talk,' croaked Rory. 'Just listen.'

I listened. Rory described Mum struggling to keep her foot on the clutch. He described his dad bursting on to the bus and having to decide who to save. He described it all so vividly I could see it as clearly as if I'd been there.

'Get him out,' screamed Mum. 'Get Rory out. I can't hold the clutch much longer. We're going into the river.'

Karl looked at Mum's foot slipping off the clutch. He looked at the charging goat. He looked at Rory writhing in agony on the floor.

He grabbed his son and dragged him off the bus.

Even before Karl and Rory sprawled into the bushes at the side of the road, the back wheels of the bus were spinning in the mud. The clutch spring had been too strong for Mum's poor crushed legs.

The bus seemed to hang there on the edge of the cliff for a moment. The back wheels flung sludge at the sky. The engine roared. Then the bus shot forward and over the edge.

That would have been enough for me. Knowing Mum had died a hero would have been enough for me. I could have lived happily with that for whatever short time my infected body had left.

But there was more.

As the bus went over the edge of the cliff, the fuel line must have been ripped out by a rock. Suddenly the engine went dead and the bus fell towards the dark swirling river in silence.

Except for one sound. Mum's voice, strong and clear.

'Dawn,' she shouted with the passion and energy that Dad reckoned had made the bedroom windows rattle when I was born. 'I love you.'

Even after the bus had disappeared into the depths of the river, and Karl had dived in after it, Mum's words still echoed inside my head and I knew that from then on I'd have to be dead to stop hearing them.

I slumped back against the wall of the ship's passageway and a storm broke inside me that would have been a match for any storm that ship had ever seen, even in the Atlantic. Tears that had been waiting five years came out in huge shuddering sobs. Tears of sadness. Tears of grief. Tears of love.

They took a long time to pour out, but when they stopped I felt more peaceful than I could ever remember feeling, including being with Dad at Dubbo zoo.

Until I heard a faint, high-pitched rasping.

Rory. He was barely breathing. He stared up at me with dull eyes. The colour and life were draining out of his poor suffering face.

I'd forgotten about the blue mould. While Rory had been telling me about Mum, my fists had been clenched tight. I opened my hands and in each palm was a sweaty lump of blue mould the size of an egg.

I broke a piece off one of the lumps. Then I panicked. How should I give it to Rory. Externally? Internally?

I rubbed the blue mould carefully on to his face. He looked at me gratefully, but the light continued to fade in his eyes.

'Thanks,' he whispered, 'but it's too late.'

I broke another piece off and gently pushed it through his lips into his mouth.

His eyes closed. His breathing slowed. The blue powder on his face was gradually turning white.

My eyes filled with tears again. 'Oh, Rory,' I said.

He was dying. He'd helped me get my mum back and now he was dying. And there was nothing I could do.

Except what his mum would have done.

I leant forward and kissed him gently on his swollen lips. They didn't feel swollen to me and I didn't feel like his mum.

I felt like a girl who loved him.

Out of the corner of my eye I saw his cheek turning blue. I'd always imagined that when I finally kissed a boy both our cheeks would probably turn red, but his were definitely turning blue.

I peered at them. The blue mould on his face was growing. It was eating the while mould.

Rory's eyes opened. 'Don't stop,' he murmured. I'd always imagined that when a boy said 'don't stop' I'd stop immediately, but on this occasion I didn't. I put a piece of blue mould into my mouth and lay down next to Rory and put my arms round him.

I only gave myself a tiny piece. With Mum's shoe gone

we couldn't grow any more. The two lumps were all we had for Karl and Eileen and Howard.

Rory and I lay like that for a long time. As the minutes passed, and Rory's breathing slowly got stronger, I thought how lucky I was to have a brother like him.

My thoughts seemed to help. His face became less twisted and the terrible marks of the infection started to fade. So I kept on thinking those thoughts and having those feelings.

It wasn't hard. It was much easier than thinking about the slobbering horror that was waiting for us at the other end of the passageway.

NINE

Dawn had kissed me. My first one. Probably hers too. With a kiss she had saved my life.

What had gone on in her mind? Kissing my revolting sagging face. It was a kiss that gave, not a kiss that took. There was nothing in it for her. It was an act of compassion. She was telling me, 'Rory, I care about you.

Rory, I don't want you to die. Rory, even though you are infected, I really care.'

She was saying, 'Rory, you are not ugly. Not inside.'

I kept touching my lips and remembering the softness of Dawn's. How could she have done it? How could she have kissed my foul flesh?

I remembered the look of love in her eyes. Not love like in soppy love stories. Not girlfriend love. But the sort of love that you have for a brother. He might annoy you. He might get on your nerves. But you don't want him to die.

And then I realised that was how I felt about her. She was daggy. Sometimes she was bossy. But she was kind. And gutsy.

I didn't love her like a girlfriend. I loved her like a sister.

And she had saved my life. She had put the blue mould in my mouth and it had started to work. I could feel it making me better. But it wasn't enough. The virus had been too strong for it.

Until Dawn gave me the kiss of life. And gave the blue mould what it needed to grow and do its work.

I wanted to ask if her feelings were the same as mine. But I was embarrassed.

'That kiss,' I stammered. 'Did . . .'

'Yes?' said Dawn.

'Did I have halitosis?'

'Rory,' she said. 'This is no time for discussing personal hygiene. We have to get that mould back to your dad. And Howard. And your mum. Before they die of the virus.'

She held up the two precious balls of blue mould – one in each hand. All that was left. But enough. Just enough to save them all. If we could get it back in time.

I suddenly felt terribly guilty. I was so pleased to be getting better and so shocked by the kiss that I had forgotten all about the others.

Dad and Eileen and Howard. They were all dying and I could only think about myself.

We had to take the mould to them. Quickly. Dawn and I were the only ones who could save them. Only the blue mould could kill the virus. And what about poor old Gramps? All alone with Dad. Trying to keep him alive.

'Let's go,' I said.

We started back along the small corridor, following the dim yellow lights. Suddenly they went out. We were in total darkness.

'Hang on to my belt,' I said.

'Why?' said Dawn.

'So we don't get separated.'

'You hang on to me,' she said.

Boy, she could be annoying. Why did she always have to lead the way? Still, she had saved my life. And kissed me. At that moment I would have forgiven her anything. I grabbed her belt and followed her along the empty black corridor.

Suddenly she stopped.

'What is it?' I whispered.

'Something's blocking the way,' she whispered back. 'The whole corridor is blocked with flat furry things. A whole wall of them. Someone, something is trying to stop us.'

I put my hand out and quickly pulled it back again. 'Yuck,' I screamed. 'Rat skins.'

'Slobberers have been here,' said Dawn. 'That's what the spitting noise was.'

I tried to pull one of the rat skins out but it wouldn't budge. The skins felt as if they had been cemented together by a sort of sticky wet dribble. It was as strong as glue.

'We'll have to go back to the sick bay and keep going that way,' I said.

Dawn started to make her way back down the corridor the way we had just come. 'I think I know where this leads,' she said. 'And I'm not sure I want to go there.'

But she kept moving on. Sometimes she stumbled. Once she fell. But she climbed back up without a word and went on. And I followed, hanging tightly on to her belt. Suddenly she stopped. And started to sniff.

'It's that smell again,' I said in a shaky voice.

'It's like I thought,' she said. 'This corridor has been going in a circle. It's leading back to the dining room from the other direction.'

'Halitosis,' I said. 'Stinking slobberer breath. Let's find another way.'

'There is no other way,' said Dawn.

I held on to her more tightly and we moved forward with trembling legs and racing hearts. The smell grew worse and worse. Oh, foul. Oh, disgusting. We were walking to our doom. Walking into the slobberers' nest. I was sure of it. But we had to go on. We had to get the mould to Dad and Howard and Mum.

Now we could hear them. Sucking, sucking, sucking. A revolting sound. The slobberers' wet song of death.

Our legs took us forward. How I don't know. We were like condemned prisoners walking to our doom. Slowly, I began to see details of the passageway. Dim light was filtering through dirty portholes. I could make out the shape of Dawn's head. Morning had arrived.

Up ahead I could just read a sign hanging above a steel doorway. It read:

DINING ROOM

'What's for breakfast?' said Dawn.

I didn't laugh. 'Listen,' I said. The sucking was much louder.

I shuddered and remembered the sucked-out skin of the dog at the wrecker's yard. But I didn't say anything.

We crept up to the door and peered around the edge.

Nothing could have prepared us for the sight. No one in the history of the world had ever seen such a sight.

A huge slobberer the size of a whale almost filled the room. It lay on its side revealing four bloated blue teats. On each teat a baby slobberer sucked greedily.

Babies. Surely they couldn't be babies. Each one was as big as a cow.

'The queen,' I gasped. 'She's feeding them up.'

I knew where that queen had come from. Howard's infected apple-man. And now the queen was gigantic. She must have eaten thousands of rats.

The queen's long wet tongue flicked around the room like the tail of a crocodile. Suddenly she flipped it upwards into the shadowy mass of pipes and pulled down a fat rat. In a second it was gone. Swallowed. Sucked out.

Phoot. She spat the skin out like a bullet and it thunked into the wall.

We crept back down the corridor. 'There's no hope,' I said. 'We'll never get past her. That tongue would suck us up in a second.'

I hung my head. It was useless. There was no other way out. Dad would die. And Mum. And Howard. And in the end Dawn and me. We were trapped like rats in the abandoned hulk.

'Listen, Rory,' said Dawn. 'We have to work together on this.' Dawn held up her fists and shook the two balls of blue mould at me.

'This would kill the queen,' she said. 'It killed the white mould. It would do the same to the queen.'

I shook my head. 'We'd never get near it,' I said. 'Not

with that tongue lashing around. And anyway, if we use the mould up on the queen there will be none left for Mum and Dad and Howard.'

'We could use half of it,' said Dawn. 'We could use one ball on the queen. And keep the other for your family.'

I remembered the frog general. Gramps had killed it by throwing salt into its cake-hole. If we could throw some mould into the queen's gob she might die too.

The thought of that slimy mouth made me shudder. Someone could die throwing the mould into it. And that someone should be me. I took one ball of mould from Dawn and held it in my hand. If the queen ate me she would eat the mould as well. And that would be the end of her.

It was strange really. The virus had nearly killed me. And now I would soon be back to normal. Looking forward to a great life with Mum and Dad. I had defeated death and now I had to face it again. There really wasn't any choice. Dawn had risked her life for me. She'd kissed me, even though she might have become infected. She'd pressed her soft lips against my rotting ones.

Now it was my turn. There was only one thing to do.

'Take off your bra,' I shouted suddenly.

'What?' she yelped.

'Take off your bra.'

'Rory,' she said in an outraged voice. 'Get real.'

She stared at me. Then her eyes grew round. She was remembering. Remembering a silly trick played by a silly boy a long time ago. Without another sound she pulled her arms inside her T-shirt and started to wriggle and jiggle like a butterfly trying to get out of a cocoon.

'Got it,' she yelled. She shot out one arm and held her bra in the air above her head. We both looked at each other, embarrassed. After all, she was my sister. My face felt as red as hers looked.

'Tie it across the doorway,' I said.

We snuck back to the door and I pushed one end over a rusty bolt near the door frame. Then I passed the other end across to Dawn. *Please don't let the queen see it. Please don't let the queen grab my outstretched arm.*

Dawn wedged her end into a broken hinge. The sucking of the babies grew louder but there was not a sound from the queen.

I put my precious ball of mould into one of the cups of the bra. Just like I had done so long ago with tennis balls.

Suddenly I leapt into the doorway and pulled my slingshot back. 'Take that,' I screamed. I released the bra and the ball of mould hurtled into the air.

The queen saw it. Her eyes darted from side to side. She opened her huge mouth. Then, like an expert batsman, she flipped the ball of mould into the air with her tongue.

It broke into pieces and fell like powder slowly downwards.

My heart fell with it. The queen had beaten us. Hit us for a six.

There was only one ball of mould left. We could try to use it to save ourselves. Have another shot. But then we'd have none left to try and save Mum and Dad and Howard.

We watched in despair as the blue powder floated down.

All over the baby slobberers.

They immediately began to squirm and jiggle. They didn't like it. It was attacking them. Sending them crazy. But they didn't let go of those teats. Not for a second. They began to suck at an enormous rate. Faster and faster. Sucking, sucking, sucking. As if they were dying of thirst. In agony they sucked. Faster and faster. The blue mould was sending them into a feeding frenzy.

The queen let out a furious howl of pain. She shook her fat body like a dying walrus but to no effect. The babies bit harder and sucked even more furiously. They grew and grew as the gorging continued.

And the queen began to shrink. Squealing and thrashing around she tried to rid herself of her terrible offspring.

Dawn gasped in horror. 'They're sucking her out,' she yelled. 'They're swallowing her innards. Drinking her guts.'

I could only nod in amazement. The babies grew larger with every swallow. Now they were the size of cars. They wallowed and wriggled and sucked, in last desperate struggles for life.

The queen gave an enormous hiss and then collapsed like a huge rug onto the floor. They had totally sucked her out. She was nothing but a giant slimy mat.

The monstrous babies continued to suck on the empty teats. But there was nothing left. The meal was over.

Boom. The first baby exploded in an ear-splitting shower of foul yellow muck. *Boom, boom, boom.* The others followed. They splattered all over the floor and walls.

A silence fell over the dining room. Dawn and I just stood there staring at the scene with mouths hanging open.

I bent down and examined the remains of the babies. 'Looks like curried egg,' I said.

We both started to laugh.

Then we ran over the empty skin and carried our ball of mould along the corridor and up the ladder into the open air.

I was filled with happiness. The mould was curing me. And we had enough for poor Mum. And Dad. And my brother Howard. Everything was great. My real family was going to be together again.

'Dad,' I screamed. 'Mum. Howard. I'm coming.'

TEN

I thought Rev Arnott was going to faint when Dad asked him for another wedding.

'But,' he stammered, 'the last one was only five weeks ago.'

'Yeah,' said Dad, 'but it was a bit disrupted so we thought we'd do it again. Plus there's a few people who couldn't make it last time. A step-son I didn't know I had. And my wife's ex-husband.' Dad gave me a grin and ruffled my hair. 'And my daughter wants to be there for the whole thing this time.'

I poked my tongue out at Dad and ruffled his hair.

Rev Arnott mopped his face with a piece of blotting paper from his desk. He did look very stressed. I realised what it probably was.

'It's okay,' I said. 'None of the wedding party or guests will be contagious. The doctors have given us the all-clear. And I promise there'll be no worms in church this time.'

Rev Arnott looked a bit relieved. I gave him a smile, glad to have helped.

I didn't mention my concern about the wedding.

Last night we had a pre-wedding family dinner. It was a bit of a squash round the table because Gramps invited

Ivy Bothwell and we invited Alex and Bob. They're the government men who've been looking after us and keeping the media away. They reckon if word about the virus leaks out there could be a national health panic. I've tried to explain to them how that probably won't happen now the virus has been eradicated, but they reckon people get very tense about health issues.

I know what they mean. A couple of days ago I asked Eileen if she was going back to her bottom exercises and she got extremely tense. I had to give her a very long hug and clean her new bike to calm her down.

Mostly she and I get on pretty well, specially when we do things together like visiting Mum's grave or laying the table for dinner like we did last night.

While we were waiting for Karl and Howard to arrive from their new place across town, Gramps was telling Ivy Bothwell about Mum.

'A hero,' he was saying. 'Gave her life to save a passenger. Pity not more bus drivers are like that.'

I grinned. Gramps had already said that to most of the people in town, including two bus drivers. He'd even persuaded the local paper to do an article about Mum. And persuaded Alex and Bob to allow them to print it as long as he didn't say anything about the goat being infected.

'Of course,' said Gramps to Ivy Bothwell, 'she got her guts and determination from me. Did I tell you about the time Rory and I wrestled a giant toad?'

'Frog, Wilf,' said Ivy Bothwell. 'It was a frog.'

Ivy told me the other day how she's really attracted to men with failing memories because they don't waste time talking about old cricket scores.

Gramps told the story about the frog again, and Alex and Bob started looking a bit anxious in case Ivy was a reporter for a pensioner's magazine. I was feeling a bit anxious too. Not about Ivy, about Rory.

He was sitting in the corner not saying anything. He's been moody and quiet for several weeks, ever since we got back from hospital. I've asked him what's wrong but he hasn't wanted to talk. Even though the doctors have guaranteed there's no virus left in his body, and his skin is as clear as Karl and Eileen and Howard's, seeing him sitting there so depressed I was worried something was wrong.

Then Karl and Howard arrived and suddenly I was a lot more worried.

Their faces were covered in white patches. My insides froze. Everyone in the room stared in horror. 'Oh no,' whispered Eileen. 'Karl, your face.'

Karl looked at us for a moment, then burst out laughing. 'Relax,' he said. 'It's just paint.'

We gawked at him.

'We've been painting the ceiling of my room,' grinned Howard. 'We ran out of turps.'

Everyone breathed out and started talking all at once.

'Jeez,' said Eileen. 'Don't do that to us.'

'There's turps under the sink,' said Dad. 'Don't get it in my lamb stew.'

'I used to wear a fair bit of camouflage in the war,' said Gramps.

'I've got some news,' said Karl when he'd cleaned himself up. Most of us quietened down when we heard this. Gramps carried on whispering to Ivy Bothwell about boot polish.

'I had a call this afternoon,' continued Karl, 'from the defence department team who are analysing the tanker at the refinery.' Now he had Gramps' attention too. 'They reckon the virus came from an area of the Persian Gulf affected by an underwater volcanic eruption. The tanker took water in there as ballast on its last voyage out to the oilfields.'

'That's just a theory,' said Bob hastily.

'It hasn't been verified,' added Alex, looking nervously at Ivy Bothwell.

We all started talking about underwater volcanic eruptions and how we'd stay well away from them in future. Except Rory. He just sat there looking sadly at Karl and Eileen.

I went and sat next to him.

'What's wrong?' I asked quietly. 'Do you want to talk? We can go out the back.'

Rory shook his head.

'Rory,' I said, exasperated. 'We've fought slobberers and killer roots together. We've saved each other's lives. We've shared a bra. Talk to me.'

His eyes filled with tears. 'It's private,' he muttered. 'Family business.' He got up and went to his room and locked the door.

This morning, when we were ready to leave for the church, Rory wasn't around.

'It's okay,' said Eileen, 'he's over at Karl's.'

But when Karl and Howard arrived here at the church, Rory wasn't with them. I wanted to go and look for him, but the adults made me stay here and Karl went.

The wedding should have started ten minutes ago. Mrs Conti is playing 'Here Comes the Bride' for the fifth time. Mr Kinloch from the Wool Growers' Association is making an origami sheep out of his hymn list.

Rory still isn't here.

Neither is Karl.

It's what I've feared.

ELEVEN

Here I am back on the bus just sitting and looking down the aisle. Nothing much has changed. The seats are still sagging and the broken windows are covered in dust like before. The same tree is growing up through the bonnet outside.

The skeleton of the goat is gone, though. Dad had come and buried it with the dog skin. Just to be on the safe side.

There's lots to be happy about.

Everyone is well again. I am healthier than I have ever been. Even my limp is improving. And Dawn and I are getting on terrifically. She still bugs me sometimes, especially when she comes into my room without knocking. But at school we always stick up for each other. Like the time Dawn put Rick Philpot in his place for repeating that false rumour about my dad being in trouble with the police. She fixed him up real good.

And Gramps. Well, he still keeps thinking he is back in the war and gets things muddled up. But he laughs a lot. He hangs around with Ivy Bothwell. And he and I go fishing together on Sundays and always have a great time. Dawn gets a bit cut about it but she's never said anything.

And Dad. That's the best of all – knowing that he loves me. And on top of that there is something else. It is still a secret but some government research scientists want to buy the blue mould from him. It turned out to be a new sort of penicillin. Howard says that Dad

is going to be rich one day. We're both going to get new trail bikes. Fantastic.

So why aren't I happy?

Because I've got a problem, that's why. I've been sitting here churning it over for ages. A few minutes ago I had just started to go over it again when a noise interrupted my thoughts. Someone was coming. A figure stepped up into the bus. I couldn't see who it was because the sun was glaring through the windscreen.

'Rory,' said a voice. 'Dawn told me you'd be here. Why aren't you at the wedding? Everyone's waiting.'

It was Dad. He came and sat next to me. Worried.

I stared at the floor. 'I'm not going to the wedding,' I said. 'I don't want Mum and Jack to get married again.'

'Why, mate? Why?' said Dad. He couldn't believe what he was hearing.

'I want them to get divorced.'

'What?'

'I want *you* and Mum to get married again,' I yelled. 'I want it to be like it was in the old days. When we all had tickle fights. And cooked sausages and eggs together on Saturdays. And went to the market. And you and Mum held hands and – '

'Rory,' said Dad. 'It was all over long ago with me and your mum. We can't get back together.'

'Why not?' I shouted. I could feel tears starting to form in my eyes.

'We don't love each other,' said Dad. 'Not in that way. Not any more.'

'So now I have to choose,' I yelled. 'I have to decide whether to live with you and Howard, or with Mum and Jack. I want you and Mum together. Just the four of us.'

Dad stared out of the window. 'Rory,' he said. 'We've already been through that. You can live with your mum and come and see me any time you want. All you have to do is hop on the bus. Or you can live one week with her and one with me. Or whatever you like. It's up to you.'

'It's not the same,' I said. 'It's just not the same.'

Dad didn't say anything for quite a bit. 'I know it's not the same,' he said. 'But it can still be good.' He looked at his watch. Then he rubbed his hand through my hair. The way he always used to. 'I have to go,' he said. 'We're holding up the wedding. Are you sure you won't come?'

I shook my head stubbornly. Dad stood up and headed off. 'I understand,' he said. 'I'm not going to force you.'

I looked out of the window and watched him walk past the clapped-out Land Rover and out of the broken gates of the wrecker's yard.

He is gone.

After everything that has happened I'm back in the bus where it all started. I want to go to the wedding. I want to join in with the others. I really do.

But I just don't think I can face it.

TWELVE

I thought Dad and Eileen's first wedding was tense but this one has turned out to be even tenser.

Fifteen minutes after the ceremony was meant to start, Rory and Karl still hadn't arrived.

My insides were in a double knot.

Rev Arnott was chewing his lip. Dad and Eileen were staring at the aisle carpet, pale and anxious. The guests were turning round in their pews, whispering to each other. Even Gramps looked worried.

I slid up next to Howard. 'Rory wouldn't talk to me,' I said. 'Did he tell you what's bugging him?'

'No,' said Howard, 'but I can guess. It's not easy, having more than two parents.'

I nodded.

'It's great having extra ones,' he continued, 'even if they're not all still around, but it can be mighty confusing.'

I nodded again. I could see Howard was thinking about the couple who had adopted him and then been killed. I wanted to give him a hug, but there are some painful feelings you have to have on your own.

Like the ones I imagined poor Rory was having.

Howard swallowed and blinked. Then he grinned bravely.

'Anyhow,' he said, 'let's look on the bright side. They'll probably turn up for the reception. Rory wouldn't miss party pies.'

I tried to grin bravely too, but I'm not as good at it as Howard.

'Talking of the reception,' said Howard, 'I hope you're going to be gentle with Gavin and Kyle Kinloch.'

I looked at him. Then I turned round and glared at the Kinloch brothers. They saw me and both blushed.

Relax, I said to myself. You've handled slobberers and killer mould. You can handle a couple of Year 7 dopes giving you a hard time because you're wearing a dress.

I knew I could. But I still wished my new T-shirt hadn't disappeared. The one I'd been planning to wear with jeans.

I gave the Kinlochs another glare and they went bright red.

Howard leant over to me. 'They're going to ask you for a dance,' he whispered.

I stared at him, speechless.

Then Rev Arnott cleared his throat and explained that the ceremony had to start because he had another one booked in for twelve-thirty.

Dad and Eileen stood up the front with their shoulders slumped and I knew exactly how they felt. How could we be a proper family if we couldn't even do the wedding right?

Rev Arnott started the service, but his heart wasn't in it. Neither was mine. I could see Dad's and Eileen's weren't. The only people who looked keen for it to happen were the Kinloch boys.

Rev Arnott said the bit about how if anyone had a reason why these two people should not be joined together in holy matrimony, speak now or forever hold your peace.

The door at the back of the church swung open with a creak.

We all turned. Standing there were Rory and Karl.

I stopped breathing. The church was silent except for the faint tinkling of Gramps' medals. I looked at Rory. Rory opened his mouth. Then closed it again.

'Sorry we're late,' said Karl.

'Don't worry,' said Rory. 'We haven't got a reason why Jack and Mum shouldn't be joined together.'

The whole congregation breathed a sigh of relief.

Dad spoke. 'I have,' he said.

We stared at him, gobsmacked.

Rev Arnott went pale.

'Me and Eileen should not be joined in matrimony,' said Dad, 'before we've thanked our kids for everything they've done to keep this family together.' He looked at me. 'Even when a certain dopey dad didn't take his daughter seriously.'

Everyone in the church breathed another big sigh of relief. Dad and Eileen came over and hugged me and Rory and Howard.

Then Karl did the same.

And Gramps.

When Ivy Bothwell flung her arms round Howard, Rev Arnott suggested that further thanks be saved until after the wedding.

As Dad and Eileen renewed their vows, and said the stuff about being a family till death us do part, Rory and Howard and I looked at each other and we knew that went for us too.

Dad and Eileen gazed at each other lovingly, and something in their faces reminded me of Mum.

This was the moment I'd been dreading. The moment that could ruin everything.

I turned and looked at Karl. The man who'd brought the virus into our lives. Into Mum's life. If I was going to blame anyone for Mum's death, it would be Karl.

I've been looking at him for a long time. He hasn't seen me because he's too busy gazing at Rory and Howard with love, and Eileen and Dad with genuine pleasure.

I don't blame him. He's just a parent doing his best. Like Eileen. Like Dad. Like Mum.

I don't know why thinking that is making my eyes fill with tears, but it is and they're tears of happiness.

Everything's going to be all right.

DAWN

Well, most of the time.

I've just noticed something about Rory I hadn't noticed before.

He's wearing my new T-shirt.